BLUE
RIDGE

BLUE RIDGE

Peter Malone Elliott

LeVel
BEST BOOKS

Praise for Blue Ridge

"*Blue Ridge* is an incredible, twisty thriller that's as shocking as it is compelling. Peter Malone Elliott brings a fresh and exciting new voice to crime fiction that's sure to wow readers. I couldn't turn the pages fast enough."—Hannah Mary McKinnon, internationally bestselling author of *The Revenge List*

"*Blue Ridge* is an impressive debut, with one of the most striking fictional murders I've ever read, beautiful writing, multiple moral conundrums, and a surprise ending that will stick with you for weeks afterwards."—Matt Witten, bestselling author of *Killer Story*

"Peter Malone Elliott's *Blue Ridge* is a breakneck thriller, reminiscent of Sam Shepard, with a twisty plot of brother versus brother that reveals itself to be so much more, with a ton of heart and an ending that literally stopped me in my tracks. Read this one!"—Lee Matthew Goldberg, award nominated author of *The Mentor* and *The Great Gimmelmans*

"Peter Malone Elliott's gritty Southern thriller transports readers to the mountains of Virginia where menace looms amid breathtaking landscapes. *Blue Ridge* has it all: nail-biting suspense, political intrigue, family drama and tragic romance. Like the character of Cillian, readers will find themselves racing to unearth the buried secrets left behind in the wake of his brother's murder."—Laura Picklesimer, author of *Kill for Love*

"Peter Malone Elliott's debut novel, *Blue Ridge*, is a fast-paced thrill ride filled with suspense and jump scares that will keep you on the edge of your seat. Told from dual POV (by twin brothers who couldn't be more different),

Peter's prose is intelligent yet accessible, and tension jumps off every page. It's an inside peek into the grueling, back-stabbing, pocket-lining world of US politics but, more than that, it's about families and the bonds that tie them together, and how our secrets, lies, bad decisions, and past mistakes can haunt us."— Camille Booker, author of *What If You Fly?*

I

PART ONE: THE UNRAVELING

"Each one separately thinks that he's the only one that's afraid. And they keep ridin' like that straight into the night. Not knowing."
—Sam Shepard, True West

Chapter One

Cillian

The last time I was there, we were hanging my beloved.

I remember the look of terror splashed across her face.

I remember the moment she asked me: "Why is he here?"

And I remember finding out the answer.

A foghorn blare from the eighteen-wheeler in the next lane over blasted me out of my thoughts. I had nearly drifted my ancient F-250 into his wheel-well. For probably the third time in the last five minutes. I'd been driving since the middle of the night—when most people were in their first REM cycle. And it was starting to take its toll.

As I halfheartedly waved my apologies—again—to the irate trucker, he flipped me off and barreled past me. All the years of pulling a horse trailer in this particular stretch of Virginia highway had taught me that there are two types of truckers—those who shepherded you along in their convoys as part of the brotherhood, and those who would have no problem running you off the road and rattling your trailer so hard in their wake that it would set the horses kicking and rearing with terror. This son-of-a-bitch was definitely the latter. Then again, I've grown accustomed to people being upset with me.

Disappointed, angry, dismissive—they're all branches from the same tree.

I took a swig of water and took stock of my surroundings. I was barreling east along 64, just about to come into Lexington, Virginia. I'd hung my hat here for a while after graduation. With Audrey. My beloved. Ahead of me were the Blue Ridge Mountains, tinged with shades of blue, purple, and green. I always say the majestic, rolling landscape of the Blue Ridge is nature's equivalent to the music of Patsy Cline—an inexplicably perfect cocktail of sumptuous beauty, haunting melancholy, and dark-edged mystery. Still about three hours off from my ultimate destination—Paris, Virginia. My hometown.

The place where it all began.

And the place where it all went to hell.

Coming from my current home base—Lexington, Kentucky—it would have been faster to have gone straight through West Virginia. But I tend to avoid West Virginia whenever humanly possible. Plus, given what I was on my way to do? I needed to put my finger to the flame and preemptively singe as much skin off as possible. A bass-ackwards, perverse preparation. And taking the long way through Virginia was the only way to do it. The smokey, foggy eyes of the Blue Ridge looked at me mockingly through the rising sun—as if they knew my own fate better than I did.

And you know what? I'd bet you the barn that they did.

I'm on my way to see my brother, Christopher. From the second he and I popped out of Mama, he's thought that he was better than me. In a way, though, he's right. He's more of something than I'll ever be. But I'd never tell him that in a million years. The fact that we're identical twins—and yet, somehow, he's about ten times more handsome than I am—doesn't help this notion in my brain.

One hand gripped to the wheel, I rooted through the mess of currycomb brushes, equine bandages, chaps, and boots trashing the cracked leather backseats of my truck. I thought I had left a pack of American Spirits there somewhere. On top of all this crap lay my perpetually sleeping, cranky-old-man pit bull, Shepard. He lazily opened his right eye, silently judging me.

4

"I know. I'll quit tomorrow," I lied. Shepard snorted and re-closed his eye. We'd been through that song and dance about a million times, and the music no longer interested him. He did love Bruce Springsteen, though—which is why The Boss had been thundering through my truck's sound system the entire ride. Audrey had loved him, too.

My iPhone ringtone—"M.I.L.F.$" by Fergie—cut through my Bruce-scored quest for nicotine. My most lucrative client, Summer, had bought me the phone a year ago and had programmed her personalized ringtone herself. She wouldn't let me change it because she thought it was funny. So, whenever she called me, I had to endure this synthesized torture to my eardrums. She had also gotten a top-of-the-line aftermarket Bluetooth system installed in my truck. She's a big shot consultant of some kind—I've never cared enough to ask—and her husband is one of those hedge-fund guys whose job is just barely the right side of legal. So, needless to say, money is never an issue for them.

And Summer? Well, she likes to spoil me. And I pay her back with fucks in the tack room when her husband isn't looking. She enjoys it most when I string her up in cross-ties. She cums in about 30 seconds flat. Which saves me the trouble of having to lie about why I can't bring myself to finish.

It was Summer calling me. Who'da thunk.

"Howdy, lovely." I tried telling her that no one actually talked like that in the South—that it was just a holdover from dumb Hollywood westerns and leftover social stereotypes. But she was a transplant to Kentucky from Greenwich, Connecticut, about five years gone. And she liked it. It tickled her right pink. And if she kept signing the checks that singlehandedly paid my mortgage? I'll talk however she damn wants me to.

"Howdy, cowboy." Summer's husky, Ava Gardner-like voice always did find a way to straighten up my spine, no matter how much I didn't want to do the pitter-pat.

"What can I do for you this bright and early?"

"Richard's going to be gone overnight. Business trip to New York. I'm thinking I'd like to take Incognito on a long canter through the valley." Incognito was really her horse's name, but that was also her code for saying that she wanted me to spend the night with her in the big house. Summer was convinced that Richard had tapped her phone and that he listened to all her calls. I tried telling her that the chances of Richard going to all that trouble were slim to none. Especially since he had been doing squat thrusts in the cucumber patch with Robert, the farrier that I work with, for as long as I had been knocking boots with Summer. But that wasn't a hill I was going to die on.

"Remember I told you I'm off this week?" I replied. "Going to see my brother in Virginia."

"No, that seems to have slipped my mind," she simpered. "Are you sure that wasn't next week?"

"I'm positive."

"Didn't you see him just a couple of months ago?" Summer had an incredible memory for a perpetually cross-faded cougar; I'll give her that. I had used seeing my brother as an excuse a couple of times previously. This was the first time that it was actually true.

"Are you saying I can't see my own flesh and blood more than twice a year?" I retorted, pretending to be playful.

"I'm saying that your brother is keeping me from consuming your flesh right now. And I resent him for that." Despite her phone-tapping concerns, every now and again, Summer's lust got the best of her, and she abandoned the code-speak she had made me swear by.

"I'm pretty sure that's just cannibalism."

"You haven't even begun to see what cannibalism is like."

I internally debated just how to respond to this simultaneously revolting yet faintly arousing statement. Once again, Summer had stumped me.

"We'll have plenty to talk about when I come back," I decided to stick to the protocol.

"Finnnneeeee," she huffed. "You know, your brother was on CNN again last night. I feel like I know him, the number of times I've seen him yakking on TV."

I'm sure a lot of people felt like that. He was the consummate politician from infancy. At twenty-six, Christopher had shocked about near all the locals when he was elected mayor of Middleburg. Two years later, he stunned the whole damn state when he became one of the youngest members of the U.S. Congress ever elected. Now, three rousingly successful terms later, he was rumored to be announcing his bid for the Governor's seat. So, he's been making the rounds on cable news, pontificating about the merits of the sweeping healthcare reform bill he had just proposed in Congress, something that made him a darling amongst the progressives while also seeming sensible to moderates. Hell, even the Republicans liked him. He had achieved the holy trinity. My brother has a knack for turning a sworn enemy into a follower with just a handshake, a smile, and a few words that went down like ethylene glycol—sweet to the taste right up until the moment you dropped dead from it.

Which I know was why he summoned me back home.

Like a lamb to slaughter.

"Summer, I'm getting a call from the vet on the other line. I'll call you when I'm back in town, all right?" I lied.

"You better, cowboy."

"See you, lovely." I nearly gagged as I hung up. I always felt like another person during my conversations with her—like I was putting on one of those face and voice-changing masks from the *Mission Impossible* movies. I looked down at my hands. My palms were lathered with sweat like a horse after an all-out gallop, slipping and sliding all over the steering wheel. Only discussing my brother could elicit this feeling—pure loathing with a healthy dollop of fear and anxiety.

I needed to get off the road for a beat.

As my stomach rumbled, I noticed the first exit sign for Lexington. I tried not to look at the marker for the Virginia Horse Center—the place where, as a young equestrian, I envisioned my life going very differently—and instead trained my focus on the diner perched in the distance, nestled adjacent to the turn-off for Washington and Lee University and the Virginia Military Institute. I didn't recognize it—it must have sprouted up after I had bolted out of the state for good. Which was perfect. Granted, I was hungry for something that a restaurant couldn't satiate—a rage torching my insides that only one specific thing, one hell or high-water act, could quell.

But for now? Pancakes sounded good.

* * *

White, fluffy, and full of artificial product—my waitress's not-subtle boob job and my flapjacks were one and the same. Annie was her name. She was a real sweetheart. She let me bring Shepard inside and even brought him a bowl of water.

"You all set there?" Annie asked me, looking at my mostly cleaned plate.

"Yes, ma'am. Thank you." No matter how subpar the food was, Dad raised Christopher and me to never be rude to servers. It was one of the only valuable things that fucker taught us before he kicked the bucket.

Annie bent over to pick up my plate and cutlery, giving me a full view of the silicone boulders fused onto her slender frame. I quickly averted my eyes. I had learned to keep my baser instincts in check. The only time I got intimate with anyone was if I had to for business, like with Summer. Genuine, honest-to-God male-female companionship wasn't something that interested me anymore.

Not since Audrey.

Annie glanced over at Shepard, who, by this point, was sitting upright in the booth across from me like the human he thought he was.

"You want to make him real happy?" I said to Annie, motioning at Shepard. "Give him that last little bit of sausage on my plate."

Annie smiled at Shepard as his tail started thumping louder than a bass drum. She tenderly fed Shepard as he gratefully slurped it down in about two seconds flat.

"He's sweet," she said as she scratched the top of his head.

"Yeah, he has it in him when he's not sleeping and farting up a storm."

Annie giggled as Shepard cocked his head at me.

C'mon man, not in front of the lady.

I reached into my pocket and pulled out a fresh pack of American Spirits.

"I'm assuming I can't smoke in here?"

Annie glanced around at the empty restaurant. It was after the usual breakfast time rush, so the only souls in the place were us.

"Will Shepard mind if I join you?" She arched her eyebrow playfully at me.

I looked over at Shepard. He was already fast asleep again, not paying us any mind.

I shook my head, handed Annie a cig, and lit her up as she slid in next to Shepard's resting carcass. I sparked up my own, and we each took a long, silent, satisfied drag before flicking our first crown of ashes into my discarded coffee mug.

"You look like you're on your way to somewhere," she said after a tick.

"Who says that somewhere isn't here?"

"No one is on their way to a diner just off 64."

"What does 'on your way to somewhere' look like, exactly?"

Annie slowly looked me up and down, her cigarette looking virginal tucked inside her ruby red lips.

"Not a lick of good," she said after a moment.

I took an inhale and blew out a smoke ring, trying to deflect from the fact that she was pretty much bang on the money.

"If it makes you feel any better, I'm in the same boat as you," Annie saved me from my thoughts.

"Where are you off to?"

"Out west. Los Angeles. A friend of my uncle is a movie producer. Says he can get me a part in something he's doing," she excitedly smiled.

Good god.

"That's exciting," I said, not knowing how else to reply. "When do you leave?"

"This is my last shift. In a few hours, I'll be out of this town faster than a horny jackrabbit."

I couldn't help but smile at the imagery. "Well, best of luck to you."

"What do you do? Besides carrying around a cloud of gloom over your shoulders like a bale of hay?"

"I work with horses."

"You enjoy that?"

I thought about how to answer that for a long while. I decided to hit her with the truth.

Fuck it. What do I have to lose? I would never see her again.

"It's about the only thing that makes my life worth living."

Annie started to say something back but thought better of it. Instead, she stubbed out the last of her cigarette into the mug and tore off the bill, setting it down in front of me.

"I hope you find what you're looking for."

"You too."

She gave Shepard a lipstick-stained kiss and me a soft smile before clearing the dishware and sashaying off.

I looked down at the check. Ten dollars for a hot meal with a side of therapy seemed low. I reached into my pocket and laid down all the cash I had on me. About eighty big ones. She needed it more than I did.

And where I was going? Money wasn't going to help me any.

I wormed my way out of the booth, snapping my fingers at Shepard. "C'mon, boy."

As Shepard and I exited and started towards the truck, I felt the dreaded stab in my knee and started to limp. Back in my steeplechase days, my horse had bucked at a particularly terrifying bush jump at the Gold Cup and dragged me almost the length of a football field. After that, my bum knee forever had a mind of its own. It chose to work only when it felt up to the task, modulating to barometric pressure.

I looked up at the sky. A looming, encased-in-gray squall line was ominously marching in my direction. It was far off in the distance still, but its funereal, deliberate pace was unmistakable.

A storm was coming.

* * *

Let's meet at Daddy's cabin up in Sky Meadows. Spend a few days together. Just you and me. The Blue Ridge is gorgeous in the fall. It'll be like old times, Brother.

Cruising north on 81, I wondered what the hell he was referring to when he said "old times" in the email he sent me. I had barely had any "times" there at all—only three other trips I could remember. My whole life. Unlike Christopher. The prodigal son.

Growing up, Christopher got all of Dad's attention. Especially after Mama died. While I was at the stable and eventing across the East Coast, Dad would drive Christopher to football practice and cheer him on in the stands during his games. Dad never questioned paying more money than he actually had for Christopher's recruiting camps and scouting videos—none of which worked, by the way—but I had to pay my own way by being a "work-student" for one of the local horse trainers. Don't go thinking it was anything academic. I mucked manure, bathed the horses, cleaned the tack, threw the feed, and stacked the hay in exchange for lessons.

After Christopher would do something "heroic" like throw a touchdown pass—which doesn't seem all that difficult, if you ask me, especially when you compare it to driving a 1,600 lb. Irish Sport Horse over five-foot stone fences at a gallop—Dad would take Christopher up to the cabin for a celebratory weekend of beer and hunting. It didn't matter how many show ribbons or championships I brought back. Christopher had always done something more impressive. The day after I told Dad that I had been invited to train with the US Olympic Equestrian team, he died. Heart attack. Part of me wonders if that happened because I had finally done something worthy enough of his approval, and the shock did him in.

I looked at the clock—it was only mid-day, and I wasn't supposed to meet Christopher until tonight. I had some time to kill.

I took the 211 exit and then the fork that headed towards Jeremy's Run Overlook. I needed some fresh air. My brain was beginning to suffocate me. It tends to do that.

As I pulled in and parked, I saw the lot was completely empty. As it should be—most people in their right mind wouldn't go on a hike when it looked like the sky was just about to sink onto our heads.

But I wasn't most people, unfortunately.

Shepard came to from his slumber and barked at me. He needed to pee.

"I know, boy, we're going, we're going," I said as I opened the backdoor for him. He darted out and immediately marked his territory.

By this point, the pain in my knee was pretty excruciating. I gingerly swung my legs to the side and tried to get out. It felt like the devil was living inside my leg, taking a jackhammer to the cartilage behind my kneecap.

I sighed, realizing what I needed to do. I reached into the pocket over the sun visor meant for sunglasses that I instead used to store my OxyContin. I hated the way the pills made me feel—what they made me think—but they were the only thing that helped in times like this.

I dry-swallowed two tablets and closed my eyes, waiting for them to take effect.

Not long after, I see Audrey.

She's riding towards me, gracefully sitting the trot on her British Warm-blood, Dolly. She thought it would be funny to name her very British horse a very American name.

It was.

She and Dolly kick up into a canter, her blonde hair billowing behind her, the way it would when we cross-country raced one another at Great Meadow. Even if Dolly was still tacked up in her dressage saddle, Audrey would kick my ass. Every time. And then we would make love. Tender and gentle—something I've never done with anyone else. And never will.

I can hear her lilting, soft voice—the one that strung together melodies in my ears.

I want you forever, Cillian.

The grass tickles our bare skin as I slide inside of her.

She and Dolly move toward me.

Closer.

And closer.

And closer.

Just as Audrey's about to reach out and touch my face, I see that her hair is drenched, coated in blood.

Her blood.

I wrenched open my eyes, unable to take it anymore.

I bellowed up at the heavens, trying to spew out the poison embedded in my soul. It didn't work.

But the pain in my knee was gone.

Shepard sat down on the ground watching me, well used to this by now. His big brown eyes peered up at me as he whimpered, filled with the kind of pity that made my heart hurt.

Hands trembling, I stepped down from the cab of my truck onto the pine needle-covered earth. I scratched Shepard's ears. "It's okay, boy. Sorry. I'm back. I'm okay," I said softly. Shepard licked my cheek in response.

I took a deep breath and shut the driver's door. I needed to remember my purpose. The reason for me pulling an Odysseus.

Walking okay now, I strode around to the covered flatbed of my truck and pulled out a small black box. I removed the brand new Bersa Thunder .380 purchased from a friend of a friend of a client of mine.

I loaded the cartridge, just like he showed me.

I had only ever fired two guns in my life—a 12-gauge shotgun and a bolt action rifle. So, I needed to practice shooting this one. Locking up my truck, I headed towards the trail, whistling at Shepard to join me.

As I limped into the dense, dark forest, the first raindrop hit my cheek as I felt the weight of the Bersa in my right hand. Even though it's one of the lightest guns on the market, it nearly made me fall over with its heft.

Because this was the gun I was going to use to kill my brother.

Chapter Two

Christopher

I just wanted people to leave me alone for two goddamn minutes. That's all.

I stood looking out the luminous bay window in the living room of my Daddy's cabin, looking down at the pond—the lone speck of blue in the sprawling swath of green. I used to go swimming in it as a boy, but my ex-wife had spent a lot of money turning it into a decorative koi pond—so swimming wasn't a possibility anymore. I tried telling her that I didn't think an exotic-inspired thing like that really fit into the country landscape, but you didn't tell Bonnie no.

I suppose I shouldn't call it Daddy's cabin anymore. After all, I've spent enough money on this place to make a Swiss banker blush, and I made sure local zoning laws were passed so that no one can build anything within five miles. It's my sanctuary. *Mine.*

Cillian was due to arrive later today. To say that my identical twin brother and I are estranged is like saying Churchill and Hitler didn't like each other: the understatement of the century. I invited him to smooth things over. To prevent him from running his mouth to the press. Anytime I want to run for any type of office, I have to play this game of chicken with him to make sure he doesn't say anything about Audrey's death that isn't public knowledge. We had done this before—when I was running for mayor of Middleburg and then again for my Congressional races. This negotiation was, to put it lightly, exhausting. This would be the first time we'd done it at the cabin since it happened, though. And this was different. This was for the coup de grâce—the Governor's Mansion.

If only that was my sole worry. Ensuring Cillian's silence ran a distant second to the other precarious position in which I now found myself.

To make things worse, it seemed like the phones were ringing off the hook every five seconds. And it was really sucking the buzz out of the second Irish coffee I was sipping. Although the fact that I was chasing it with Pepto-Bismol to settle my stomach probably wasn't helping my angst, either.

Bzzzzzz.

Bzzzzzz.

Bzzzzzz.

I turned around to the hand-carved teak coffee table resting in the middle of the living room. Everything in this house was bought from American companies, I'm proud to say. Sure, some of them outsourced their labor to Bangladesh, but my constituents didn't need to know that. I make good money as a silent, off-the-books partner in my college buddy's Silicon Valley tech start-up—every month, my offshore account in the Caymans is filled with about three times what I pull down in my yearly government salary—but a man has got to cut corners somewhere, right? I'm not a Rockefeller. But I am smart—everyone laughed at Zander when he said he wanted to create a new mobile payment service. Not me. I sold my car to give him his first seed money. Now, over 75% of all e-commerce businesses in America use it. And I had reaped the benefits. And then some.

I shook my head, forcing myself out of my preening loop of thought. Ever since I had arrived at the cabin a few hours ago, my three cell phones laid out on that coffee table had been vibrating nonstop. The first was my personal line, the second was the one linked to my Congressional office in DC, and the third was a direct line to the Godmother, the alpha female of all political consultants, the benefactor who was backing my soon-to-be-announced run for Governor. It wasn't the end of the world to miss a call here or there from the first two, but not the third.

You *never* missed a call from the Godmother.

She wielded the kind of influence that made straightforward power seem like an innocent little schoolgirl. On a daily basis, she made or broke whole lives before she'd even sipped her first cup of freshly ground Italian espresso. She was the political equivalent of a Black Ops team—you knew the end results of her work, but never the ruthless methods she employed. I was her first Democrat. Most of the time, it made me proud to be someone's first. Not with the Godmother. But no one was better—if you wanted to win, you hired her. And I had wanted to win. You'd think that in this day and age, we'd be beyond the "Kingmaker" cliche of a powerful influencer pulling the strings behind the curtain.

But you'd be wrong.

She had called me ten times in the last twenty-four hours. And I had ignored every single one of them. Somewhere, I imagined that she was simultaneously combusting.

It had been the Godmother's suggestion to invite Cillian here. To try and negotiate some sort of once-and-for-all cease-fire truce before I ran for executive office. When I told her that I'd held executive office before when I was mayor of Middleburg, she just laughed and patted my cheek like I was an infant. I also tried telling her that my relationship with Cillian wasn't something you could simply wave a white flag at, and then everything would be jake. But she persisted. So, I reluctantly agreed. There were bigger fish to fry.

But given what I had just found out about her? The fact that I had taken *any* counsel from her—let alone the seven figures of under-the-table seed money—made my stomach churn. Hence, the whisky-coffee-Pepto cocktail. Which, I can tell you with absolute certainty, is the vilest combination of liquids a person can put into their body.

Luckily, it wasn't the Godmother this time. Just a FaceTime call on my work line. I breathed out a sigh of relief. The only person who ever FaceTimed me was Ada, my chief-of-staff. She would be a sight for sore eyes.

Act like everything is normal, asshole.

16

I plastered on a smile and injected the whisper of a good mood into my voice. By this point, I had gotten that down to a science. Politicking 101.

I grabbed the second phone on its last vibration. Ada's delicately controlled features sharply contrasted with her electrifying blue eyes that looked like they were charged up by the wrath of Zeus.

"This is Congressman Clark. And who do I have the pleasure of speaking with today?" I answered in a mockingly serious tone.

"Whenever you answer the phone like that, it sounds like you're trying to sell me an internet/cable/phone bundle," Ada shot back. Poor soul, she was perpetually frazzled, doing the job of about three staffers put together. She ran my life for me, and she did it without a single complaint ever. I didn't deserve her. She had been with me since my mayoral campaign, and the Godmother had advised me that I should consider replacing her with someone more "weathered." That was the word she used. Fat chance of that ever happening. Ada would be with me until the day I died.

"Sorry to disappoint you," I teased.

"You're damn right, you disappoint me. I hate Verizon. I'm ready to drop them like a slippery fish in a creek bed," she cracked an amused half-smile and rolled her eyes.

"Speaking of disappointment, how was your date last night?"

Ada let loose a long, fatigued sigh. "Put it this way: talking to you is like a bright, shining star," she quipped in her warm-as-fried-apples-in-cinnamon Lynchburg twang.

"C'mon, it couldn't have been that bad."

"She's a paralegal for an oil company. We ran out of things to talk about after five minutes."

"One of these days, you've got to ditch the app dating and let me set you up with someone. I know plenty of nice ladies."

"No, you don't."

"No, I don't. Was the food at least good?"

"Top notch, thank you. Giorgio sends his regards."

"You know, I can always get at least a half-hour's worth of material out of the food. An hour with a good bottle of wine."

"Because that's what every girl wants—a sixty-minute conversation about the quality of Virginia-grown Cabernet Francs."

I cracked a smile at Ada's retort. "And what can I do for you on this glorious day, Ada?"

"Three things. Congressman Williams called again about co-sponsoring his upcoming education bill—"

"Good lord, that guy will not let up, will he?" I interrupted. "Set up a lunch with him next week." Williams was a blowhard that made Bernie Sanders look easy-going, but going in on the bill with him would be a good look for me. It didn't stand a chance of passing. But between Williams' bill and the healthcare legislation I had just proposed on my own? That should shut up the people in the party who thought I wasn't progressive enough.

Ada grabbed a pen from her never-ending supply and started scribbling on a yellow pad. She only ever used rollerball pens. Give her a ballpoint and be prepared for a twenty-minute rant about them. I always teased her about the fact she didn't take notes on a computer—that she only used Staples brand yellow legal pads. There were probably hundreds of them stacked around her desk. For her birthday one year, I thought it would be funny to buy her some stock shares in Office Depot. She didn't laugh.

"Ari Melber's producer asked about having you on the show this Thursday?"

"Call Chris Hayes and leverage it to get onto his."

"I thought you liked Ari?"

"I like him fine. His time slot is garbage. I need prime time."

More scribbling. "Last thing: you need to settle on your campaign manager before we announce at the end of the month."

"We? I didn't realize you were my running mate, Ada."

"Oh, please. You'd be chasing your own tail for eternity if I wasn't there to tell you where it is."

"I'd certainly have a less cluttered office, that's for sure."

"I love it when you attempt humor."

"Who said I was attempting and not succeeding?"

"I did. The campaign manager?"

"I'm narrowing down the candidates. There's still a lot of old white men to choose from, after all."

"Ms. Fisker said she wants your decision by the end of the week, or she'll pick for you." Ada mentioning the Godmother's given name wiped the playful smirk clean off my face.

"At this point, why doesn't she just pick herself?"

"It seems like that might be on the table."

"I see."

"She wanted me to tell you that she's had trouble reaching you." I recognized Ada's tone—it was half sympathetic warning, half what-the-fuck-are-you-doing Christopher.

I swallowed down the anxiety bubbling up my esophagus. I couldn't tell Ada the reason why I had been ducking the Godmother's calls.

That, three days ago, our dinner together had unleashed an emotion I had never felt before in my life: unfettered, unfiltered fear.

That a mere five days ago, I had confirmed who the Godmother really was. That I had unwittingly become a part of something revolting—something that would be the end of my career, of my life as I knew it, if I didn't soon figure out how to wriggle free of its grasp.

"I'll deal with her," I managed to croak out. Ada was innocent in all of this—the less she knew, the better. She could still have a future in politics if this all went belly up. "Thanks, Ada. Talk soon."

I slowly hung up my phone, feeling the panic attack beginning to crackle through my body like popcorn in my veins.

I needed to clear my head before I met with Daniela. I needed to be on the straight and narrow when I confessed to her.

To the only person I could trust to save my skin.

* * *

I tried to momentarily distract myself from the life-or-death importance of the meeting with Daniela by thinking about the other thing burning a hole in my gut. The small little matter of the impending arrival of my brother.

So, I decided to go for a run.

I glanced at my Apple Watch as I traversed the lush loop that circled the back end of my property, bordering on the edge of Sky Meadows State Park. I was on track to crush my best 5k time by a good amount. I covered ground more quickly when I had something to divert my attention—something other than the chattering of *Pod Saves America* or the blaring electronic stylings of CHVRCHES and Marshmello that I usually had flooding my AirPods. This time, my mind was projecting a double feature of worry. First up: how would I break the ice with Cillian?

What would I even talk to him about? The last two times we had done this dance, I barely knew anything about his life. I knew even less now.

He still blamed me for Audrey's tragedy. Still. Eight years later. He never said so, but he didn't have to—his silence, and the way he would look at me the once-in-a-blue-moon times we did see one another, spoke for him. Assuming I was able to extricate myself from this mess with the Godmother, I was still planning on running for Governor. After all, I had worked my ass off to get to this position. I deserved it. And for that? I would need Cillian to shut up and stay quiet.

Calm down, asshole. One thing at a time.

Quickening my pace, my five-toed running shoes squelched in the wet muck. It had poured last night, so it was muddier than an alligator's private parts. These shoes were going to be ruined after this—but that's okay. I had five more pairs in my closet.

I was approaching the predetermined meet point, where the edge of my property intersected with one of the Park's hiking trails—a beautiful scenic overlook that gave a hawk's eye view of the eastern slopes of the Blue Ridge. Yesterday, I called Daniela on a prepaid phone I bought from a gas station. Given what I had learned, I had to assume that my three cells were being monitored by the Godmother and her cronies. Everyone whines about the NSA, but it's private security contractors that people should really be afraid of—they have zero oversight and absolutely no accountability to anything or anyone. And the Godmother's people certainly fit that bill. And then some.

I had kept things vague enough to protect both of us in case Daniela's phone records were eventually subpoenaed but tantalizing enough to get her to fly down from New York. If politics had taught me one thing, it was how to lay bait for singularly minded, driven go-getters. And Daniela was definitely that.

At the precipice of the overlook, I came to a panting halt. My exercise-induced asthma flared even more in the crisp autumn air. I raised my hands to the top of my head, trying to flood some oxygen into my lungs as I took in the vista below. I challenge anyone who doesn't believe in God to come to Virginia and look at the Blue Ridge. No chance that something like that is explained solely by tectonic shifts in the ground. Something this exquisite? It's painted by the brush of a presence not fully explainable by human logic.

It was when I hit the stop button on my Nike Run Club app that I heard her voice.

"Next time, you should pick a better meeting place. This view fucking sucks."

Her smile dripping with sarcasm, Daniela Langer joined me at the overlook's edge. Her cuts-through-glass New York accent always made me chuckle. The underlying abrasiveness of her. The way she spoke, her heterochromia, and her biracial heritage had made her stick out while we were undergrads at the University of Virginia. We became fast friends after she brought her homemade Mofongo to a potluck dinner for the Entrepreneurship Club, a secret recipe that had been passed down for generations on her father's side. It had been a while since we had seen each other in the flesh, but we swapped the occasional email here and there. The *New York Times* was lucky to have her. Every newspaper worth its salt needs a bulldog for an investigative journalist. Especially when that bulldog has been nominated for a Pulitzer for going toe-to-toe against gargoyles like the Klan.

"Want me to get those for you?" I pointed at the still-on store tags dangling out from the neckline of her brand-new running ensemble.

"Absolutely not—I'm returning them the second this meeting is over."

"I doubt the store will take back your sweat-stained clothes, Daniela."

"If you complain loudly enough, anyone will take anything back."

"I had forgotten how good you are with people."

Daniela shielded her eyes from the sun as she approached me. "I doubt you called me up here to preach retail return policy to me."

She always knew how to cut right to the chase.

"Remember when we talked about the number of active hate groups in Virginia?"

"Yeah?"

"There's another one to add to that list."

She straightened up, curiosity piqued. "What makes you say that?"

I slowly met her gaze for the first time. "Because their leader is bankrolling my run for Governor."

* * *

I cool-down jogged back towards my property, in no real hurry as my conversation with Daniela replayed in my ears. I had told her the few things I had been able to find out about the Godmother's organization—that they weren't anything like your "typical" white nationalist organization.

Instead of angry, neck-bearded yahoos, they were polished, high-powered, and even higher-moneyed titans of industry. They were slowly and secretly subverting the government of Virginia with their checkbooks. They had been poisoning the well for years. They had been slowly tilting a portion of the state in a direction that was so grotesque I could barely bring myself to believe it. Charlottesville in 2017 was no one-off. Worse things *were* coming.

The Organization had dozens of elected officials in their pocket—local councilmen, local election officials, congressmen, state senators—and now, with me, they were making a play for the Governor's Mansion. Some of these officials were true believers, fanatics for the cause. Others were like me—dumb, ignorant saps who didn't realize who they were dealing with until it was too late. Saps that The Organization had dirt on—skeletons in the closet that, if brought to light, would end them—and thus, were blackmailed into silence.

I refused to become a casualty in that way.

I picked up my jog into a half-speed run.

Even though I couldn't yet tell Daniela just how I came about the USB drive I gave her, nor about how they were holding the sordid Audrey business over my head as collateral, it felt good to unload what I could share—flush out the parasites that had been gnawing away at my soul. Daniela, given that this wasn't her first rodeo, pointed out to me that, even though she believed me, none of this was enough yet. That, if we published now, we'd get buried in a mountain of libel lawsuits, and our careers would be over faster than you could say 'boo.' That we needed concrete, indisputable evidence that ties *directly* back to the Godmother. That we needed to nail her to the wall and not leave any chance of her being able to wriggle free. She also pointed out to me that, no matter what I did, I might be charged as an accessory at the end of all of this. She wasn't a lawyer, but...I had already taken their dirty seed money, after all.

Fuck.

I increased my speed once more.

Daniela laid it out for me: we would build a case together. Slowly. Methodically. I would operate as originally planned—allowing the Godmother to steer my campaign. But I would be acting as an inside man, slowly infiltrating her Organization. I would document all their illicit activities and pass them on to Daniela. Once we had gathered a comprehensive file on just how deep their roots ran, then—and only then—would she publish.

You can do so much more damage from the inside, Christopher. Think about it.

It was easy for her to say that.

She wasn't the one who had to dine and drink with the devil.

She wasn't the one risking life and limb.

Double fuck.

I was in an all-out sprint now, shoes slapping, fallen leaves kicking up clouds of brown and orange.

In.

Out.

In.

Out.

In.

Out.

My breath slowly drained out the bottom of my lungs. I kept going, redlining my inner odometer.

In.

Out.

In.

Out.

In.

Out.

I was starting to see spots. I could end it all here. Save everyone the trouble.

In.

Out.

In.

Out.

In.

Out.

Just as the spots threatened to turn my eyeballs into a permanent kaleidoscope, I ran smack into a low-hanging branch, knocking me to the ground, forcing me to catch my breath.

Not today.

I barely felt the vomit and bile exploding out of my mouth as I came back to reality.

Get. Your. Shit. Together.

I wiped my mouth and slowly stood up, getting my bearings. I had made it to my backyard.

It'll be fine. I just need a shower, a shave, and a drink. Multiple drinks. I could even call up a local lady friend. I still had some time before he got here.

But as I circled around the back of the cabin towards the front door, I saw Cillian's truck cresting over the top of the long driveway.

My brother was early.

Chapter Three

Cillian

Every time I see that fake-as-a-three-dollar-bill smile on his face, I want to take a currycomb brush soaked in bleach and scrub it right off him.

I knew underneath that smirk of his was fury—he *hated* when people didn't show up exactly when they said they would. He always had his days planned out to the millisecond. So I showed up three hours early. Just to fuck with him.

As I pulled the truck in front of the garage and Christopher did his best 1950s sitcom-waving impression of "welcome to the neighborhood," I considered just doing it. Right here, right now. I thought about how easy it would be to roll down the window, whip out the Bersa, blow his head to kingdom come, and drive off.

Stop it. You have a plan. You have to wait for the right moment. Even if it takes longer than you want.

I looked back at Shepard, who was standing at attention, nose pressed up against the glass of the back window while his tail swished back and forth. For some inexplicable reason, Shepard liked Christopher. I thought dogs were supposed to be able to tell when someone was good or not. Or, at the very least, when they have a soul. But I guess when someone makes a habit of greeting a dog with bacon bits—even if they've only met a handful of times—that person will linger in that dog's memory and make them lose their moral compass. Or all sense of…well, sense.

Sure enough, when I pulled open the backdoor, Shepard tumbled out and made a beeline for Christopher, who crouched down with his arms outstretched wide.

"There's my buddy! There he is." I hate when people talk to animals and babies in that high-pitched, whiny voice that sounds more like a radio frequency than a human.

I stepped out of the driver's seat. Shepard and I were still damp from the storm back at Jeremy's Run. I rounded my truck to where Christopher and my Judas of a dog were, my heartbeat thundering through my rib cage like a metronome hooked up to an amplifier.

We locked eyes.

Fuck me. Biding my time is going to be harder than I thought.

Finally, my brother stood up, breaking the silence.

"The two of you are soaked! What'd you do, walk through hell while Satan was taking a shower?"

"Nah. He knew I was on my way to meet you."

And the dance begins.

"You're early."

"I thought we said five?" I lied.

"Eight."

"Oh. I can come back."

There was that billboard-worthy smile of his again. "Don't be silly. I just wish I had known. Still had some preparations to make." Christopher pointed at Shepard, who was expectantly sniffing around the pockets of his running attire. "I could have fried something up for our friend."

"He'll be fine."

"Daddy always said bacon makes a dog's coat shiny."

"How many beers in would he be when he said that?"

"That doesn't make it false."

"Shep'll survive."

"Surviving and living are two different things, Brother."

"Don't I know it, Brother."

A roll of thunder rumbled in the distance. The storm that I had already weathered was rapidly approaching us. But that was nothing compared to the agitated, low moan that shook loose from Shepard as he continued to search for something edible in Christopher's pockets. I did my best to prevent a grin from tugging at the corner of my lips. I knew that sound, and I knew what would come soon after that sound if he wasn't placated.

Just needed to buy some time.

"Will Bonnie be joining us for these few days?" I knew full well that he and Bonnie had split about a year back, but it had been long enough since we had seen one another that I could reasonably claim that I didn't.

A flicker of something—maybe sadness, maybe relief—tore into the phony mask that Christopher was currently wearing. "No. I'm afraid that she and I aren't together anymore."

"Oh. Shame. You normally have such a good eye for people."

Wrath crinkled the corners of my brother's eyes. It wouldn't be perceptible to anyone else but me, but I knew what to look for. I knew what he was imagining doing to me at that moment. Problem is, he needed me. And I needed to keep him on the tit just long enough to be rid of him forever. So, we were at a stalemate. Until one of us decided to blink first.

And that sure as shit wasn't going to be me.

The thunder got louder, along with Shepard's irritation.

Christopher motioned at the cabin. "We should probably get inside. Rain's about to hit."

I looked at Shepard, recognizing the glint in his eye.

Any second now.

I nodded in agreement. "Yeah. It's a real frog strangler." I mirrored his beckoning to the front door. "After you."

Just as Christopher tried to pick up and move, Shepard pinned his front leg on Christopher's right foot, lifted his hind leg, and did what any reasonable animal would do in this situation. I could barely stifle my snickering as Christopher shouted out and recoiled in disgust as he shook himself loose from Shepard's iron grip and propulsive stream of urine.

"What the fuck?!" bellowed my brother. Shepard did his best John Wayne impression as he sidled back over to me, swinging his hips domineeringly.

"Sorry, Brother. I don't know what got into him," I feigned innocently.

Shepard sat down next to me at attention and licked his chops, knowing full well what he did and not caring one bit.

Looks like Judas was on my side after all.

* * *

While Christopher showered off Shepard's piss, I ambled around the cabin, taking stock of my brother's palace. I barely recognized anything I saw—things had changed quite a bit since I was here last. Designer furniture, wallpaper, and rugs that probably cost more than my entire house back in Kentucky. I barely knew my brother anymore, but even I knew this décor wasn't suitable for him. Not representative of where he came from. Where *we* came from. This chichi shit—stuff that he had clearly spent a small fortune on to try and give the property a clean slate after what had gone down—was to impress a crowd of people that was never going to pick up what he was putting down. No matter how high in government he rose, he was always going to be seen as poor white trash made good—a cancer in this neck of the woods if there ever was one. I almost felt sorry for him.

Almost.

I drained the last of my coffee that Christopher had insisted on pouring for me and set the empty mug on his expensive-looking coffee table. No coaster. Because fuck him. He had spent about two minutes explaining to me that it was some specially imported blend of Colombian beans. Or maybe he said Arabica. I couldn't remember. About five seconds in, I had turned off my ears. Putting down the mug with no coaster seemed a fair punishment. The coffee was delicious, though. I'll say that much.

Shepard's buzz saw snoring made me snap back to my surroundings. Stepping over my beached whale of a dog, I looked outside through the living room's new, larger-than-necessary bay window. The storm was shifting between two gears: raining so hard that it made the whole house sound like a rock drummer hopped up on cocaine and a slow drizzle that looked like a movie star trying to cry their way to an Academy Award. It seemed God couldn't decide whether or not he wanted to wipe us clean off the earth, washing away the mistakes he made when creating us.

I heard the shower shut off and the curtain rings grind against the rod as Christopher finally stepped out. I checked my watch—it had been thirty minutes since he had gone into the bathroom. I have never met a man who takes as long in the shower as he does.

The bathroom door burst open as a freshly changed Christopher stepped out, steam billowing out behind him.

"Woo boy. Nothing better than a long, hot shower. You want in?" He hooked his thumb behind him.

Yeah, there's definitely hot water left after that Greek tragedy of a shower. Dickhead.

"I'm fine."

"Are you sure? Don't want to spritz the horse smell off you?"

"I didn't think I smelled."

"It lingers."

I clenched my jaw. "That smell is in my blood, Brother. No chance of getting it out now."

"Anything is fixable if you try hard enough, Brother."

"Didn't realize I needed to be fixed."

Choosing not to respond, Christopher pointed at my coffee mug.

"More coffee?"

I snatched it up before he could get to it. It delighted me to see that a faint ring line had been left on his precious table. "I'll get it myself."

I strode over to the galley kitchen that had been renovated just enough that he could claim it was a "chef's kitchen" and poured myself another cup out of the stainless-steel pot. Trying to look anywhere but at my brother, I intently studied the murky liquid that was steaming out of my porcelain mug.

"I was thinking I'd fix us some dinner here in a bit. How do you feel about

steak tartare? I got the recipe from this restaurant on the Hill that I go to..."
Once again, I tuned out Christopher's voice as he rambled on, changing the
channel in my brain to something else.

Anything else.

I looked up from the coffee through the small kitchen window. God had
downshifted the weather into second gear for a beat, so I could see into the
backyard.

And that's when I noticed it.

The Red Maple where my beloved's body had swung in the wind.

*The bastard told me he was going to cut it down. He promised me that he was
going to chop it into mulch-sized pieces. And, like an idiot, I had believed him.*

My hands shook as my fist curled around the mug like the Ouroboros.

*He changed everything else about this fucking house, but he couldn't be bothered
to change the one thing that actually needed to go?*

Tighter.

And tighter.

And tighter.

When I kill him, I'm going to make it slow. And painful.

"What the hell are you doing?!" Christopher yelled at me.

I looked down at my right hand. My grip had cracked the mug down to
bits and gashed open my palm. Not deep enough to warrant a trip to the
hospital, but deep enough that it wasn't nothing.

I let my blood drip down onto Christopher's hardwood floor, making no
attempt to stop my DNA from sullying it.

"Jesus, Cillian!" He practically shoved me into the sink and under the cold,
running tap water before dropping to his knees in a vain attempt to prevent
my blood from forever soiling his domain.

As the frigid water slowly brought me back down to earth, I set my jaw,
reigning myself in. It took a minute before I could bring myself to speak. "I
need to lie down."

And with that, I spiked the shards of mug into the trash, wrapped my hand
in a towel, and strode into the guest bedroom, slamming the door behind
me.

Christopher's raw meat would just have to wait.

**

The sound of tightening rope woke me up from my nightmare with a jolt.

I lurched up out of the guest bedroom's bed, my forehead dripping in the sweat of fear.

There's nothing on this green earth that I wouldn't do to cut that memory out of my head.

I checked my watch. There was still some dried blood on the strap from before, and the old towel I had used to wrap my wound was now permanently red. It was a little after 1 AM, and the cabin was wrapped in a misty film of darkness. I rubbed my temples, trying desperately to stop them from pounding.

After the earlier incident in the kitchen, I hadn't gotten out of this bed, save for one time when I heard Shepard scratching at the door. Shepard got rather insistent when a door wasn't opened for him immediately. Now, he was curled up against the radiator, claiming all the heat for himself. I think in a previous life, he was a tyrant prince. Or maybe a Hollywood producer. From what I hear, they're two sides of the same coin.

I swung my legs horizontally over the bed frame, touching my bare feet down on the floor. Unlike the rest of the house, the guest bedroom flooring was the cheap, laminate stuff that only appeared like it was wood. I guess Christopher chose to cut corners in a place he knew most people wouldn't see. I'd say there was a metaphor of some kind in that.

I ran my tongue over my cracked, dry lips. They, along with my parched throat, needed to be satiated. Oxycontin tends to make me thirstier than an alcoholic at a brewery.

I would need to step foot outside my stronghold.

I slowly opened my door and tip-toed out into the living room, taking great care not to make any noise that could potentially rouse my brother. I didn't want to have to see his smug face again until morning.

I peeked at the crack beneath his door frame. No light emanating from within, far as I could tell. I pressed my ear lightly against his door. I could hear the faint sounds of his snoring interlaced with his noise machine that concocted sounds of a babbling brook streaming through a forest.

Sleep tight, asshole.

I padded to the kitchen and poured myself a glass of water, taking care not to look out the window at the thing that had taken a buzz saw to my nerves in the first place. I drained the glass and repeated the process. As I felt the ice-cold liquid sliding down inside my chest, I recognized something else creeping in the back door of my brain: doubt.

Once I did what I came here to do, there was no going back from it. My brother's death wouldn't go unnoticed. And I would be the prime suspect unless I executed everything perfectly. But if I missed one thing, slipped up on one point? I would be trading my own life for his. It's not like I had experience doing this, after all.

And for murdering a high-profile Virginia politician? Life in prison. Was that a risk I was willing to take?

As I feebly tried to extinguish the bonfire in my brain, I noticed, for the first time, my brother's fridge. Unlike everything else in this godforsaken place, it looked like someone with a soul had decorated it. It was covered with photos, as well as a few quirky magnets. One in particular caught my eye. It was the head of a bear—mouth wide open, baring its teeth—that had been fashioned into a bottle opener. Underneath the head was the catchphrase in all caps: BEAR WITH ME WHILE I OPEN THIS BEER.

I couldn't help it. That made me chuckle.

My eyes cycled through the photos. Most of them were of Christopher shaking hands with various state and federal government figures. I recognized a few. There were a couple with Dad, and then a couple more with some of Christopher's college buddies that I vaguely remembered. The type of guys who were no doubt still caught up talking about the good ol' days—save for the geeky-looking one on the far right. That was the tech wiz that hit it big with Christopher's initial backing. The guy that paid for everything in this house.

But it wasn't them that caught my attention.

32

In the top left corner, so small and faded that if you blinked, you'd miss it, was a picture of us. We were about eight years old, arms wrapped around each other as we cheesed in front of Funland, the small outdoor amusement park on the boardwalk in Rehoboth Beach. My front two teeth were missing. His too.

I pulled off the photo to get a closer look. Mama loved Rehoboth. We went there all the time before she passed. I remembered Funland. It was one of the few memories I had left of my early childhood—the times before Christopher and I grew apart. I remembered us smashing into each other with bumper cars, laughing up a storm, and then getting frozen custard where the cones had enough sugar in them to last us a week.

One time, we waited in line for nearly a half-hour for one of those delicious treats, and when we finally got them, a neighborhood bully I had some tussles with came up and knocked the cone out of my hand. Christopher, in solidarity, didn't eat his either. But that was mainly because he jammed it on top of the bully's head before giving him a shiner. After the bully staggered away, he helped me up and told me that 'brothers looked after brothers.'

For a split second, I wondered if my face would ever again carry the unadulterated delight that photo captured. Or if either of us would tell the other something like that again. But then I realized all that was a distant memory—something that could never be reclaimed.

No matter how hard I tried.

There was no chance of my going back to sleep now. So, I quietly unlocked the front door and let myself out.

It was time for a walk in the night.

***

Walking at night relaxes me more than it probably should. There's something oddly freeing about not being able to see more than a few feet in front of you. You're completely surrendering everything over to the universe and its twisted sense of humor. The ultimate roll of the dice in this bullshit game of craps that we call life.

It was completely clear overhead now—the storm had passed, leaving the kind of cloudless night where the moon is shining so bright it's practically burning a hole in the sky. It was the kind of moon where, as a boy, I'd climb the tallest tree all the way to the top just to get a look at it and pretend I was Jimmy Stewart about to lasso it down.

I wasn't a boy anymore.

He had probably planted that photo there in preparation for me coming. There's no way a guy like him would hang onto that photo for any other reason...right?

I tried to remember if I had ever seen it before. I honestly couldn't recall—I had done everything in my power to erase my memories of this place, like an addict flushing all his drugs down the toilet.

Stop it. Don't let him win. Manipulating people to get what he wants is his profession. He doesn't deserve to come out of this unscathed. He doesn't deserve to come out of anything unscathed.

I needed to shut the fuck up and listen to what my brain was trying to tell me. Drown out what my heart, the foolhardiest part of me, was attempting to get me to believe. The part of me that had prevented me from carrying out my plan of retribution all these years. The part of me that secretly wished my brother would accept some sort of responsibility for what had happened with Audrey—so that we—my brother and I—could perhaps, maybe, find some sort of common ground again. A truce.

I stopped and looked around, getting my bearings, not exactly sure how long I had been walking. I did know it was just a straight shot back to the cabin, though, and I knew I was high up on a mountain. Off the proverbial beaten path—hell, I'd gotten to the point where trails were but a distant memory.

Which made it weird that I saw a fresh set of hoof prints in the mud in front of me.

Frowning, I crouched down to get a better look. The indentation marks were light, which meant two things: the horse didn't have a rider, and it wasn't shod. No one would be riding up here in the night, anyway. It had probably jumped its fence. A runaway. An animal that was looking for a way out of its circumstances by any means necessary.

I followed the tracks to see where they led, only to find they dead-ended in an open grassy plateau. I let out a series of low whistles, trying on the off chance that I could lure the horse out of hiding. No luck. As I wet my lips to try again, I stopped myself short.

Why would I want to stop this horse from achieving what it really wanted? Horses are herd animals—they don't run off unless the life they've been living is so awful that braving it alone in the wilderness seems like the only possible alternative.

I chuckled ruefully as it suddenly occurred to me—this horse had the stones to do the thing that I had been too chicken to do all these years. The burn-all-of-your-bridges battle charge was the only thing that would actually give me what I wanted: some sort of finality, maybe resolution.

I needed to take a page out of this horse's book—hop the wall that had been boxing me in and gallop off into the night. Untethered by doubt.

I turned heel and practically double-timed back to the cabin.

I had failed to protect my beloved from him. I had been the ultimate coward.

But now? I was going to make him pay. For all of it.

I got back to the cabin in what felt like no time at all.

Then I saw that the front door was wide open.

And that my brother's corpse was splayed on the steps, his brains splattered all over the front porch.

Someone had beaten me to it.

Chapter Four

Christopher

God, my brother had such a penchant for theatrics.

fter he had cut himself open like he was in a horror movie and then stormed off to his bedroom, I knew I wasn't going to see him for the rest of the evening. Looks like the conversation that we were both dreading would have to wait until the morning. I really wanted to do it nice this time—even make us a meal. Pretend that we were civilized. But you can't cook a chicken that doesn't want to be plucked.

I carefully extracted Cillian's red poison from my brand-new floor with baking soda and white vinegar. That would be at least one thing the bastard wouldn't be able to ruin. I looked up from my handiwork to see Shepard staring at me, his brown eyes trained on me like an assassin. A hungry assassin.

"You peed on me. You don't get anything from me now. That's not how it works." Shepard simply licked his chops and laid down in front of me, head tucked on top of his folded paws. I couldn't help but chuckle at him. If I ever had kids, I was doomed.

Kids. Cillian never understood how desperately I wanted to be a father.

Not wanting to go down that road, I bopped Shepard's nose. He bared his teeth, but in a playful way that dogs do when they want you to do it more.

"I guess both of us have got to eat something, right?" I reached into the fridge and pulled out the steak I had salted and left covered for a couple of hours in preparation. Shepard had gotten gray around his eyes and snout since I saw him last. And I had no idea when—or if—I'd ever see him again. So why not spoil him a little? I slapped the steak on the counter, along with the other tools and ingredients that I'd need for the tartare: a sharp knife, olive oil, salt, pepper, shallots, capers, eggs, and ciabatta bread.

My life was going to shit in basically every single capacity. But damn it, I was going to make a meal. And I was going to enjoy it.

As I went over to the sink to rinse off the steak, I glanced at the Red Maple out back. The place where the police had cut down Audrey's limp, swinging-in-the-wind body. I knew that was what had set off Cillian—I'm not an idiot. But I didn't care. You can't just get rid of things that trigger you. You don't grow and improve as a person that way. You learn to face them head-on, expose yourself to them until they no longer bother you. In time, Cillian would understand that. Maybe even realize that I was trying to do him a favor. Or appreciate the lengths—and great expense—that Ada and I had gone to pay off and blackmail the right people in the right places to make the whole issue go gently into that good night.

But I wouldn't hold my breath.

I started trimming off the large tendons and pieces of fat from the steak. Normally, those are my favorite parts of a steak, but for a tartare, they are meaningless. You need to get to the heart of the meat—the lean center—and strip away all the excess. There's a good life axiom in there somewhere. But I was too focused to search for it.

It was Audrey who had first got me interested in cooking. She showed me how to make some of the dishes I still make today. She introduced me to Gordon Ramsay. We laughed together as he yelled at the idiots on *Kitchen Nightmares* while we drank Pinot Noir she had stolen from her father's walk-in wine cellar. He was the kind of guy who would buy several cases of expensive vintages during a visit to a winery and then forget he had them until ten years later. So, he never caught her.

Something that Cillian always seems to conveniently forget is that Audrey and I were friends. And not just because she was dating my brother. We really enjoyed each other's company. It crushed me when, out of jealousy, Cillian told her that he didn't want us to see each other anymore. It had been completely platonic, mind you—it was just nice to have someone in my life who wasn't a meathead ex-football player or an overachieving former beauty queen vying for my affection.

What we had was magical. And then we were nothing.

All the fat now trimmed, I started dicing the meat by hand. It was easier to do it with an electric grinder, but I enjoyed the challenge. The texture and taste felt different when you went the extra mile—like you had really earned it. As I sliced, my Henckel knife gleamed in the spotlight from the atmospheric mid-century overhead light fixture.

I was destroyed when Audrey passed, like someone had popped a hole in my back tire while I was driving through the desert, leaving me to rot in the hot sun for good. But, unlike my brother, I didn't give in to that feeling. Instead of running off to Kentucky like Cillian did, I did everything in my power to stay the course. I pushed my proverbial wreck of a car, with every ounce of force remaining in my body, until I got to a service station—a therapist. I got myself fixed up. I moved forward. The therapist was nice. Her office smelled like lavender. Of course, when I was all straightened out, I paid her off to destroy any records of my being there. Ada watched her do it—and wouldn't leave her office until the last page had been shredded. Voters will forgive a lot of things—screwing hookers, sketchy tax evasion schemes, and sexist diatribes—but God forbid you ever admit you were depressed.

I diced with more intensity. My knife was practically humming it was moving so fast.

You didn't know her like I did. She confided in me about how controlling you could be. How she didn't feel like she mattered as much to you as the damn horses. She wasn't the one who was—

FUCKING SHIT!

I had nearly cut off my damn finger—blood was shooting out of my pointer faster than a boy losing his virginity. It flooded through the meat, turning it from a warm pink to a deep crimson.

What a surprise. Something else ruined.

* * *

I love the sound that a square ice cube makes when it's in a rocks glass. That clinking it makes as you tip back your drink? It's the opening movement of a beautiful symphony.

After draining the last gulp of John J. Bowman Single Barrel bourbon from my Waterford Double Old-Fashioned glass, I looked over to the bar cart positioned in the corner of my office.

The orchestra was waiting for its conductor.

After ruining my feast, I had thrown together some breakfast-for-dinner munchies for Shepard and me. He wolfed it down in about two seconds flat and then abruptly ditched me to go to Cillian's room. No matter how hard I tried with that dog, his allegiances never changed. All I was to him was a glorified vending machine. He was smarter than I gave him credit for, I guess, because I fell for it every time.

I had retired to my office for a drink or five. Bonnie had thought I drank too much. As a result, I had soundproofed the entire room, so she couldn't hear when I was throwing a few back. I figured that was the considerate thing to do. I used to love going to bars. Not the classy cocktail establishments that I would occasionally go to now for dinner and drinks with fellow politicians. I'm talking about the down-home saloons where the floor is sticky, and all they serve is Jim Beam and PBR. I enjoyed the atmosphere, the harmless flirting with the denim-clad lady bartenders, the camaraderie with the fellow barflies. The folks who would stomp the mud off their boots before rubbing shoulders with one another. But I had to retire from that scene once I got into politics. It's funny, isn't it? Once you enter the public life, everything else about you has to become private.

I finished pouring number three and settled back into my Eames chair. I used to only drink Tennessee whiskey—I practically peed Jack Daniels when I was younger. But I had learned my lesson about that—successful politicians only drink local product. Directly at eye level across from me, hung up on the wood-paneled walls, was a framed print of Ernest Hemingway. The crazy bastard was pointing a gun directly at camera, one eye closed as he took aim at someone's chest.

Believe me, Ernie. I feel you. More than you can imagine.

As I sipped the beautifully potent Virginia-distilled liquor, I couldn't help but burst out into a rueful fit of laughter.

What a mess.

As if on cue, I felt the side table next to me vibrate. All the color drained from my face. It was her. The Godmother. Calling the phone that, when she first gave it to me, she'd deadpan dubbed "the Batphone." I don't think she was joking at all.

I took a deep breath as Daniela's words rang in my head. I couldn't dodge her anymore—I had to resume business as usual. Even if that business made me want to hurl.

I answered on the last ring. "Ms. Fisker, ma'am, how are you this evening?"

Her soft, carefully demure voice practically purred through the receiver. She brought new meaning to the phrase "speak softly and carry a big stick." I don't think I'd ever heard her raise her voice once—but she never needed to.

"I've been trying to reach you. Are you aware of how many times I've called you?"

"I'm not exactly sure—"

"This is the eleventh time."

"I deeply apologize, ma'am. No excuses. It won't happen again." I knew she didn't like bullshit, so I always tried to be upfront with her. I nearly choked on the irony of it all—her requesting that I always be honest with her when she had done anything but with me.

There was a long silence on the other end of the phone. "Fine," she finally uttered. "I should hope not."

I could hear the faint spark of her lighting up a cigarette. She smoked using one of those long, bone-white ivory cigarette holders. There was something simultaneously elegant yet unsettling about someone who engaged in a vice like tobacco but didn't want to get her hands dirty. "All is forgiven."

"Thank you, ma'am."

I heard her sigh. "Whenever you call me ma'am, I feel as though you're adding about ten years of dark circles under my eyes. If you're not careful, you're going to make me look like an old bloodhound."

I needed to lightly flirt with her. That was our dynamic before, and I needed to keep up appearances to maintain my cover. "Well, the wisdom of years has only honed your beauty."

There was her sing-song burble of laughter. "I'm in your neck of the woods. There's someone I want you to meet."

"Who?"

"Someone good to know."

"What about my brother?"

"Is he a baby in a locked car?"

"Well, no—"

"Then I think he'll keep, don't you?" It wasn't a question.

"Of course. Where are you?"

"You know The Ashby?"

I checked my watch. It was half past 10.

"Sure. But they're closed now."

"They'll open it for me."

I couldn't help but laugh. There was nothing I could do to escape her. "Why doesn't that surprise me?"

She took another long drag of her cigarette. "I think nothing about me should surprise you at this point, Congressman."

My heart dropped into my scrotum as I tried to interpret what the fuck that oblique statement meant. Whether or not she knew that I was on to her. Whether or not I was on the edge of a precipice.

Breathe, damn it. One step at a time.

"Don't you dare tease me, Anika. I'm on my way." I hung up the phone and looked over to my drink.

My ice cube had completely melted.

* * *

When I got to the Ashby, the high-class yet rustic bar area was completely vacant, save for her. The first thing I saw was the back of her white pantsuit—the only pop of light in the otherwise dimly lit, mahogany-ensconced room. Her get-up looked like it cost more than a car. And it probably did—every time I saw the Godmother, she was wearing something different, and then I never saw it again. I never understood that aspect about ladies' fashion—that if you wore it once, it was somehow radioactive and couldn't rest on your body again. Then again, there was…a lot I didn't understand about humankind's superior gender.

She was drinking her usual, a White Lady—a gin cocktail for which she would order just the ingredients, specifying measurements as precise as the edge of a protractor, and then make it herself wherever she was sitting. The attending server or bartender would always make a stink face when she did that, and then, at the end of the night, when she tipped them 80% of the total bill amount, they would fall all over themselves to smooch her backside.

But tonight? It looked like the Devil in a New Dress would be stirring my drinks, too.

Steadying myself, I took a deep breath, my heartbeat practically rattling in my ribs. I had to remember my purpose. Why I was here. Why I was doing what I was doing.

You lie for a living. You can do this.

I broke out my best campaign grin. "Of all the gin joints," I said as I slid onto the stool next to her.

She smiled as she turned to face me, locking onto me with her Alaskan wolf-gray eyes. I swear she could make a man go into cardiac arrest with those things. "One of these days, you're going to have to come up with an original opening line."

"Classics never go out of style."

She arched her eyebrow playfully. "I won't argue with that."

I took her in. She was practically a Roman statue come to life. Perfect symmetry, immaculate bone structure, and toned muscles. Once, I asked her what she did to make her face so unblemished and pure. She just laughed at me. I didn't realize I was being funny—I use three facial products a day, and my complexion had never even come close to looking like hers.

It was her voice, though, that always threw me for a loop. Before the Godmother, I had never met someone who had no discernible accent or faint traces of regionalism of any kind. It was almost as if she was a machine that had Googled what a human should sound like and adopted those characteristics. And the softness—I had never heard her raise her voice once. The volume was just a few notches above a whisper, yet you could hear it for miles.

"You changed your hair." I motioned at her jet-black, freshly bobbed hair.

"Do you like it?"

"You looked fantastic as a blonde. You look even better like this."

"Oh, good. I wouldn't want to do something you didn't approve of." She stared at me icily for a moment before allowing a half-smile to crest across her lips. I had to teach myself not to soil myself whenever she did that. It wasn't easy.

She rose and strode behind the bar. Without asking, she reached for the Old Rip Van Winkle 10-year-old and poured me a glass. A bottle of that stuff usually went for about $1,000.

She reached into her handbag and removed her vintage Hermes cigarette case. Out came that ridiculous bone ivory holder of hers with a cancer stick to match. I automatically reached into my pocket to grab the Zippo lighter I kept on hand specifically—and only—for my meetings with her. She nodded her thanks as I lit her up.

Gazing at me for an excruciatingly long time, she sized me up in a way that would make Clint Eastwood blush. She was doing her best Theia impression—examining the lights within my soul, debating on whether she should keep them going or extinguish them for good.

Deep breath. Drink your bourbon.

Stay.

Calm.

Finally, after taking a drag that would have decimated the lungs of the Marlboro Man, she broke the silence. "I've picked a campaign manager for you."

I had to stop myself from emitting an audible sigh of relief.

She didn't know. She wouldn't be talking strategy with me if she did. "Ada told me I still had some time to select a candidate."

"You lost the right of choice when I couldn't reach you."

"Is that who you're having me meet tonight?" I asked.

"You're talking to her right now."

I raised my eyebrow. I couldn't help but be intrigued. "Is that right?"

"Of course, we'll hire someone to be the public face for the cameras, but he'll just be an extension of my reach."

"Why is it that you're so camera shy, Anika? You certainly have the face for it."

There was Dirty Harry again, murdering me multiple times over as she exhaled smoke like Drogon. Finally, she allowed herself a smile and flicked her ashes into an empty glass. "Do you remember our first meeting, Congressman?"

I uneasily shifted in my stool. "Of course. It was at the party Zander and I threw after we took his company public."

The Godmother nodded. "I was invited by a friend. I had only intended on making a brief appearance out of respect, but then I saw this handsome young man working the room with an aplomb that immediately caught my eye. He was charming yet commanding, knew exactly how long to talk with someone and what conversational buttons to push to make them feel like they were the only ones that mattered—and want to pull out their checkbooks. It was a masterclass in fundraising gladhanding—raw talent that most of the political figures I work with could never even come close to achieving, even with all the training in the world. I watched this young man for close to an hour…and then he barreled towards me like a heat-seeking missile."

I flashed a grimace that, to the untrained eye, would look like a genuine smile. "I know money when it enters a room."

If only I had known what she actually was.

"You also wanted to fuck me."

I cleared my throat and nervously chuckled. She wasn't wrong, mind you—it was just a bit unnerving to hear it so plainly stated.

"You needn't be embarrassed, Congressman," she continued. "I found it flattering. But there wasn't any world where I was going to let that happen. A dalliance like that would present too many potential liabilities for my business. But after we got to talking, it became clear to me that you were a star in the making. Someone who wasn't going to be happy with just working behind the scenes at a tech company. Someone who had...limitless potential."

Queasiness started to coat the inside of my stomach. "You were the first one to encourage me to run for office besides my Daddy. Told me that when the time came for something bigger, to give you a call."

There was that deeply unsettling half-smile of hers again. "And the rest is history."

Self-loathing pinpricking my spine, I cranked up the wattage of my phony smile to match hers. Revisiting our origin story made it even more clear that the Godmother had played me perfectly. She had immediately recognized the cavernous well of ambition and greed living inside me, knew that my moral fortitude could be manipulated. That if she dangled the carrot of prestige, power, and prominence, I would take the bait faster than a starving mule. She hadn't put a gun to my head—all she did was give me the tiniest of nudges. And this entire situation I now found myself in? It was all a disaster of my own making.

The thick silence sat there for an excruciating moment like an uninvited house guest before the Godmother finally broke it with another probing question.

"Do you play chess, Congressman?"

"I always preferred checkers," I said in an attempt at levity. It didn't take.

"My father taught me to play when I was five. At first, it was just a lark—a way to commune with the old man. Eventually, it became more than just a pastime. I started playing in tournaments. I became ranked nationally. Every child has their thing, you know. And strategic warfare disguised as a parlor game was mine."

"I didn't know that about you."

"It's not something I talk about much." She walked back around the bar and re-took her place next to me. "But then, I stopped."

"Why's that?" I wondered where the hell she was going with this.

"When I was seventeen, I had won enough matches that I had a shot at becoming the American junior champion. I buckled down and got all the way to the quarterfinals. Three wins away from being the #1 US player in the world. I was ecstatic. My opponent was this little shit from Arizona. Couldn't have been more than thirteen. He drank soda and burped when he played. But I didn't underestimate him, didn't go in cocky. I treated him like I had approached all my other enemies. I prepared rigorously. But it didn't matter. He defeated me in ten minutes. I never stood a chance."

She stubbed out her cigarette.

"So…did you play him again?" My heart was palpitating in my chest like I was at one of those Diplo concerts I went to during college.

"Quite the contrary. That was the last game of chess I ever played. I realized that I had hit the ceiling. I had gleaned every morsel of knowledge and experience that I could possibly get from it. No matter what I did, there were going to be people better at it than I. And it was a thought that I couldn't bear. So, I moved over to politics. And I've found in that arena? *No one* bests me. Or even comes close."

"I'm sorry, Anika, but I'm having trouble following you." I feigned ignorance at what she was building to, even though I knew full well.

She lightly rested her finger on top of my hand like a spider, marking the anchor point of the web she was about to weave. "The most powerful piece on a chess board is the Queen. All the other pieces have importance, serve a purpose. But the Queen knows all. The Queen is almighty. All the other pieces support her moves. And can be sacrificed for her greater good. I need you to understand that you are an entity that serves at my discretion. And nothing more."

Before I could conjure up any sort of reply, she seized my hand and twisted it around with the precision of a Krav Maga expert. I howled in agony—I knew that if she bent it five more degrees to the right, it'd be more broken than our penal system. The pain was excruciating, a searing sharpness that was cutting through the entire right side of my body.

"You have an objective. A function. But you can be taken out of play if I see fit. Do you understand what I'm saying to you?"

"Yes. Yes!" I managed to blurt out.

She studied me for a beat before releasing me.

"Good boy. Go home. Get some sleep. Once you've dealt with your brother, call me, and we'll proceed as planned."

"What about the rest of your people?" There was no point in playing coy now.

"What about them?"

"I need to know exactly who I'm dealing with here."

She gazed at me for a tick before letting out a howl of laughter.

"The male ego—its constant need to feel in control even while it's inferior—never ceases to amaze me. The future, Christopher. You're dealing with the future."

As she left the bar, I looked down at my quivering hand. If only that was the only part of me that was trembling. I was barely cognizant driving home. It's a goddamn miracle I didn't crash into something. Or someone.

I could feel panicked hysteria trying to ring my bell.

I just needed to sleep. That's all. I would know what to do in the light of dawn.

Please, God. Let that be true.

* * *

I surfaced from my slumber, gasping for air, drenched.

As the fog cleared, I wiggled my toes. They squished. I groaned, knowing what this meant.

I had wet the bed.

It was a humiliating condition to have an overactive bladder. Especially at my age. I had been given a prescription that, about 90% of the time, took care of the issue. But, on the nights like tonight when I forgot to take the pill? It was anybody's ball game.

I tapped my iPhone to glance at the time. 1:16 AM.

Ugh. Getting back to sleep now was going to be near impossible.

I gingerly stepped out of bed and stripped my bedding. Might as well throw it in the wash while I grabbed a new set.

I padded out into the hallway and saw that Cillian's door was ajar and his bed empty. As I poked my head in curiously, Shepard squinted open his eyes, pissed that I intruded.

"I know, I know. Sorry," I said to him as I backed away. I briefly considered looking for Cillian, but I lost the energy about three seconds into the thought. He had a habit of going out for late walks when we were kids. Chronic insomnia had always plagued him. Sometimes, he would wake me up when he rose, and when he did, he'd always check to make sure my sheets were dry. If they weren't, he'd help me change them. If they were fine, he'd tuck me back in and tell me to go back to sleep.

That was back before we were enemies. When we were just brothers.

Shaking off the bittersweet memory, I slid open the laundry closet and popped the sheets into the washer, quickly starting the machine before reaching up and grabbing a fresh set from the shelf above.

I was just about to turn back in when I heard a faint tapping at the front door.

The damn fool had probably barreled out without thinking and locked himself out. Fuming, I stormed over to the front door, ready to give Cillian a good hollering at, when I saw that it wasn't him.

This was a pleasant surprise.

"Oh. It's you. What on earth are you doing here this late?"

And that's when I saw the gun.

Chapter Five

Cillian

So this is what murder really looks like.

I tried my best to process what I was seeing in front of me—my identical twin brother's head mushroom-clouded into a thousand splatters. In the movies, death is always portrayed in a neater way. An otherwise intact body, with a perfectly sculpted pool of blood underneath the specific area of the gunshot wound, and that's it.

This wasn't that. This was reality.

No one deserves to go out this way. Not even him.

I slowly approached what was left of Christopher, crouching down to get a better look at him. I thought about taking his pulse, just to confirm he was actually dead. I had read that, in times of crisis, focusing on simple, basic mechanical acts helped people cope.

What the fuck is wrong with you? His heart isn't going to still be beating when parts of his face are on the other side of the lawn, you goddamn moron.

I retched. I hadn't eaten anything since that diner stop, so nothing came out, but that didn't stop my body from trying its damnedest to purge itself.

This is what I had wanted to do to him. To my own flesh and blood. What kind of an animal does that make me?

I forced myself up and shoved away the self-loathing. I needed to think practically. Logically. Nothing would be helped by just standing idly with my dick in my hand. I took a deep breath and glanced around to see if there were any shells or casings from the weapon used to shoot him. Something that would help the police track the murderer.

No dice.

Who the hell would do this to him? To us? To me? Audrey's family seeking revenge? Her old man putting out some old-fashioned vigilante justice?

No. That couldn't be it. Given the dirt that Christopher's chief-of-staff, Ada, had dug up on Audrey's father—the disturbing double-life he had been leading that Ada used as insurance to make sure they didn't ask too many questions about Audrey's death or conduct an autopsy—I knew they weren't the culpable ones here. They wouldn't dare risk all that coming to light. And it's not like I had any real enemies or friends to speak of anymore. I broke off all ties when I went to Kentucky. For my sanity.

Think, damn it. It's not like there were any neighbors that could be the culprit. What in the fuck—

Shepard's wild baying yanked me out of my tailspin.

Shepard. Thank God. They hadn't taken my dog from me.

"Shep! It's me, boy. It's okay. C'mere!" Shepard crept through the front door, trembling. I had never seen him shake like that before. "It's okay," I called. Shepard looked at Christopher's corpse, then at me. He was too terrified to move.

"I know, boy. I know. C'mere, it's okay," I repeated more softly, trying to coax him past the most traumatic thing he's seen in his short life. Finally, he worked up the courage, skirting around my brother's remains before bolting over to me and pressing up against my legs, whimpering. I wrapped him in a bear hug and rubbed his stomach, like Mama did with me to calm me down to fall asleep when I was young. Shepard leaned into my embrace, but his gaze never broke from what was left of Christopher. I forced myself to bring my gaze to where my brother's campaign-winning smile would have been. Now it was just an empty cavity of blood and teeth.

My brother. My kin. My ally. Or at least, he was once. That felt so long ago now. There was never going to be any chance of us reclaiming what we once were. I knew that. He knew that. But...he was still my brother.

And now? He was immortalized as my enemy instead of my blood. Nothing could ever be resolved. The boys, the comrade-in-arms that had stomped the boardwalk of Rehoboth, were buried in the sand forever. The kid who would distract Dad on the tail end of his benders and take double the beating from him, just so I could slip out the back door and avoid the crack of his belt, was now a pile of remains. I'll never be able to wipe the image out of my head of Christopher proudly showing off the collection of purple bruises Dad gave him after one of those episodes. Whenever I would try to apologize, Christopher would cut me off and just say, "Nah. These are just my warrior wounds—I'm a knight in battle. Arthur doesn't have shit on me." Then he'd slug me in the shoulder and wink at me.

And you had wanted to wipe him off God's green earth by your own hand, you piece of garbage.

Remorseful regret started to strangle me. I worked my hands through Shepard's fur, trying to distract myself. That's when reality sunk in: I needed to go back into the house. Not to call the police—although I'd need to do that sooner rather than later—but to see if there was something, anything, that would clue me into who would want to blow my brother's head off.

Besides me.

Crreeeeeeaaakkkk.

The sound was coming from inside.

Crreeeeeeaaakkkk.

My heartbeat thumped its way into my eardrums.

Jesus, was the killer still in the house? Camped out inside, ready to blow me to kingdom come, too?

Crreeeeeeaaakkkk.

Adrenaline surged through me like venom serum.

Fuck that. I wasn't going to go gentle into that good night. Not for this. Not because some asshole had a gripe against my brother. I was going to get this bastard.

"Stay here, boy," I commanded Shepard. He obediently laid down, his head resting in his paws as he watched over Christopher. Hands balled into fists, ready to brawl, I moved back towards the front door as stealthily as I could—which wasn't an easy task, given that I was squelching through my brother's innards. It took every ounce of control I had not to projectile vomit again right then and there.

How could I effectively protect myself if I couldn't get to my gun? What else could I use? The only option seemed to be one of Christopher's ridiculously overpriced stainless-steel knives from the block in the kitchen. Could I get there without the killer jumping me? I had no idea where the fucker was.

If this sadist was lurking in the shadows, a knife wouldn't be much in the way of protection. But it was better than nothing. I had to be careful. Vigilant with every step, like I was playing an adult version of Christopher's favorite game: "The floor is lava."

I took a breath.

The floor is lava.

I still could hear Christopher's shrill, louder-than-a-megaphone voice screaming and whooping whenever we played it when we were kids. Every time he fell to the ground and "died," Christopher would shout "Yippee Ki Yay, Mother F-er" like he was John McClane.

But this wasn't a game. This was real. This was—

Crreeeeeeaaakkkk.

I frantically cycled my gaze through the living room to my left and the mud room to my right. Nowhere to hide in there. Safe to go onward.

I pressed forward to the kitchen. The well-oiled door opened without a sound. Christopher's obsessive renovation of the cabin was coming in handy. I grabbed one of the knives from the block. I cursed myself at the *sccccrraaattchhh* it made as I unsheathed it. But now I was armed.

Crreeeeeeaaakkkk.

The sound was louder than it was before. Quicker. Heavier. It was coming from somewhere to my left, directly across the way from the kitchen table.

You can make this right. Right here, right now. You can make a one-for-one trade. Slay your brother's murderer by your own hand. Go out with a sense of principle. With a sense of nobility.

As I started to follow the noise, my bum knee buckled from under me. I dropped the knife in a clatter to the hardwood as I collapsed in a heap.

Don't do this to me now.

I slowly pulled myself up, using the kitchen island for leverage. I nearly chomped straight through my lip to stop from crying out in pain.

Crreeeeeeaaakkkkkk whomp-whomp-whomp.

What in the <u>fuck</u> was that?

Before, the sound was like the claw of a hammer scraping against a car's paint job. This was different. This was guttural. Deeper. Like an otherworldly beast flopping around the bottom of the ocean. It was almost like—

Wait a minute.

I limped over to the closest closet, knife back dangling in my right hand and threw open the doors. The sound was coming from the load of laundry cycling in the front-loading washing machine.

Jesus, Cillian.

Adrenaline leaking out of me like oil from a punctured tank, I canceled the wash and opened the drum. One of the sheets had gotten caught in between the metal lip of the machine, causing the internal motor to grind against itself. I almost laughed at the symbolic, bad murder-mystery nature of this.

Obviously, the killer wouldn't still be here—the job was done. What did you think this was, a shitty slasher movie from the 80s? Pull. Yourself. Together.

A rueful laugh escaped my lips. It was all too perfect. It would be near impossible for me to convince anyone I wasn't Christopher's murderer. Not unless I found something. Not unless I unearthed the secret that my brother was obviously carrying. Not the one that I was fifty percent responsible for and cemented both of our places in hell—but the one that resulted in such a cold-blooded, calculated execution.

I needed to get more of an idea of what I was dealing with. And then I would call the cops. Do the right thing. The thing that Audrey would want me to do.

The thing that I failed to do for her.

My eyes flickered over to Christopher's office. My brother's lair was the perfect place to start the search.

* * *

I had been searching Christopher's fortress of an office for nearly an hour now, and I found diddly squat.

That's not completely true—I had found *things*. I had found enough paper clips to open an office supply store, for instance. Which made no goddamn sense, given that the only actual papers I found were the blank ones lying in the paper tray of the printer. But it wasn't the time to puzzle that one out.

I pushed back from my brother's desk in frustration, slamming shut the drawer I had just opened. I should have known that the bastard wouldn't keep anything of note lying around for prying eyes like mine to find. He was too smart for that. Or devious. Take your pick—with Christopher, intelligence and cunning felt like two sides of the same coin.

I was about to be crushed by a boulder of anxiety—the one I had been straining to hold in place since I started this search—that was starting to crash down the hill of my mind. I could feel an avalanche of panic rumbling in the distance.

This had to be a setup.

It was all too coincidental. And given the timing of the kill? They had probably been lying in wait in the mountains for hours, watching for the perfect time to strike—knowing I would storm out of the house full of rage steaming at some point.

And if I couldn't find anything? I was suspect number one.

From the outside looking in, it was an open-and-shut matter. It wouldn't take much digging to discover that Christopher and I were estranged and antagonistic. A few simple interviews of locals and past acquaintances would do the trick. It wouldn't be a huge leap to assume that I had some kind of motive to do the deed. I was alone with him, the closest person was at least a ten-minute drive away, and the gun I had bought three weeks ago was nowhere even close to legal. Hell, if I didn't know me? I wouldn't believe that I was innocent of the murder. Even Shepard, my perpetually placid canine, had long abandoned his post in front of Christopher's body to pace back and forth throughout the house. You knew things were bad when that bacon-groveling SOB was nervous.

Damn it, Christopher. There must be something in here that won't turn me straight into barbecue. Some sort of saving grace.

I rubbed my temples. I was working on a tension headache that was grinding toward a vision-stopping migraine. And this was no time to be blinded. I tried applying the pressure point on my hand that Audrey had shown me way back when. Whenever she did it, the pain in my head slipped out of me quickly like an Irish goodbye. Whenever I did it, I just pinched the skin on my palms. Now was no different.

I stood up, hoping it would get the blood flowing and wash away the throbbing, and walked into my brother's meticulously maintained mid-century modern palace. Christopher had obviously sunk a lot of cash into this room to make Don Draper feel at home. Hell, he probably thought he *was* Don Draper.

That's when my eyes hit the bar cart.

It had crossed my sights when I first came in, but I had tried not to pay it any mind. I've been sober for eight years now. Alcoholism is the gift that keeps on giving in the Clarke family. And it would be a lie if I said that whiskey didn't look like the perfect medicine right now.

I picked up the bottle. Christopher always preferred bourbon. I was a rye man through and through. Rye is spicier and less accessible in its notes, while bourbon is sweeter and mellow—easier going down. I suppose it was fitting, in a perverse way, that booze perfectly summarized our differing personalities.

Don't go down this road again. Not this time. You're on a clock here. Don't be an idiot.

Putting the bottle down, I took another look at the office. There had to be something in here that I could use. I could feel it in my bones.

So why hadn't I found anything?

Just as I was about to turn tail and give up, I realized that I had left one rather large stone unturned: his computer. I'm still one of the few holdouts from the digital age. I send in my taxes by mailed hard copy. I don't trust anything that I can't hold in my own two hands. I like knowing the weight, the texture, the feel of everything before I attach my name to it.

I resisted the urge to whack myself in the face.

Of course he wouldn't keep anything as loose and untethered as hard copies, you dipshit. Look at this godforsaken house. It was pristine, sterile, nothing out of place—an OCD patient's wet dream.

I flung myself back down in his chair and urgently shook the mouse, bringing the computer back to life. The user menu was password-protected. My mind did anxiety-fueled jumping jacks through the potentially endless possibilities of what that could be.

Then I thought about the type of man my brother was. How, like every single secret he had held close to his vest, his password would probably be some sick irony, the last thing that anyone would ever think of.

Something that only he knew about.

Something that I only knew.

I typed out my beloved's name. *A-U-D-R-E-Y.*

Bingo.

My vision clouded as my blood cooked. I managed to not put my fist through the wall. If I had my way, he would have never been allowed to utter or use Audrey's name in any capacity.

Stop. That isn't going to help you now. Focus on the task at hand.

His desktop now fully loaded, the first thing I was met with was a half-finished Word document. It was a draft of a letter to someone—a Mrs. Applebaum. I combed through the folders of my brain to see if I knew an Applebaum. It didn't take long to find it—Mrs. Applebaum was our fifth-grade teacher. A saint of a lady if there ever was one. She made us dinner for a month straight after Mama blew her brains out. I skimmed through Christopher's letter. He had kept in semi-regular touch with her from the looks of it. I'd be lying if I said that didn't rip out my heart. I saved the letter before quitting out of it. I know no one would probably ever see it, but it felt wrong of me to just delete it.

That sorted, I clicked on the finder folder. Even though I didn't like computers, I knew my way around them decently enough. But I had no idea what I was looking for. I skimmed through the hundreds of folders in his documents, all of them meticulously labeled. And all of them worthless—least as far as I could tell.

Panic flaring up again, I turned off the computer and started to think through what would happen next. I would call the police, they would come, and it would be an uncomfortable few days while I was their prime suspect. They would shove a microscope up my behind faster than green grass through a goose. But then the truth—my innocence—would eventually come out. Because...well, it had to, right? As long as I got rid of my gun, they wouldn't have anything on me. I would just have to ride things out.

Get rid of the gun. Right.

I torpedoed into my bedroom and opened the drawer where I had been keeping it. And my heart about near dropped out the soles of my boots.

Because the Bersa was nowhere to be found.

That didn't make any goddamn sense. I had a crystal-clear memory of putting it in this drawer. I wouldn't absent-mindedly misplace it. No way.

Throwing cautiousness out the window, I ripped apart every single inch of the room, searching. It didn't make a lick of difference. Despair gripped me as I choked back a moan of anguished recognition.

The killer must have taken it.

No doubt it would be found on the Shenandoah riverbank nearby a couple of days from now, conveniently ready to be spotted by any pimply preteen tuber coming to float the river. My fingerprints would be all over it. The final nail in my immaculately constructed coffin.

I can't explain why but, right then and there, I had a sixth sense that there was something waiting for me in Christopher's bedroom.

I dragged myself to his door. Opened it wide. And that's when I saw it.

On the wall above his bed, smeared in blood, was the message: *THIS IS WHAT YOU DESERVED, BROTHER.*

I didn't even bother wondering anything different. That was his blood on the wall. In handwriting that eerily looked like mine. I knew what needed to happen next.

I needed to run.

II

PART TWO: THE SQUALL

"All I see is a picture of you. You and her. I don't even know if the picture's real anymore. I don't even care. It's a made-up picture. It invades my head. The two of you...it cuts me so deep I'll never get over it."
—Sam Shepard, Fool for Love

Chapter Six

Cillian

Something was wrong with Audrey and me. And I didn't know how to fix it.

I clenched the steering wheel of the used F-250 I had just bought off old man Farragut, trying my damnedest not to nervously glance at Audrey through the corner of my eye. I had gotten what I paid for—he hadn't even bothered to clean it before selling it to me. The interior still reeked from the stench of his pipe tobacco.

But also, tension. Mostly tension, in fact.

I couldn't resist anymore. Audrey's emerald green eyes were glinting in the early morning sun. I know she felt me looking at her, but her mind was elsewhere. She scanned the rolling horizon like she was looking for its soul as she absentmindedly rubbed the belly of Shepard, the pit bull that we had adopted together a couple of months before. She'd named him for Sam Shepard, her favorite playwright.

I had no idea who Sam Shepard was before I met Audrey. She had all his works, and she loaned them to me to read. The one she loved the most was *Fool for Love*. Mine was *True West*—the first one she handed me. *True West* is a play about two brothers who are perpetually engaged in a game of one-upmanship until one tries to strangle the other with a telephone wire. I've never read anything that nails brotherly hatred so accurately—except for the attempted murder at the end. Shepard took some dramatic license there—no brother would want to kill his own blood.

But it was Audrey's penciled-in notes to herself in the margins of all of them that really made me smile wide. She was so goddamn smart—sharper than I ever had hopes of being. I loved that about her. She made me better.

I ended up devouring Shepard's stuff. I read every single damn one of them over the course of a long weekend. Practically the only times I got up were to pee and to feed myself. Some were better than others—I'll admit, getting through his earlier experimental works with its disjointed dialogue was a tall order—but in one way or another, they all dealt with people on the fringes of society, people truly on the edge. I liked that.

When I asked Audrey why she loved Shepard so much, she paused for a lick before saying that there was a "palpable tragedy" to everything he wrote—a deep-seated sadness and longing rooted in every single one of his characters. She said that near all the male characters in his work reminded her of me—wounded animals from the rough and tumble that, with the right amount of TLC work ("tenderness, love, and care," as she called it) could be brought back to life. That didn't quite sit right with me when she said it—the implication that I was something that she needed to "fix." But I chose the path of least resistance. Why look a gift horse in the mouth?

And now? I feared to God that she had grown tired of that work.

Shepard's snoring sharply snapped me out of my reverie. Audrey and I thought that the joint responsibility of caring for a dog together would make us close again. But it was just a flash in the pan—a temporary spark—instead of the permanent reignition we were hoping for. Even so, I couldn't help but smile at the sight of the two of them. Shepard loved soaking up sunbeams while he slept—he was like a giant kitten in that way—and Audrey was so gentle with him. She was going to be such a good mother one day.

I forced myself to take my eyes off her. We had agreed to not talk for twenty minutes, to give us time to cool down from the screaming match we'd just had. I couldn't even remember what had started the fight—I was angry, but I couldn't even begin to tell you about what. I'd reckon she'd probably say the same. The way this past year or so had been, I wasn't sure where one argument ended and the next began. It was a good rule in concept—us "breaking" for twenty minutes after a fight—but one both of us had trouble sticking to. Patience wasn't Audrey's particular brand of vodka—and Lord knows it wasn't mine, either. But here we were, trying to drink the damn stuff. Trying to be better. For ourselves. For each other.

And even despite our lingering troubles, there was something else nipping at Audrey. I couldn't explain it. I just knew. Some other something gnawing away at her heart while breathing melancholy into her lungs. She was good at hiding it and would flick it away like a thoroughbred does a fly whenever I asked her about it. But I could see it in her face every so often. I would catch her in the mornings after getting out of the shower staring at herself in the mirror—her eyes were elsewhere, like she was looking for a secret embedded deep in her skin. It was the same look that Mama had in the months leading up to her suicide. And that terrified me.

Just open your mouth and say you're sorry. Don't be an idiot.

I started to speak, and then I reined it in. We had agreed to take space. I needed to respect that and give it to her.

Audrey and I had been together for long, long while—but we had known each other for even longer than that. We first met when we were fourteen, at a Prelim eventing competition. We were both the youngest riders in our division by a country mile. She was the only girl.

Eventing—dressage, stadium jumping, and cross-country—is the triathlon of horse-riding. Dressage is about restraint, subtle fluidity of movement in a confined space. Stadium jumping is like being a conductor—you have to have metronome-like precision as you count the strides before vaulting a fence and then shifting on a dime to coax your horse to change its lead. Cross-country, the thing that I truly lived for, is all about brute strength and endurance—pounding across hills and water to fling yourself over stone walls on a horse galloping at breakneck speed. If you excelled in all three? You had achieved the holy grail of an equestrian. I used to make fun of dressage, calling it horse-prancing. I wanted to cut my tongue out for saying that once I saw Audrey do it. It wasn't just a silly dance with her—it was ballet. And that's not even mentioning how good she was at the other two.

That first competition, she came in first, and I was in second. It was like that in near every single event we faced off in. And that was fine by me.

Soon as we graduated high school, we moved down to Lexington together. Her parents had forbidden her from seeing me, and escape was the only way to be together. Her family put the blame square on my shoulders. But hell, it was her idea to flee to that neck of Virginia. Like some sort of modern-day Romeo and Juliet. It was bliss at first. Both of us pursuing riding full tilt, me spurring her on, and vice-versa. Then Audrey's parents formally disowned her. They took everything back that they had given her. I still remember when the trailer came to cart off her beloved Dolly back to her parents' estate. I thought Audrey might never recover. She had to start completely from scratch.

I was lucky—Rip, the trainer that I worked for all those hours in middle school and high school, had given me my horse as a graduation present. Apollo was an older thoroughbred that wasn't quite the right fit for track racing, so the owners that had him before had dumped him for a song. Their neglect was my gain—even though he wasn't good for racing, he was a natural for eventing. I had never seen an animal that could take the kinds of cross-country jumps he did with such joy. And I had worked out a deal with a stable owner in Lexington—I worked around the barn in exchange for free board. So, my overhead was practically nothing. I tried to set Audrey up with a similar gig—but she wasn't interested.

Even though she had grown up around horses, there's a difference between just riding and also having to deal with all the dirty grunt work that goes into taking care of a horse. And going from never having to think about money to being as poor as dirt is something that I don't think she was ever going to be ready for. Eventually, Audrey became so discouraged that she became a veterinary assistant at a local horse clinic and a mere weekend pleasure rider. It was like watching Michael Jordan hang up his basketball sneakers to go play baseball. But she said it was what she wanted. So, I didn't fight her.

I should have.

Meanwhile, I kept competing. And without Audrey opposing me? No rider could touch me—I crushed every single competition I entered. I won enough of 'em that I'd been asked to join the US Olympic team a year and a half ago. She was so happy for me. Her dimples were on full display nearly all damn day. She told me that she could still compete vicariously through me. She baked me a strawberry rhubarb crumb pie and apologized that it was all she could afford to do. I told her that was silly—that the pie was the best I'd ever had.

Then, a week before I was supposed to start training with the team, I got dragged halfway to hell. Doctors said the way my knee was torn and mangled, I'd be lucky to walk again, never mind compete. I wasn't even supposed to be riding in the Gold Cup that day—a friend's jockey went AWOL, and I filled in at the last minute as a favor. It's amazing how long you can spend working on your dreams and just how quickly they can be crushed. In just one goddamn split second, nothing was the same. For good. I had to get reconstructive surgery and do six months of intense rehab. I hadn't wanted to at all—if I couldn't ride, what the hell was the point, right? But Audrey convinced me that I had to. "Inaction is the greatest sin, Cillian," was what she told me.

Fuck if I was gonna argue with that.

Even despite that, though, that time was a real rough patch. I barely spoke to anyone during that time. And the ABC store attendant got to know me well. It got to the point where I didn't even have to say a word when I walked in—he'd just pull the Templeton off the shelf, and I'd silently give him cash and leave.

I treated Audrey real poorly in that stretch, too—I'm man enough to admit it. I never laid a hand on her or anything like that—if you ask me, anyone who hits a woman should have their nuts hacked off. But I said some right awful things—comments that I'd give my kidney to take back. I'm a mean drunk. I knew that. She knew that. She made me promise not to drink anymore. And that was a promise I intend to keep. It's been difficult to find a steady job. I've been knocking around from barn to barn, getting work as a stable hand wherever I could. I'd do things like exercise horses to keep them fit and limber for weekend riders. I'd become an opening act to a rich brat getting his first riding lesson. It was humiliating. But I had to do something.

And horses are all I know.

Once I healed enough that I could casually ride, Audrey and I would occasionally go out on the trail with one another. But the magic was gone— it was a hobby for her now, and I was bitter. Hell, I still am. We'd both lost our North Star—the thing that'd been driving us our whole lives—and were relegated to simply surviving. We'd stuck together when most couples would have split, especially those our age. We were committed enough, though, that we chose to close our eyes at the thing staring us down—that our best days were probably behind us at age twenty-six. Committed or just plain stubborn—it's sometimes hard to tell the difference between the two when you're in a long-term relationship.

Stop it. Don't go down the rabbit hole. Stay in the moment.

I tried to concentrate on our surroundings. We were nearly halfway to our destination, in the stretch between Harrisonburg and Mount Jackson, where there's not much of anything save for the broken dreams and regret of farms just trying to live long enough to see another season. Even the cornfields had given up hope and were withering two ways past Sunday. It was me who had proposed taking this trip—a reset of sorts. I didn't have the money for a hotel, so I suggested a weekend getaway to Dad's hunting cabin up on the Ridge overlooking my minuscule hometown of Paris. Sky Meadows was to the east, the Shenandoah River to the west, and the Appalachian Trail a stone's throw away. I'd only been to the cabin twice before, but I knew it as beautiful and peaceful—two things we were in desperate need of. Even though she'd already been driving up to the equine center in nearby Leesburg a ton recently for work, Audrey was in favor of the idea.

Hell, I would buy magic beans from a homeless man on the side of the road if I thought it would help our relationship.

Even though the trip had been my idea, that doesn't mean it still didn't make me squirm. Dad had bought the cabin after Mama died, and he spent so much time there that we became a family of two households—the place where Mama killed herself, and the place where Dad got to let all his inhibitions loose, his children be damned. It got to the point that Dad only came back to Christopher and me when he was out of underwear and beer. Mostly beer. He only shared his sanctuary with his favorite son, my brother. The two times I had been there previously only happened because Christopher demanded that Dad bring me along, too. That was back when we were best friends. Now the cabin was Christopher's—he inherited it after the old fuck had walked into the mist for the last time.

I'll admit, it was considerate of Christopher to let Audrey and me have it for the weekend. I'm guessing he could hear it in my voice—the tone of a man who was trying to bail out a sinking ship with a two-gallon bucket. I'd wanted to vomit at asking him for a favor. But Audrey and I always traveled together well. Maybe this would keep the flood water at bay.

God, please let that be true.

I glanced back over at Audrey. She had closed her eyes for a spell. Her delicate, long eyelashes fluttered in the gentle gust of the A/C. Even when she was sleeping, her beauty had the ability to reach inside my chest and flip on all the lights, brightening every dark cavern in me. Tame my temper. I fully admit that. Audrey could cool my jets without uttering a single word. When I first met her, I wondered what deal with the devil she had made to gain that skill. But then I decided she was just a heaven-sent angel. And I had just yelled at that heavenly woman for something that I couldn't even recall.

Fix this, you ungrateful asshole.

I couldn't talk to her, though—that would break the "fair fighting" rules we had set up. So, I needed to figure out a way to communicate *with* her without actually talking *to* her. Now was one of the infinite moments where I wished relationships came with an instruction manual.

I reached into the console and removed Bruce Springsteen's latest album, *Wrecking Ball.* We had driven all the way up to D.C. in April to see him perform it live. Dancing wasn't good for my knee, but I'll be damned if I wasn't going to rock out to The Boss with my lady. It didn't even matter that he was playing the Verizon Center—a terrible concert venue if there ever was one. Who wants to see a show in a massive sports arena with terrible acoustics that tall athletes sweat in for a living? But it was magic. Everything that night made sense. I'd do anything for us to have that night again. Even just once.

I slid the disc into the CD player and cranked up the volume. As the percussive, driving intro of "We Take Care of Our Own" boomed out of our speakers, both Shepard and Audrey's left eyes cracked open simultaneously. Their tendency to do that together, as if on cue, never ceased to amaze me.

"I been shooba-looba-dooba which holds the throne!" I bellowed intentionally off-key, replacing parts of the actual lyrics with nonsense word salad shouted in my cartoonish Bruce impersonation that never failed to make her giggle.

Shepard's tail started thumping against Audrey's stomach.

"I been hubba-dubba-rubba that leads me home!" I took my hands off the wheel and waved them just slightly off-tempo above my head, knowing that Audrey always teased me that I looked like a middle-aged Dad when I did it.

Both of Audrey's eyes were open now, and a reluctant smile was spreading across her face. She shot me a playful, mock annoyed look as she theatrically rolled her eyes. No traces of the unknown murky malady. Just pure, radiant sunshine.

Here we go. I got her.

"I been heeba-deeba-lubba turned to stone!" My pitch was ear-splitting now. But it was offset by the gentle chime of her laughter—the thing that sounded like what I imagined the bells of Heaven would be.

This time, as the song roared into its anthem-like chorus, she joined me, and we both exclaimed the real honest-to-goodness lyrics at the top of our lungs. Neither of us was a good singer, but we put our backs into it as we barreled down the highway.

The darkness had been lifted.

At least for the moment.

* * *

After belting out a few more Bruce tunes, we decided to stop for a bite. I asked her what she was in the mood for, and she pointed at a greasy truck stop and said that she was craving a burger. That was one of my favorite things about her—she didn't have a pretentious bone in her body. And that was a miracle, too, given her family. Her folks are old money—country gentry living in an 1800s-era stone manor with seven fireplaces on a hundred acres near Upperville. They were people who rode to the hounds, fox hunting in their pinks. They reminded me of the rich British folk from Audrey's Jane Austen books.

The first time they had me over for dinner, they informed me that they were bringing out the "nice china." I made a joke about not wanting to meet the china that was mean. It didn't go over well. But Audrey had laughed so much water came shooting out her nose like an adolescent on a Slip N' Slide. But she didn't drop the Waterford crystal glass she was holding, so I chalked it up as a victory. She took my breath away—the way she could laugh so hard and yet look so poised and elegant.

We set up in the flatbed of my truck, eating in the parking lot as we gazed at the Shenandoah Valley across the 81. Its vales were no Blue Ridge, mind you, but that didn't mean it wasn't a thing to look at with admiration. If we were comparing them using the superior gender as an analogy? With its gold hayfields and placid basins, the Valley would be a sunny blonde, while the Ridge, with its wild, mystical, auburn-orange foliage and rolling hills, would be best described as a fiery redhead.

Shepard was sprawled out at our feet, doing the pooch version of manspreading. Meat juice dribbled down Audrey's chin as she bit into the cheeseburger that was about the size of her head. I was always amazed how she managed to eat things like that and not spill all over herself. I had gotten the same thing, and I already knew that the shirt I was wearing was a goner.

"You can always tell the quality of a burger by the amount of grease it leaves on the wrapper. The more, the better." Audrey arched her eyebrow at me as she swallowed down her beef with a sip of strawberry milkshake. This wasn't the first time she had said this, but I realized that this was her way of making conversation, breaking the ice. So, I pretended it was the first time she'd ever uttered it.

"The Surgeon General might disagree with you. I think he'd say that was a one-way ticket to heart disease," I countered, teasing.

"Joke's on you. The Surgeon General is a woman."

"Well, then I promise you that she'd definitely know better."

"How's that, now?"

"It's been my experience that women know more than men about most everything."

"And that's the right answer! Open wide." She picked up a fry and, without waiting for me to ready myself, threw it in my general direction. Instead of arcing into my mouth, it bopped me on the nose and fell to the ground. Before I could reach down to pick it up, Shepard hoovered it up.

"Shep's got to learn the etiquette surrounding the five-second rule."

"Lots of things for us to teach him and not enough time to do it."

The unintended ominousness of Audrey's statement hung there thicker than the humidity of a balmy Virginia summer's day. Finally, I broke the silence.

"I'm sorry we fought." I cupped my hands over my face like a visor so I could look her in the eye. Show her I meant it.

She returned the favor. Or at least, I thought she did—she always had sunglasses on during days like this—a practical, smart decision that I never seemed to remember to make. "Yeah. Me too."

I gauged her face and body language, trying to figure if this was the correct time to ask her what I really wanted to know. The knowledge that would save us. The knowledge that would save me.

Screw it. No guts, no glory.

"We've been fighting a lot recently." I needed to tread lightly, slowly dip my toe into the pool instead of cannonballing in with no grace like I usually did.

Off this, Audrey removed her aviator shades. Her eyes were a darker shade than they usually were, having been blocked from the light. "I guess."

"There's something bothering you."

Damn it. That sounded accusatory. Not the way I had wanted it to.

Her face tightened. I knew that expression well. "Are you implying that all of our arguments have been my fault, Cillian?" She was so well-bred; even when she was mad, she spoke all prim and proper-like.

I bristled. I could feel my self-defense mechanisms cinching tight over me like armor. "No, Audrey. That's not what I meant. Please give me the benefit of the doubt, would you?"

She crossed her arms over her chest. "Enlighten me, then. What did you mean?"

"There's been something wrong with you—"

"I'm sorry?"

"Wait, hold on, I didn't mean for it to come out like that—"

"I'm so glad to know that you think that I'm such a problem—"

"I never said that. You know I'm not good at this—"

"That I'm such a broken wretch of a person—"

"If you would please let me finish—"

"I would love it if you, just once, actually took responsibility for the things you say—"

"Audrey, I'm just trying to figure out what has been laying you so low—"

"Have you ever thought for a minute that it's *you*?"

I felt my blood starting to boil. The rage monster was rising. "Yeah. I'm the problem. I ask out of concern what's wrong, and I'm the enemy. Maybe it's just *you*, darling."

"And you know how much I love sarcasm."

"It would certainly explain why you use it to guilt me all the time."

I noticed out of the corner of our eyes that people were starting to stare. My cheeks flushed with embarrassment. I don't know why it bothered me as much as it did—I wish I could be one of those people who didn't care what others thought. But that wasn't me.

"Now you're going to tell me to calm down, right?" She probed.

"God damn it, I didn't say anything!"

Audrey turned to the few truckers who were gawking at us. "Fuck right off up a tree, why don't you?!" The truckers scattered like mice being chased by a barn cat. Audrey really had it in her to holler when she wanted to—prim and proper right out the window.

I felt my anger starting to propel me off the ground. "How about we both take a deep breath and talk about this like adults."

Audrey was matching my fury-fueled levitation herself. "I will when you do, Cillian Matthew Clarke." She only full-named me when we were fighting. And we had been sparring so much recently that I had grown to hate the sound of my own name.

"What is this really about? What are we fighting about here?"

"I wish I knew." Her tone hit me as hard as a right cross from Floyd Mayweather Jr.

"I'm trying to be civil here, and it seems like you're not interested in that."

"I'm being perfectly civil, Cillian. It's you that's perpetuating all of this."

"You were just screaming at bystanders, and *I'm* perpetuating things?"

"I wasn't screaming, Cillian, I was just being *passionate—*"

I felt like I was going to near drop over, blinded by the wrath flying through my head. "I suppose I just need to make my peace with it. You don't love me anymore. You'd rather be with someone else. Someone who's successful and not a mess like me. Someone like Christopher, right?"

She stared at me, dumbfounded. "Oh my God. I can't keep having this fight with you."

"We wouldn't have to if you actually answered my questions."

"That's because none of your questions have been worth answering!"

"Before I made you an ultimatum and drew a line in the sand, you two spent more time together than you and I did! And you did that even knowing how I felt about my brother. Every time I opened our goddamn front door, there he'd be sitting on my couch. How do you think that made me feel, Audrey?!"

"It's called having friends, Cillian. Just because you don't have any doesn't mean that I shouldn't either."

"It's not about not having friends, Audrey, it's about how weird it is for you to spend so much goddamn alone time with my brother! You chose to spend your free time with him instead of me. You were choosing *him* over *me!*"

"Well, I stopped seeing him, didn't I? I haven't seen him in three years! Just as you commanded!"

"Only after I got down on my hands and knees and begged you. Which

I'm sure you *loved!*"

"Listen to yourself, Cillian, you sound like an infant!"

"I'll stop sounding like an infant when you stop being a bi—!"

THWACK! The sting of her hand seared my cheek.

And it was almost immediately followed by the sound of Shepard whimpering while he wet himself.

That deflated the both of us. Our nonsense had scared our canine child. What a disgrace. Wordlessly, she held him as I wiped up the mess with my napkins while she patted him dry with hers. This wasn't the first time we had done this to him, so we had it down to a science at this point.

Jesus. What the fuck was wrong with us?

I knew I needed to say something. But I had no idea what. Finally, the words found their way to my lips.

"I'm sorry for what I said. No excuses. It terrifies me that I can't fix us. I can feel you slipping through my fingers, and I don't know how to stop it." I couldn't bring myself to look at her when I felt this small. When I felt this ashamed of myself. "I see the sadness having its way with your heart, and I just want to fix it."

I didn't need to tilt my gaze up to know how she was looking at me: it was her gaze that was the perfect cocktail of resentment, deep-seated anger, pity, sadness, and love. Something that you only come to recognize when your relationship is on the rocks. "Not everything can be fixed, Cillian. Love doesn't work that way."

And with that, she turned away and stepped back into the passenger seat of the truck.

She hadn't finished her burger.

* * *

We drove the remainder of the trip in complete silence. No music, no nothing save for the sound of Shepard's anxious panting and the rumble of my truck's engine. Both sounded like they were held together only by sheer determination and rubber bands.

It had been a long time since I had been back to Paris. Not since I moved out. Left it all behind. That was almost eight years ago now. Out of loyalty to Mama, I hadn't gone to Dad's funeral. Not after it came to light what he'd been secretly doing to her all those years. It made me sick. And Christopher gave him a pass for his degeneracy and abuse. The fucker. That's when the fracture between us really got entrenched deep. We'd always been competitive and rivals—but this was the straw that broke the camel's back.

But that's a story for another time.

Not to my surprise, it looked like no time had passed at all in Paris. The main road skirting our town was still named after John Mosby, the Confederate commander whose riders crossed the Ashby Gap all the time— the naming was never appropriate to my thinking and, for some ungodly reason, hadn't been changed yet. Mosby was nicknamed "The Gray Ghost," and Paris certainly took after that title, relegating itself to a faint whisper of a place.

Besides the picturesque embrace of Ol' Blue on the outskirts of town, The Ashby Inn was still the only real thing to sniff at, besides maybe the Trinity United Methodist Church. Tourists always marveled at its Gothic Revival architecture. I lost count of the number of times that, as I would walk by on the way to the corner market, I would be asked to take photos of strangers with that in the backdrop. On days when I needed a laugh, I would purposefully frame them out of the shot, instead opting to take a picture of just the landscape. Then, I'd walk away before they could say anything. Those days became more frequent the older I got.

Passing Paris on my left and chugging up the growing incline of the Ridge itself, I came to the turnoff road, Liberty Hill Lane, that led up to the cabin. Calling it a road, though, was generous. It's more a path of gravel that slices up through the mountains for a couple of miles before reaching its destination. My truck's suspension squealed as it made the climb—the perfect score to the simmering tension between Audrey and me.

Finally, we plateaued onto even terrain. The cabin was now in sight.
We made it.

Sensing that we were approaching our destination, Shepard's tail started flicking back and forth. Audrey smiled, too.

Why the fuck was she smiling? Had she been here before? Did she have some sort of memory here without me? With him? Did he take her up here like some kind of—

I wanted to slap myself. I needed to stop pouring gasoline on my brain and filling in blanks that I didn't even know for sure existed with dynamite. For all I knew, it could be—

"Wow. Look at that view," she exhaled breathily, pointing at the magnificent vista in front of us. The cabin itself wasn't much to look at it, but the panoramic views it gave along the Ridge, the lush paradise of blue and green below, was truly something to behold. Dad had always said this was his nest in the sky. And he wasn't wrong. For a wretch of a man, he had a poetic turn of phrase in him every now and again.

This was going to be just what the doctor ordered for us. It had to be.

"Yeah. It's really something else, isn't it? Almost pretty as you," I replied. I hesitantly reached over to hold her hand, uncertain she would be open to my touch. She let me. I smiled, relieved, as I rubbed my thumb against the folds of her palm.

Her soft skin felt good in my grasp. It felt <u>right</u>. The only thing that I was ever supposed to touch. It was—

That's when I saw Christopher's car in the driveway.

And there he was, raking leaves shirtless in the front yard, his tanned, chiseled physique golden in the early afternoon sun. I was strong enough, but I could never get my body to look like that. No matter how hard I tried.

After seeing us pull to a stop, my brother tossed down the rake and gave us a shit-eating grin and wave. No one else would be able to tell because he hid it real well, but I knew him. And I could see that he was drunk.

Audrey uncertainly turned to me. "Why is he here?"

I had no earthly idea.

Chapter Seven

Christopher

Only seven goddamn souls wanted to hear what I had to say. That's pathetic.

I shifted uncomfortably behind the makeshift portable podium that I had slapped together with some old plywood. There Ada was, standing at the back of the crowd, dutifully holding her clipboard, posture the spitting image of perfect.

Was it really a crowd, though, if I could count them all on two hands?

Ada had practically never left my side since we formally declared last week. I had my pick of potential campaign manager hires—not because of who I was, but the amount of money I was able to offer. I didn't want a political mercenary, though—I wanted someone like me. Someone who had earned everything through willpower and ambition. Someone who was as hungry as they were crafty. Someone whose ways weren't set in stone. I didn't know anything about her past or her upbringing—but I didn't need to. Ada checked all the boxes. So much so, in fact, that I was able to forgive her for the fact she was a Virginia Tech Hokie to my University of Virginia Cavalier—the ultimate affirmation of her talents, if you ask me.

Ada nodded encouragingly at me. She had such a wonderful smile—simultaneously bright, warm, and telegenic. She probably should be running for office and not me. But she said, right from the jump, that she never wanted to be the face—she only wanted to be the one pulling the strings on my grin. It was a slightly odd thing to say—especially since it was unprompted by a question from me—but I appreciated her honesty. She offhandedly mentioned that her mother had taught her that. I didn't push to learn more—Ada didn't seem to care for her too much. And I knew better than most about the treachery of familial bloodlines.

I had been the one to pick the front of the Upper Crust bakery as the spot for my first campaign event for Mayor of Middleburg. Ada had wanted a bit more formal of a setting, something like the Red Fox Inn & Tavern. I thought the bakery's proximity to the center of town and being next to the Safeway seemed like a good bet to lure in prospective voters. But the real reason? Upper Crust's homemade cookies were the best I've ever had in my life. And since I was paying for the whole campaign out of my own pocket? I had final approval.

Yeah, that really sounds like Mayor material—a man who picks campaign spots based on cookies. Idiot.

I was nervous. Which was incredibly dumb. I'd done much harder things than this. I'd thrown touchdown passes in front of thousands and spoken to angel investors worth hundreds of millions. I'm excellent with people. I'd been told that my whole life—by people who both adored and despised me. But now? My underwear was so sweat-soaked that it felt marshier than a swamp down there. All because of seven measly souls—a couple of whom looked like they belonged in a 19th-century oil painting more so than real life. But in a town of under six hundred people? I'd need every single last damn vote.

And I wanted to be Mayor. I wanted it bad. Not because I was head over heels for Middleburg. If my hometown of Paris was actually big enough to have a mayor and wasn't just an unincorporated slice of heaven, I would have thrown in my hat for that. But it wasn't. So, the close-by Middleburg would have to do. I'd been living in the town for the past year since I moved back to Virginia after my lucrative stint in San Jose, and Middleburg had grown on me quite a bit. But that's not why I wanted the position. I wanted it because of what it represented: the first step to getting what I desired most: respect from those who had forever turned their noses up at me and my family. After all, if a boy who grew up poor in Paris could become ruler of the old-money fiefdom that was Middleburg? Anything was possible.

I gazed out at the audience—the noun perpetually in air quotes.

These people could swing the election single-handedly. Put on your game face, Clarke. This moment is what you've been eating your Wheaties for.

"I want to thank y'all for coming out to see me today. Gorgeous morning, isn't it?" I got a few half-smiles and nods. I recognized those looks. On the surface, they seemed polite and civil, but underneath, they were "blessing my heart" about six ways over. Which, if you're unfamiliar with the South, is...not what you want.

"For those of you who don't know me—I'm Christopher Clarke, and I'm going to be the next Mayor of Middleburg!" I checked in with Ada, whose eyes looked like they were about to pop out of her head. She had specifically told me to avoid statements like that—ones that could be potentially misconstrued as arrogant. But she quickly covered it with a smile and a round of applause. The seven onlookers tepidly joined in to keep up appearances. Old Virginians are polite that way.

I cleared my throat anxiously and returned to the talking points Ada had devised for me.

"I bet I know what y'all are thinking. Who the heck am I? Why vote for someone that's young enough to be your son or date your daughter? I get it. I'd feel exactly the same way if I were you. Here's the thing, though—you may not know me yet. But I know you."

I scanned the faces in front of me to see if I was making any headway with the onlookers. Only just.

"I was born and raised in Fauquier County. I did some time out west— enough time to make a little money, but realized that California isn't for me. And don't get me started on Los Angeles. Lucifer himself would spend twenty-four hours there and need to take a bath." That garnered a few ripples of laughter. Progress.

The advice that Ada gave me before this rang in my ears—*local politics is about one-on-one connection. Making the person you're pressing flesh with feel like the most important person on Earth.*

Now was the part of the performance where I was meant to prove my man-of-the-people mettle. I stepped off the podium and strode over to the first audience member—a belle in her 50s who still dressed like she was in her early 30s. I had to stop myself from smirking. Ada had seated her in the first chair because she knew me well enough already to know I thrived with middle-aged ladies like her, making her the perfect person to open with.

I slyly smiled at the belle as I stretched out my hand to her. "I do believe you're Miss Devar?"

She blushed slightly as she took it. "Call me Delia," she replied.

"Delia. Thank you. You own the beauty parlor on Madison, right?"

Her eyes crinkled with surprise. "That's right."

"Now I heard that you went and bought that property some 25 years ago. You were about my age when you turned an old, worn-out used car parts store into the thriving community cornerstone that your salon is today— while pregnant with your firstborn, no less?"

Delia's eyes shined proudly as she nodded affirmatively.

"What a tremendous accomplishment. I'm sure you probably had a lot of people tell you that you were foolish to take on such a monumental task. That you didn't stand a snowball's chance in hell?"

"You're not wrong."

I amped up the wattage of my smile. Time to lay it on thick. "You wanted to make a difference. Make your mark on the world. Prove to everyone that you were more than just a beauty pageant queen."

"Oh, I never competed in any pageants."

I feigned surprise. "No? Well, if you had, I bet you would have won every single one of 'em. And I know you know where I'm coming from. I'm just a young gun itching for the chance to prove his naysayers wrong. Just like you were, ma'am. And still are." I shot her a wink and released my hand as she tittered and nodded.

One vote in the bag.

I moved on to the gent sitting next to her—Alfred Leviathan, a man who definitely had dust falling out of his briefs. He owned the rare bookstore just 'round the corner from here.

"Time is dead as long it is being clicked off by little wheels; only when the clock stops does time come to life." I grasped Alfred's pruned-up hand in mine as I quoted William Faulkner. "Mr. Leviathan, only when I set foot into your store does time come to life for me. I've spent many an afternoon browsing the stacks, combing through the wonderful selection of first editions you have at your disposal. My personal favorite is anything by Faulkner."

Alfred gave me a yellowed smile, stained from years of smoking tobacco out on porches. *"The Sound and the Fury* is my favorite out of all of William's works."

The pretentiousness of the shopkeeper calling Faulkner by his first name only about near bowled me over. "Your lovely niece Elizabeth mentioned as much."

That wasn't technically a lie. I had already known his Faulkner preference before I walked in for the first time. The lovely Liz, who ran the day-to-day of the shop, got to talking with me and told me all about her quirky old Uncle from Mississippi. "It would be my honor to take you to dinner, sir. We could discuss your store and all things Faulkner over steaks and brandy?"

He nodded affirmatively and gave me a friendly pat on the shoulder. 2 for 2.

Just before continuing down to number three, I caught eyes with Ada. She gave me a thumbs-up and mouthed, "perfect."

I was just getting started.

* * *

You simply haven't lived until you've eaten an Upper Crust Bakery triple-decker cookie sandwich.

I should probably clarify—a triple-decker cookie sandwich doesn't actually exist. Just a little something I made up when I was a kid. It's exactly what it sounds like, nothing fancy—just three "Cow Puddle" cookies stacked on top of one another. Cow Puddle was the Upper Crust name for a Butterscotch

80

and Pecan cookie. And it's the most divine thing you've ever put in your mouth. And a triple-decker of Cow Puddles? It's a dentist's nightmare but an absolute treasure for your tastebuds if you can unhinge your jaw enough to swallow it. But you should only do it when the cookies are fresh out of the oven—so melty that, as you bite into your handcrafted tower of crumbly goodness, they blend into one massive, not-too-crunchy but not-too-gooey, cavity-inducing blob. After all, if you're going to indulge, you might as well go full-on glutton.

Ada and I were sitting out back in the patio area, celebrating our first success. Each of those seven people had pledged their votes to me. It was small. But it was a start. And Delia offered me a free haircut. Among other things. The Bakery's outdoor chairs and tables were all sorts of rickety. But I didn't care. I was feeling right good about myself. And the ceramic cow figurines they had placed all over always made me chuckle.

And most importantly? I had my triple-decker.

"Are you sure you don't want anything?" I motioned to Ada with my Puddle-slimed fingers. "They have pie, too. If you're into that sort of thing."

Ada looked at me as I devoured my hard-earned treat like a starved hippo, bemused in a way that must be how a scientist gazes at a test subject. "No, thank you, I'm on a diet."

"A diet? Why? You look great."

"There's always room for improvement."

I chewed thoughtfully for a moment, debating how best to reply to that. There was absolutely no need for her to lose any weight—anyone with an ounce of sense would be able to tell you that. My heart went out to her, thinking about the demon inside her head that made her think she didn't look terrific the way she was. I cursed the source of that pain on her behalf—most likely some overbearing parent. "Well, I think you look wonderful. And anyone who tells you otherwise will have to deal with me." I took another chomp of my triple-decker.

Off this, Ada arched an eyebrow at me. "I need you to promise me something."

"What's that?"

"Never eat in front of a voter. Ever."

"I think Miss Delia wanted to take me out to dinner." I chuckled and jammed the remaining portion of the cookie into my mouth.

"Now I know what it feels like to be a passenger in an evil vehicle cruising through Paradise."

That made me stand at attention for a spell. I knew Ada was well-read—but referencing an obscure piece of fiction by Sam Shepard like that in casual conversation was a trick and a half. The only other person capable of such a feat was Audrey.

And I couldn't bring myself to think about her right now.

What was Ada getting after?

"I only know one other lady that can quote Shepard off the holster like that."

Ada demurely nodded. "Sounds like someone worth knowing."

You have no idea.

I cleared my throat, eager to get off the topic, masking my thoughts with a chuckle and a smile. "I'm an evil vehicle, huh? I don't get any points for not spilling on myself?"

"No."

"You're no fun."

Ada pulled out a miniature hand sanitizer bottle from her purse and handed it to me. "Tomorrow, we have the pancake breakfast event at the Middleburg Library."

"You know you can just call it the 'library,' right? Given that we're in Middleburg, and there's only one in town?" I squirted some sanitizer onto my palms.

She snatched back the hand sanitizer. "Eight a.m. Sharp."

I mock saluted. "Affirmative, Lieutenant."

She cracked a smile. "At ease, Private. You did excellent work today. Congratulations."

"Wouldn't have been able to do it without you, Consigliere. Walk you to your car?"

"What a gentleman."

As I escorted Ada to her automobile, I basked in the beautifully crisp, yet sunshiny day of autumn laid out before us. It was that perfect temperature—the kind that makes you want to sit out on the lawn with a blanket and a book while wearing a sweater and drinking a hot cider. My favorite time of year.

So far, today was impeccable. A success if there ever was one. Nothing could possibly ruin this—

I was shoved out the window of my sweet ride of thoughts by the music of a passing car's sound system. My feet stopped functioning when I recognized the tune they were playing: "Poison and Wine" by The Civil Wars. The stirring, tight harmonies of Joy Williams and John Paul White were unmistakable. It was the song that made my chest ache with regret.

It was the song that Audrey and I shared together.

"Are you okay, Christopher?" Ada gazed at me with concern.

I didn't know Ada well enough yet to show her my sensitive side, to give her a window into the part of me that had been inconsolable for the last month. The part of me I was desperately trying to bury.

Lock it up, Christopher.

I forced a smile. "All good, Lieutenant. I just remembered an errand I have to run. I'll see you tomorrow." I waved to her and turned heel, back in the direction that I came from. I could feel her questioning gaze probing its way between my shoulder blades. But I didn't want to think about that now.

Because right now? I needed a drink. The beautifully melancholic chorus of The Civil War's ballad rang in my ears. It was burned in my memory—the perfect film score to my sorrow. I needed something strong. Stronger than strong.

I needed something that would help me with the toughest task of all: washing away the taste of the girl whose mouth was like wine. The girl who was now heading in my direction.

But not to see me.

* * *

The prophetic words of The Civil Wars playing in my head were my only company—save for the glass of Jack Daniels in front of me. And Ol' Jack was already half-empty, his suitcase packed with one foot out the door.

Even my liquor was running out on me.

I was the only one in the bar. After all, it was only a little after 1 PM on a weekday. I could feel the bartender's judgmental gaze blazing on me like hot sun rays on the beach. And it only intensified when I asked him to leave the bottle on the counter. But I didn't care. I at least had the foresight to go outside of Middleburg. I was somewhere in Leesburg. About twenty minutes away from the prying eyes of any potential voters. Away from the future. For now, I just wanted to drown in the amber-colored water of the present.

When my brother had called me a few days ago, asking if they could use my cabin—I hung up before giving an answer. I needed to think about how to reply first. I couldn't just give in to the part of my body that was screaming, 'absolutely fucking not.' I needed to be measured. Calm. Rational. He wasn't doing anything wrong. He was asking his sibling for a favor. Reasonable enough, right?

But I was in love with my identical twin brother's girlfriend. And she had broken my heart. And he could never know.

Audrey had made that very clear when she broke off contact about a month ago. That she loved my brother and that she wanted to work on things with him. And that, if I really cared about her, we would keep what happened just between us.

What she really meant was that I was a mistake. And that she didn't love me the way I loved her.

I snatched up the bottle and emptied out a fresh pour into my glass. I had been holding it together pretty well until I heard that song on the radio. I had respected her wishes—I left her alone. No calls, texts, nothing. I deleted every single message we had exchanged. I kept moving. I had to—otherwise, I would collapse in a heap of misery and despair.

About three months ago, I got a text from Audrey out of the blue. She was going to be up at the Marion duPont Scott Equine Medical Center learning about new treatments for a torn suspensory, and she asked to see me, on the account of it was just a stone's throw away. It had been close to three years since we had last seen one another. Cillian had forbidden Audrey from spending time with me, which was lunacy—given that we were just friends and had never laid a finger on one another. But when Cillian got an idea in his head, he wasn't about to abandon it for something as trivial as common sense or reason. So, when she texted me, I asked her what Cillian would think about us meeting. She replied that she didn't care about that anymore. So, I invited her to my place for dinner.

I was excited. I had money now, and I was looking forward to impressing her in ways I couldn't before. We'd eat, laugh, and have some wine. Like old times. But better. I was on her level now—her family's level—monetarily speaking anyhow, and I could prove it to her. The Cape Cod-style house I had just bought wasn't a mansion or anything, but it was significantly nicer than anything she'd ever seen me in before. And I had bought it in cash. No mortgage required. That had to impress her, right?

Audrey was wearing immaculately pressed, rolled-up denim and a red blouse when I opened my bright blue front door. I always marveled at the way she managed to look effortlessly classy and sophisticated, even in casual clothes. She reminded me of Grace Kelly in that way. Except I thought she looked even better than Princess Grace, may that angel of a woman rest in peace. Audrey was holding a bottle of Cabernet Franc—not as nice as the kind we used to drink after stealing it from her Daddy's cellar, but that didn't matter. I cooked an avocado pasta recipe I had stolen from a restaurant I liked in San Jose, but without the tomatoes. I knew she was allergic. We picked up right where we left off. I couldn't remember the last time I had laughed that much.

As the night started to wind down, we moved to the living room, where we got to talking about Cillian. Things weren't good, she said. They were arguing all the time, she said. They didn't seem to have anything in common anymore, she said. Like a good friend, I just listened and affirmed the way she was feeling, asking questions at the appropriate intervals. My heart about broke when she told me that Cillian wouldn't go dancing with her. So,

I asked her to dance with me. Right there in the living room. She laughed shyly but agreed. I rooted through my collection of vinyls for the perfect accompaniment. I flipped through a medley of classic crooners—Frank Sinatra, Ella Fitzgerald, Billie Holiday—before settling on something more modern: *Barton Hallow*. The Civil Wars' first LP. I dropped the needle on the album's fifth track. I took her hand and moved her to the middle of my hardwood floor.

"Poison and Wine." The perfect song to slow-dance to. Like the world was giving us the green light to act on something we hadn't ever dared to.

"Is this okay?" I asked as I wrapped my arm around her waist.

She nodded.

We held each other, silently listening to the music as we rested in each other's arms.

"Is this okay?" she asked me as she put her head on my chest.

I nodded.

My heartbeat started doing double time.

Her hair smelled like vanilla and lilac. I stroked her cheek. We looked at each other. The song crescendoed. I leaned closer into her. Her into me. Her lip balm tasted like strawberries. Her skin like cocoa butter.

She lifted my shirt over my head. I slid off her jeans.

She nibbled my neck and whispered the magic words into my ear.

"Take me."

She moaned as I entered her. Gripped onto my pecs as I stroked her while she dripped on me. Gasped my name into my ear as I finished.

And nothing was ever the same.

"Hey mister, my shift is about to end. Mind settling up?" The bartender's words forced me back to reality. I was still the only one in the bar, but I had been sitting there for a good couple of hours, judging by the clock.

I nodded and threw down some cash. "Give me a to-go cup." The bartender's eyes flicked uncertainly from the bottle up to my face, then back to the bottle again. I set down some more cash. He got me a Styrofoam cup with a lid. It was the size of a Big Gulp. If my two years in Silicon Valley with Zander taught me anything, it's that everyone has their price. And everything is for sale. Especially when it comes to rules and so-called better judgment.

I stumbled out the back door and heaved myself into my Chevrolet Volt. Some people around here made fun of the fact that I owned a plug-in hybrid, calling it a "wind-up toy car." Simple-minded people make fun of what they don't understand. I didn't care—I loved her. She was cherry red with off-white leather seats. And she was good for the environment. I named her Joanie after my favorite character from *Mad Men*.

The alarm on my iPhone blared. A text reminder flashed on my screen: *text Cillian about cabin keys.*

Given what Cillian had told me, they'd probably be arriving in the next hour or so. Without thinking about it, I silenced the alarm and dutifully started typing out a text to Cillian telling him where I hid the spare key. About halfway through, a single thought thundered through my head.

What in God's name was I doing?

I had willingly agreed to give my cabin to him. So he could try and resuscitate his relationship with the woman he didn't deserve—the woman that he treated poorly enough to force her to turn elsewhere for affection.

So he could eat *my* food and drink *my* liquor.

So he could fuck her in *my* bed.

They'd be rolling around in *my* sheets. Abusing the springs of *my* mattress. Wiping their sweat-glistened faces post-climax with *my* pillows.

No fucking chance.

I slammed the push-start button of Joanie. This wasn't going to stand. I pounded down another swig of Mr. Daniels as I tore out of the parking lot.

I couldn't have her myself. Fine. Not everybody gets what they want in life. I understand that. But if I couldn't be with her? Then neither could he.

And I was going to make damn sure of that.

Chapter Eight

Cillian

"It's a goddamn beautiful day, isn't it Cillian?"

I'd known a lot of people in my day, but I hadn't ever heard one voice that could top Christopher's in the volume department. It was the voice of the man who had gotten every single fucking thing in his life with ease—a person who didn't just *want* to be heard, but also felt that he *deserved* it.

I glanced over at Audrey and Shep. His wet nose was pressed up against the window, tail thumping at the sight of this new potential friend. Audrey's expression was, for the first time since I had known her, devoid of any tell-tale signs of anything. I wondered what that could mean. That she was secretly happy to see him? Or maybe she was as pissed as I was to see his stupid, smirking face and was cloaking her real feelings in a mask of politeness? Either way, there was no chance that I was going to let Christopher ruin my weekend.

Our weekend.

I hopped down out of the truck and hung a hook around the flatbed to meet him on the lawn. "What are you doing here, Christopher?" It looked like he'd done two hundred push-ups moments before we'd arrived, his pectoral muscles were so large. And knowing how vain he was? That probably wasn't too far off. If I had money to gamble with, or if I had eyes in the back of my head, I bet I'd see Audrey sneaking a peek at his exposed torso.

Christopher put his hands on his hips, like a cartoon superhero. "It's always good to be greeted so warmly by your own flesh and blood. I'm great, Cillian. How are you?"

I heard Audrey's side of the truck open, but I was too locked in to pay it any mind. He smelled like he had taken a long soak in a bathtub of Jack Daniels. "Little early to be drinking."

It was an ability of his that I had always envied—no matter how much he drank, he always seemed in control. He never got sloppy. I wish I could say the same for me. If I put more than two drinks down my gullet? Things usually got messy. But I wasn't drinking anymore. I had promised Audrey.

"I was celebrating with my campaign staff. Our event today was quite the success. Just blowing off some steam," Christopher said.

"I think you can go ahead and flick off the kettle now."

"I don't recall asking you, now did I?"

Our showdown was interrupted by Shep bounding towards us, playful doggy energy finally uncorked after the long car ride. Sure enough, he made a beeline straight for Christopher, who crouched down and embraced him like a dad in an L.L. Bean commercial. Despite it all, I had to try hard not to smile—Shep was so funny-looking when his panting tongue hung out to the side like that.

"Well, now, who is this ruffian?" Christopher said as he scratched the top of his head. "He might just be about the sweetest thing I've ever seen."

Jesus. Even now, loaded out of his mind, he's in campaign performance mode with his brother. Did he have some sort of power cord I could yank out?

"His name is Shepard," Audrey said. She was now at my side, politely smiling.

"Cute. You always did love old Sam."

"And I still do. Despite your insistence that he can't hold a candle to Tennessee Williams." I recognized the warm-as-a-hot-toddy inflection she used when she was intellectually aroused. I rarely heard it directed towards me.

"Oh, c'mon! Look at them side-by-side. Your guy is speaking 5th-grade English, and my guy reinvented the entire goddamn language! After all, it's not insistence if it's a fact. Isn't that right, Brother?" Christopher shot me a playful wink.

A fucking wink. He was shoving my nose in it. The fact that I couldn't keep up. And why was she talking about Sam Shepard with him?

"It's nice to see you, Christopher," she replied.

"Likewise, Audrey." Christopher arched an eyebrow in my direction. "See now, Cillian, *that's* how you properly greet someone." He smiled at me, half playful and half not so much, making sure he never broke eye contact with me as he handed Shep back to Audrey.

"What brings you up here?" Audrey asked.

A wave of relief washed over me. That was the air Audrey put on when she was talking all decorum-like, but really thinking the exact opposite. It meant that, despite it all, she was on my team.

Christopher reached into the back pocket of his jeans and pulled out an old bandana, taking great care to wipe the perspiration from every inch of his face and upper body, including his cut-from-stone abs. "Well, I just wanted to check on everything up here before you came, of course. Only the best for my brother and his betrothed."

"We're not engaged," Audrey shot back. Despite my feelings about marriage, I didn't care for how quickly that came out of her mouth.

"No?" Christopher questioned. "After all this time, too? Seems like that'd be the next step, wouldn't it?"

"We don't need a piece of paper telling us—"

"Well, I'm sure you know what you're doing; don't mind me," Christopher interrupted as he gestured at my truck. "Why don't I help you with your bags, Cillian? Give that knee of yours a rest."

"That'd be fine, Christopher, thank you," Audrey answered for me.

Christopher met my eyes. "You heard the lady."

I stared back at Christopher, envisioning the sixty-six different ways I could pummel him, before finally stepping out of his way.

He yanked open the backseat of the truck with a fervor and removed our two bags—a small overnight bag for me and a full-on packed large suitcase for Audrey. Despite how no-nonsense she was in other aspects of her life, she always packed way more than necessary for trips. She had backup clothes for her backup clothes. It didn't bother me—it was just a funny little quirk I had noticed. And it came in handy sometimes. There was a camping trip we took down in Luray where I ran out of underpants. So...I put on one of Audrey's. It was strangely comfortable. I wasn't—and still am not—sure what to do with that knowledge.

Christopher took Audrey's suitcase in one hand and gripped my bag in the other. "I was thinking that it'd be nice if I fixed us all a meal before heading back into town?" Christopher glanced back and forth between Audrey and me—not quite telling, but not quite asking neither. "After all, it'd be rude for you to come to my neck of the woods and for me not to provide some sort of hospitality. At least, that's how I was raised."

My neck of the woods. Like I didn't grow up here, too. *At least, that's how I was raised.* Like I was a goddamn barn animal. Like I didn't share our parents' DNA. Although, I'm sure Dad probably would have preferred that. God, in so many ways Christopher was just like the old man. Arrogant as the day is long and about as full of wind as a corn-eating horse.

"We wouldn't want to put you out," I replied.

"It's not putting me out if I'm offering. What do you think, Audrey?"

There was that sphinx-like expression on my beloved's face again. "What were you thinking about making?"

"Avocado pasta."

Her lips tightened. "Cillian doesn't like avocado."

Fuck that. If Christopher and Audrey both eat it? I'll shovel enough of that frou-frou shit into my mouth to make me a goddamn avocado tree. I've seen him drop on a single meal what I spend on groceries for an entire month. I wasn't going to be outdone by him. Not this time.

"I don't mind it so much, darlin'." My jaw tightened as I squared up to my kin. "That sounds good, Chris. Thank you."

I smirked as I saw the thunderclaps roll across his face. He *hated* being called Chris. And me? Well, I *loved* whipping it out of my holster every now and again.

"Well. It's settled then."

91

The thick silence of our three-way standoff was broken by a loud belch from Shep. Despite it all, that earned a laugh from all three of us. I swear, that dog was born to be a tension-breaker if there ever was one.

* * *

If you had told me that Dad's cabin was going to look *exactly* the same from the last time I had set foot in here? I would've laughed in your face and called you some sort of name. But here we were, and I was proved to be the fool. It looked like Dad was still tromping the floors—that Christopher hadn't changed a goddamn thing since Dad gave up the ghost. Not the ugly-as-a-bandicoot, peeling plaid wallpaper that made the entire house look like a flannel button-up from The Gap. Not the beer-stained linoleum floors in the kitchen from when Dad was too loaded to notice he was spilling. Not the taxidermy heads scattered all over the living room that he bragged about bagging all over the surrounding property—even though there were "Do Not Hunt" signs posted everywhere, plain as could be. It was like a fucking shrine to him. It about near made me vomit.

Not Shep, though. He made himself right comfortable straight away on the living room couch, snoozing up a storm. About the only saving grace in the damn place were the candles Christopher had lit, which filled the entire place in the sweet-smelling film of tobacco and vanilla. Mama had liked that smell, so I liked it too. I wonder if he remembered that, or if it was just a coincidence.

"What an absolutely charming place, Christopher!" I couldn't believe what I was hearing escape from Audrey's lips. "It's got so much character."

I took an enormous glug of the iced tea Christopher had insisted on pouring for us. She actually liked this shithole? What was next, that she thought Maryland was a better state than Virginia?

"Thank you kindly, Audrey," Christopher said. "I keep thinking that maybe I should change some things around. But I just can't bear it yet. Not so soon after Daddy passed. But I will. Thankfully, I've got the cash to do it when the time is right."

That elicited a politely sympathetic 'I'm sorry' from Audrey, which about made my hair stand up on end. "I don't know if you can still say 'so soon' after more than a year," I said.

"Cillian, don't be rude." Audrey spat out at me.

"That's okay, Audrey. Cillian is entitled to his opinion. Perhaps he may even be right." Christopher shot me a smile that, to anyone else, would look like a brotherly expression of acknowledgment. But I knew the truth of it—that he was probably imagining shoving a hot poker into my eyeball.

Christopher hooked his thumb behind him, motioning to the second bedroom. "I set y'all up in there. Why don't you get unpacked, and I'll dart over and borrow some ingredients from The Ashby? I've become friendly with the owner."

Audrey arched an eyebrow at me as she raised her glass of tea to her lips, silently urging me to speak up. I took the hint.

"Is there something wrong with the master bedroom?"

Christopher folded his arms over his chest. "The mattress in there has got a massive case of bedbugs. I've ordered a new one. But you know how it is. Things take a long time to be delivered out here."

"Right."

"You can make do?" Christopher shot us a faux look of concern that I saw right through.

"Sure."

Christopher clapped his hands. "That settles it, then. I shall return." With that, he bundled out the front door.

Audrey turned to me. "He's really making us sleep in the other bedroom?"

I nodded, the hot blood of contempt snaking through my veins. "Looks like it."

"You really think he's got bed bugs?"

"No. But you really wanna take that chance?"

"Not particularly."

The afternoon sun poked through the half-drawn blinds in the kitchen, dancing a two-step with Audrey's halo of gold hair. "You sure seemed happy to see him."

God damn it. I did it again. The thing I was thinking in my head came out in a completely different way than what I meant.

Audrey's eyes clouded over. But it wasn't just with anger. It was also that unknown murky malady sinking its claws into her soul.

Nice, Cillian. Look what you did, you sack of shit. Fix it. Now.

"This was a mistake coming here." Audrey's gaze met mine as she spoke. The way she said it floored me. I could tell it wasn't meant to argue or fan the flame. It was just simply saying what was.

"No, it wasn't, darlin'. I'm just…all sorts of mixed up. I'm being unfair to you, and I'm sorry. We'll humor Christopher, let him cook us dinner, and then he'll leave. We're going to have a wonderful weekend. I promise." I slowly approached her, arms outstretched. "Can I give you a hug?"

Audrey looked at me uncertainly for a beat. Finally, she nodded. Just as I was about to wrap her in my arms, her face changed.

"Audrey, what's wrong?"

She looked about six shades of nauseated. "Do you smell that?"

I looked at her curious. "Smell what, darlin'?"

Her eyes darted over to the candles. "The candles."

I wasn't following her. "Yeah, they've been lit since we came in. Want me to blow 'em out? I'll go blow 'em out."

She gripped my forearms as I started to pull away. Sweat was pouring off her brow. "Cillian, wait—"

And with that, she convulsed and unleashed a geyser of vomit onto my chest. Every single morsel of that burger and milkshake that she had consumed earlier was now dripping on my t-shirt. I probably should have leaned back or gotten out of the way. But truth be told, I was too shocked to move a muscle.

Jesus. I didn't think it was possible for this much vomit to come out of a human.

After she was finished, the way she looked at me nearly broke my heart in two.

"I…I'm so sorry, Cillian. I'm so sorry." Audrey's lower lip started to tremble.

"That's alright, darlin'. Feeling ill isn't nothing to be ashamed of. Don't give it a second thought." I took off my upchuck-slimed shirt and balled it up onto the floor. I guided her head to my shoulder and stroked the back of her neck with my thumb and index finger, the way I knew she liked.

That's when she started crying.

I honestly don't think that 'crying' is an adequate word for it, though. When I think of crying, I think of a few soft tears falling down a cheek, like a spring drizzle. Audrey's crying here was something different. This was a hurricane—the levee had finally been snapped by whatever the pent-up demon was that had been banging on inside of her.

As she bawled into my shoulder, I racked my brain for something I could do, besides just giving her shelter and waiting for her to dry herself out.

Then it hit me. I could sing.

Not in the goofy way I did back in the car with Bruce. There wasn't anything silly about this. She was stripped bare emotionally, so I knew I had to match her earnestness. I put my lips to her right ear and gently swayed her back and forth as I crooned the lyrics of "You Are My Sunshine," soft and low, willing every ounce of calm I possessed into my voice. I pecked her earlobe as I felt her melt into me. She cinched her arms around my torso as tight as the turns she used to make in the dressage ring with Dolly.

And that's when I heard the magic words float from her lips. The ones that made me feel like I could take on an entire army by myself. "I love you, Cillian. More than anything. You know that, don't you?"

I pulled her face off my shoulder, brought her to my muzzle, and gave her an Eskimo kiss, not caring about her vomit breath. "Not as much as I love you, Audrey."

Maybe this weekend would turn out okay, after all.

* * *

The guest room, to put it lightly, was a piece of shit. Just like I remembered. All there was in the room was a crappy, cheap fabric bureau you get from IKEA or Walmart and a mattress that had seen better days yesterday plopped on the floor. It felt more like a prison cell than a spare bedroom. But nobody had wanted to visit Dad, save for Christopher, so I suppose he had no reason to care. At least Christopher had made up the mattress with fresh sheets. That's something, I suppose.

I tucked in my beloved and kissed her on her forehead, sliding in Shep next to her like an emotional support teddy bear. She was already half-asleep and looked to be slipping off even further. I pressed the back of my hand to her forehead. She was burning up—like the devil was frying eggs on her temple. But she didn't have a fever. I did the thermometer check twice. I leaned back, perched on the corner of the mattress, wondering what the hell was going on. Maybe it was food poisoning from the cheeseburger she had earlier. If it was, though, why hadn't I been barfing up a storm next to her?

Was there something she wasn't telling me? Some secret that was scooping out her insides with a rusted spoon?

I brought my brain to a halt. I needed to stop the locomotive before it ran off the tracks. So, I turned out the light and closed the door behind me, leaving Audrey to her slumber. I went to the kitchen to grab myself a drink. Opening the door, I saw that there weren't any options save for water, the remnants of the iced tea we drank earlier, and a 24-pack of Pabst Blue Ribbon. My lips salivated off the last one.

I need to take the edge off. What's one beer on a Saturday? Especially when I had to deal with Christopher for a whole goddamn dinner. With a beer in my gullet, I could handle that. I have self-control. I can stop after one. I can handle my business. I wasn't in the headspace that I was in before.

Damn it, Audrey, I deserve a drink.

Justification achieved, I removed a bottle. Beer wasn't rye whiskey—my preferred potion—but it would do. I had forgotten how good a cold bottle of beer felt in your hand on a sunny day, like an extension of your palm and your fingertips. I popped the top. That sweet foam came sweating out. I stared at it. It was the ultimate temptress, begging me to taste her juices.

I tipped it back. Jubilation coursed through me as I felt the first sips slide down my throat. Before I knew it, I had crushed the entire bottle. I gasped for air, like a scuba diver breaking through the surface after a long dip. I closed my eyes, savoring every single morsel.

Fuck. I had forgotten how good this feels.

As soon as my eyes opened back up, though, reality hit me over the head. I had broken my promise to her.

You are a piece of shit. No, you're worse than a piece of shit. At least a piece of shit is something. You're worthless. A big helping of nothing with a side of fucking prick.

I stumbled around to the sink underneath the window, looking out towards the backyard. I put the bottle down on the counter beside me and gripped the sink's porcelain basin.

A real man wouldn't give in to temptation. How could you do this to her?

I glanced out the window. Maybe the world would give me some sort of answer. Nada. Just the forested landscape that I had seen before.

Wait.

My eyes focused on the one thing that was new since the last time I'd been here. Just down the slope from the driveway out back was a freshly planted Red Maple tree.

My heart stopped. It was show-stopping gorgeous. Its foliage was blazing red with a splash of orange. It stood alone amidst the sea of browning oaks on the property. It looked like a flare signaling to the heavens above that there was life capable of true, unadulterated beauty down below.

From another vantage point, though? It looked an awful lot like a splotch of fresh blood on a canvas of camouflage.

The front door opened.

Christopher was back. I slowly turned to face him. His eyes fell to the bottle, then back to me. Then the son-of-a-bitch smirked as he asked me the one thing that I didn't need to hear.

"You want another?"

Chapter Nine

Christopher

I recognized that look in his eye.

It was the look of a man who knew, with every fiber of his being, that he wasn't supposed to be doing what he was doing.

And I had caught him.

The game is afoot.

"You want another?" I asked him again.

He couldn't even meet my eyes he was so ashamed of himself. "I...don't think I should," he said.

"Don't be silly. What's a beer amongst brothers? I won't judge you. In fact, I'll have one with you." I slapped him on the back and pulled out two more from the fridge. I cracked his open for him and jammed it into his hand. "Bottoms up."

I swigged down half of my PBR in one gulp, while he just held his, looking at the bottle like it was a ticking time bomb. Audrey had mentioned that he struggled with booze. Especially after his accident. And Lord knows, I knew full well that he couldn't hold his liquor worth a damn. When I gave him his first beer when we were fifteen down by the creek, he ended up stripping down buck naked and splashing around like an infant taking a bath for the first time. Which was all well and good. But then he thought it was a good idea to go running around the neighborhood hollering about how good he felt, his pecker flapping in the wind. I don't think the eighty-seven-year-old

Mrs. Jamison, who lived a couple doors down from us, was ever quite the same after that.

Anyway, Cillian had tasted the forbidden nectar. And he wanted more. He was wrestling with the beast of temptation, right on the precipice.

All he needed was a good, firm push.

"Where's the lady?" I asked him.

That got his attention. His beady little eyes finally snapped up to look at me. I saw fear and guilt dancing behind them like they were doing the tango. "She's lying down. Not feeling well. Shepard is in there with her, too."

"Oh. I'm sorry to hear that. I'll hold off on cooking dinner for her, then."

"You meant 'us', right?" Cillian was never good at disguising his emotions, and I could feel the jealousy catapulting out of his mouth.

I smiled. He had fallen into my trap. Now, I knew for sure that he was pumping hot, which would lead to some rash decision-making on his part.

Which is exactly what the doctor ordered.

"Of course that's what I meant, Brother. Silly me." I not-so-subtly glanced over his shoulder at Audrey's bedroom door, then back at him. "I'll tell you what. She's not looking, and I'm not going to tell a soul. It'll be our little secret. So why don't you go ahead and give in to your worser angels and drink that thing down? Then we can have some fun. Like we used to when we were kids."

I paused for a moment. Like any politician worth his salt, I knew that I needed to sprinkle in some truth with the lies.

"I know we've grown apart these past years. But it didn't used to be that way, right? There was a time when we used to enjoy each other's company. I remember. Let's put everything on hold. Just for a moment here."

Uncertain, Cillian looked at me. His expression softened a bit. I was making some headway. But I could see that he wasn't all the way convinced. So, I dialed it up a notch.

"Look, Cillian. You've already broken the seal, right? Popped opened the can of worms. Hell, they're all over the place now. You've done the thing that you weren't supposed to do. You can't change that. So…what's one more? You're already going to have to apologize to her one way or the other. So, make it something really worth apologizing for." I drained the rest of my beer and put the bottle aside. Still, Cillian hesitated.

Time to bring in the big guns.

"You and I both know you want me to get the fuck out here, right? I get that. I'd probably feel the same in your shoes. But there's something that I wanted to show you up here. You know—brother to brother. Have this beer with me; then I'll dart off into the night and leave you two to your business. Scout's honor. That a fair trade?"

After maybe a half-second of consideration on his end, Cillian chugged the entire bottle and heartily slammed it down on the counter.

This was going to be easier than I thought.

"What is it you have to show me?" He nearly spat out the words as he wiped his mouth.

I smiled as I reached into the fridge and grabbed two more bottles of the frosty stuff.

"Where I buried Daddy."

* * *

I cracked open my other bottle as I walked Cillian out to Daddy's burial ground. It was underneath the Red Maple tree out back. Even though his death had been sudden, he had always talked about how he used to climb Red Maples when he was a boy. How there was a particular one in his backyard that he would climb up and hide in to avoid his father's belt when he was on a bender. It was one of the only places in the world where he felt safe. And how he wanted to be buried under one when the time came. So, when he passed on? I had one transplanted here. I spent a small fortune getting one that wasn't fully grown but was well on its way. One that would be a fitting shade for Daddy and not a freshly planted, little dinky one.

Daddy was a flawed man. But underneath it all, he was a good person. He had been abused and lived in a time when therapy wasn't an option for a strapping young man. So, he dealt with it the only way he and his contemporaries knew—through sheer willpower and the crutch of a good drink. Cillian would have understood that if he had been a good son and hadn't played Casper the ghost. Or even just been any kind of son at all.

The selfish, wallowing-in-pity prick.

"This is where we put him to rest." I pointed at the small little headstone wedged in the ground up against the tree's trunk. Draped a few feet over Daddy was the Maple's lowest hanging branch. So even on the hottest days, Daddy's soul could grab some shade and cool off for a spell. I thought he'd like that. After all, he was the one who always told me that I was born to lead. That I had a voice that commanded respect—and that if I didn't put that to use in politics one day, I'd be doing a disservice to the world. He encouraged me to reach for greatness—that I was *able* to achieve it. Which made everything else he did irrelevant. He deserved to rest peacefully. For everything he gave to me.

"That's...great." Cillian's voice trailed off as he glared at Daddy's grave. I marveled at how Cillian's choice of words always made me want to pound him—no matter how few he uttered. In a way, it was a gift. I almost respected the skill of it in a perverse way.

"That's it? That's all you got to say?"

Squinting to avoid the sun, Cillian slowly shifted his eyes at me. "What is it I'm supposed to say, exactly?"

God damn, the fucker was really asking for it.

"I don't know, maybe show some respect for the dead? For the man whose funeral you couldn't be bothered to show up for? For the man who raised you?"

Cillian's wry, sarcastic laugh echoed throughout the property. "Maybe he raised *you*, Chris. But not me. All he was to me was a drunk who didn't give a damn about me and treated Mama worse than dirt."

I cringed at the mention of our mother. No matter how much I loved Daddy, there was no way of getting around the fact that he had done Mom wrong. "I won't fight you on the last part, Cillian. But he did care about you. He loved you. As best he could."

"Well, his best wasn't good enough."

"He didn't understand you, Cillian. You and your horses and all that—"

"Me and my horses and all that. Well said, brother," Cillian spat out.

"Well, goddamn Cillian, what did you expect? Daddy was a lot of things, but he wasn't a Rhodes scholar. It intimidated him that he couldn't keep up with you and your world. He didn't even know where to begin on how to relate to you! And don't you think it embarrassed him that he couldn't pay for any of it? It's one thing to scrounge together some loose change for secondhand pads and cleats—but it's a whole goddamn other thing to buy and care for an animal that costs more than a Mercedes."

"You don't have to be a Rhodes scholar to love your own kin."

"That's a little bit of the pot calling the kettle black, isn't it?" We locked eyes, neither of us wanting to budge from the showdown. Finally, Cillian cut through the silence by ripping the twist-off from his cold one and taking a long swig.

God, this was easy. I was playing him like a fiddle. Time to get to the heart of it, now.

I motioned back up at the house. "Things aren't going so great between you two, huh?"

Cillian's expression morphed into something like a feral wolf—teeth bared for the kill. "Why? Did she say something to you?"

I played dumb. "Calm down, Cillian. No. Just the way you sounded on the phone. I know you well enough to know when you've got a bee in your behind. And you just took another drink. So that's got to mean something, right?"

"You handed it to me."

"That doesn't mean you had to drink it."

He studied me for a beat before dropping down his guard slightly. I don't know if he believed me, but he didn't look like he wanted to kill me. So that's something.

"Things have been…challenging, as of late. Yeah," he said. He looked down at his shoes as he uttered the next part. "So, I really appreciated it when you said we could use the cabin—"

I feigned a look of shocked surprise to cut him off. "Wow. That must have twisted you up in a knot to admit that."

"—but then you actually showed up. I hadn't realized that was part of the deal." There was that withering look of Cillian's again.

"That's the thing about family, Cillian. It never leaves you. No matter how hard you try."

Off that, Cillian guzzled the last of his beer. I could tell it was already going to his head.

"Except you're going to leave now, aren't you? You promised me that you would." Back during the rare times when Cillian and I would drink together, Cillian's voice would get extra whiny when he got tipsy. Some things never change.

"Yeah, Cillian. Sure thing." I pointed at his bottle. "Why don't you give me that? Cover up the evidence of your transgression."

Cillian's face burned with self-loathing as he handed me his empty, and I slipped it in my back pocket. A hiccup burp escaped from his lips. I swear to God, it was like drinking with a kindergartner.

"You going to be all right, there?" I asked him. But I knew he wasn't going to be all right. That was the whole point of this—to drive a wedge between him and the woman that he didn't deserve. But I had to at least pretend, right? "You're probably going to want to brush your teeth ASAP. Or at least chew some gum or something."

He took a deep breath and ran his fingers through his hair. Couldn't even look at me. "Just go," Cillian said quietly, barely above a whisper.

I gave him a condescending clap on the back. "Okay, Brother. Whatever you say."

As we started to head back towards the house, we saw Audrey and Shepard come out the front door.

"What were you two doing out here?" She asked in a pleasant enough tone, but her green eyes were thundering with something fierce and dark. Meanwhile, Shepard sleepily walked next to her, looking pissed at the intrusion into his siesta.

"I realized that Cillian had never seen where Daddy was buried." I hooked my thumb behind me at the Maple. "So, I showed him. You want to join us?"

She waved me off. "That's okay. I remember him plenty well enough."

"How are you feeling, darlin'?" Cillian asked Audrey, eager to change the subject. He stumbled as the 'darlin'' slid out of his mouth. It was ever so slight—you'd only notice if you knew what you were looking for. If you'd spent years around alcoholics.

Audrey arched an eyebrow at Cillian, sizing him up. She had noticed it. But, unlike me, I could tell she had doubts about its cause. "Better, thank you," she said. It wasn't quite snappy the way she said it, but it certainly wasn't warm and friendly either. I had to stop myself from smiling. She was definitely suspicious of Cillian.

It was working. The shoe was going to drop.

"I should be heading off." I started towards my car. "Great to see y'all. Enjoy my cabin."

"Don't be silly—you promised us a meal. And you're going to give us one." Audrey smiled as she reached into her pocket and held up my keys. "Besides, we would be irresponsible if we let you drive a car right about now."

Cillian stepped up next to me. "Darlin', I've seen Christopher much more drunk than this. He's a tank. He'll be fine." I was actually impressed. Cillian, the lightweight, managed to pull himself together enough to convincingly hide his imbibing. He now sounded perfectly fine. Maybe he was a better liar than I thought.

Audrey stared at him a beat. I could tell she was trying to suss Cillian out. After a tick, it looked like he passed her inspection, so she flashed him a smile that was warmer than before, but still not all the way home. "I think the least we can do is make sure your brother eats and sobers up. He is letting us use *his* house for the weekend, right?"

I stifled a laugh as I imagined Cillian mentally smothering a banshee-like yell. To try and mitigate the potential of revealing his relapse, I knew he'd be willing to bend over backwards to anything Audrey said.

"You know best, darlin'," he muttered.

Jackpot.

"Well, if that's what you two want," I answered, "then who am I to stand in the way of your wishes?"

I could see Audrey take a deep breath before saying the next part: "And there's something the three of us need to discuss later on."

Both Cillian's and my ears pricked up at the mention of that. It was news to us. To say the absolute least.

What in the fuck did she need to talk to the both of us about? This was the first time all three of us had been together in...well, I can't even remember.

The silence hung there for a spell before I interjected: "Fine. After we eat, you talk, and we'll listen. Easy as 1-2-3. Right, Brother?"

Cillian forced a smile on his face as he motioned to the door. "Sure. After you, Brother."

* * *

Now let there be heard a great gnashing of teeth.

Daddy always said that if the only sound heard around a dinner table was chewing—like it was right now—then that meant that everyone was too busy silently thanking the cook to actually speak. But that wasn't the reason for the stone-cold hush suffocating the table today.

That said, though—I knew I had done well with this meal. I had replicated the same avocado pasta recipe that I made Audrey on that magical night, plus added a few twists I had picked up since then. I had found adding cilantro to the sauce had given the dish the slight kick in the pants that it was missing previously, for instance. I had picked up a bottle of a crisp New Zealand Sauvignon Blanc—which was just about the perfect pairing possible, in my experience. Cillian made a joke about the wine—saying that he never understood people's obsession with it. That it was nothing more than juice with some alcohol in it. I saw Audrey noticeably shudder when he said that.

Yep. You definitely chose the right man, Audrey. My brother the simpleton with the palate of a toddler. Well done.

I had poured myself and Audrey a glass each, but I noticed she hadn't touched it since the meal began. That was strange—I had never known her to turn down a good glass of wine at mealtime. At least not when we broke bread together.

Looking down at her food, though? She had joined the clean plate club.

I wonder if Cillian had ever bothered to make her a meal. Hell, I wonder if he even knew how to cook anything other than a baked potato.

"That was lovely, Christopher. Thank you," she said as she wiped her mouth daintily.

"My pleasure," I replied. "Glad to see you're feeling better and your appetite's back."

She shifted her gaze away from mine. "Thank you."

"Yeah. Me too, honey," Cillian said. He stretched out his hand and placed it over top of Audrey's as he glowered at me.

God. What was next? Was he going to pee on her or something equally as foul to mark his territory? Because that's definitely how people like to be treated—like possessions and not flesh and blood.

I felt a nudge at my knee under the table. Lo and behold, Shepard was poking me with his wet nose, begging for scraps with eyes that looked like they should have belonged to *Shrek's* Puss-in-Boots. "I really can't give Shepard anything?"

Cillian's eyes hadn't left mine for a millisecond. "No. We don't want him learning things that can't be untaught."

I thinly smiled at Cillian's barbed statement. Judging from his nearly empty plate, it appeared that he had enjoyed my cooking, too—much to his chagrin. "Looks like you like avocado after all, huh?"

"I'll eat anything if I'm hungry enough."

Jesus Christ. He couldn't even let me have that small victory.

I took a long sip of my wine. The silence simmered as the three of us danced around the inevitable. Cillian met my gaze, silently daring me to back down. I had no such intention. So, I pushed my chair back and put my hands behind my head. The universal sign that you were planning on sitting a while.

Cillian's jaw cinched tighter than a woman's corset in Dickensian times. "Well. Thank you, Chris." He stood up and started to clear everyone's plates. "I'll tidy up while you tell us what you need to tell us, honey."

I saw Audrey's face cloud over with dread and anxiety. "Oh, we don't have to talk about it right now—"

"Leave the plates, Cillian. I'll do them later. There's still dessert, after all," I interrupted.

"I don't want dessert. Audrey, you said you needed to talk. Let's talk."

I put my feet up on the neighboring chair, hunkering down. "What's the matter, Brother? I've never known you to skip dessert. What happened to that sweet tooth of yours?"

Cillian took all the dishes to the sink and started scrubbing fervently as he filled the sink up with soapy water. If he was a cartoon, steam would have been coming out of his ears. "Things change, Brother."

I turned my gaze to Audrey. "Did Cillian ever tell you about how many sweets he ate as a kid? He was *insatiable.* The poor fool was practically at the dentist every month he had so many cavities. It was a miracle he wasn't a thousand pounds."

A small half-smile flickered across Audrey's lips. "Really?"

"Oh yeah. His favorite was..." My voice trailed off as I pretended to pull it from my memory—but I knew exactly what it was. "...Hostess cakes, if my memory serves. Isn't that right, Cillian?"

Cillian didn't answer. He had already finished the plates. Now he was on to furiously scrubbing the pots and pans I had used.

I laughed as I leaned back in my chair. "Yeah, that's right, Audrey—the man you chose loves that artificial, processed garbage that you can get at a gas station. Can you believe that?"

The half-smile that had appeared on Audrey's face quickly vanished. She knew what I was doing. At this point, though? I didn't care. Needling Cillian was too much fun. "Me? I've always preferred things where you can pronounce the ingredients that are in it. Or even just know what the hell they are. I think that's a far superior way to live if you ask me. But you and I have always been different, Cillian."

Cillian slammed down his handiwork, the faucet still running. "Audrey, how about it? What did you need to tell us? The meal's over."

I had him now.

"Well, I don't know about that, Cillian—"

"It's over," he declared firmly. "Enough is enough. Audrey—"

"Fuck's sake, Cillian, can't you give her a goddamn minute? Maybe at least let her digest for a second before you go making her do your bidding—"

"Make her do my bidding? I didn't want *any* of this! You're the one that's been manipulating this whole goddamn day so you could stay as long as you pleased!"

Despite myself, I couldn't help but blurt out a laugh. "Am I not capable of doing a nice thing for a member of my family without having some sort of sinister intent?"

"No. You're not. Not in my experience. Not unless something is in it for you!"

Cillian and I were so preoccupied going at each other's throats that we had been ignorant to the fury slowly building on Audrey's face—a fact that immediately rocked us to our core as she slammed her hand emphatically on the table to shut us up, like a judge thumping her gavel down to deliver a life-altering verdict.

And that was when she said the thing that made every single courtroom drama I'd ever seen seem like a light-hearted comedy.

"I'm pregnant. And Christopher is the father."

Chapter Ten

Cillian

Christopher is the father.

If Lucifer himself had thought of the four words that would haunt me for the rest of my days? This would be about five times worse than whatever he would have come up with.

I didn't even notice that the sink I had been washing the dishes in was now completely overflowing onto the floor.

I must not have heard right. It was a joke. It had to be. I couldn't have just heard what I thought I just heard.

"What did you say?" I managed to croak out.

Audrey looked like she was racked by guilt but also relieved of the deepest burden a person could feel. "I'm pregnant. And it's his," she said as she motioned at Christopher.

Him. The rot that was currently infecting my entire life. Our entire life.

I made myself look at Christopher. Judging by his expression, he looked about as shocked as me.

"When did this happen?" My voice started to shake. I could feel my temper boiling up, scorching my insides.

"How long have you known, Audrey?" Christopher interjected.

"This doesn't concern you," I shot back. "Sit down and shut the fuck up."

"I am sitting down, Cillian."

"Then do a better job of the other thing."

"Very clever. And this *does* concern me. Or did you not hear what she just—"

"Both of you shut up!" Audrey commanded us.

Audrey took a deep breath. I could see the sweat starting to trickle down her temples.

Me and her both.

"I've known for about a month and a half now," she said to Christopher. Then she turned to me. "And it happened when I came up—"

It occurred to me that I had no interest in hearing the nitty gritty details of when my brother knocked up my lady. I put my hand up, silently begging her to stop.

"It was just the once, Cillian—" Her voice drew to a halt as I raised my hand even higher. It was shaking now, too. She obliged me.

I slowly brought my gaze from the ground to hers. I could see that she was practically stewing in perspiration now, so I tossed her a dishrag to mop her brow. As I stepped around and my feet squelched in the river of dishwater that was forming on the kitchen floor, it occurred to me that I needed to turn off the faucet unless I wanted to drown myself. Which seemed tempting, to be honest with you. But I turned it off anyway.

"*Why* did this happen?" That was the agonizing question that I really wanted answered.

Audrey didn't break her stare for a moment—her green eyes shimmered with that murky malady I'd been seeing for a while. And now? I finally knew the cause of it. "I haven't felt happy in our relationship for a long time, Cillian."

That about made me fall over with despair. And shame. And regret. For a moment, my pity for my beloved overwhelmed my blinding rage.

I was her man—and she didn't feel contented being my partner.

That had to be my fault, right? It was my responsibility to make her happy. But still—

"Sleeping with my brother made you feel happy?" My voice cracked.

Tears started to form in her eyes. "It wasn't like that."

I wasn't sure what to do with the mess of emotions I was being dealt here. Confusion, anger, shock. But sorrow quickly won out as I felt the salty sting of tears start to run down my cheek. "You told me you weren't ready to have a baby."

Maybe what she meant was that she wasn't ready to have a baby with me. That I wasn't good enough to be a father. That I wasn't—

"Maybe she was just waiting for the right person, Brother," Christopher said as he cut through the maelstrom. "And that's not something she should have to apologize for or explain. Sometimes things just happen." He got up from the kitchen table chair and stepped chin to chin with me, his shoes splashing in the puddle that was now on the kitchen floor. "When someone is desperately unhappy? Truly miserable? All bets are off."

I felt the roar of blind rage ricocheting through my chest.

"That right, Chris?" Behind me, I reached into the sink and wrapped my fingers around the handle of the stainless-steel frying pan I had just washed.

"That's right, Cillian." He sneered at me.

I sneered right back at him. "Then I guess I won't need to apologize for this."

CLAAAANNGG!

I whipped the backside of the frying pan against the side of Christopher's head. He crumbled to the ground like a deer hit by a car.

"Cillian, stop it!!!!" Audrey's voice ripped through the room. But I barely heard her or the sounds of Shepard barking and whaling from under the table.

Sorry, my love. I'm not driving the bus anymore. My lesser angels are stomping on the gas—we're all just passengers now.

I knelt close to Christopher as he writhed and groaned and whispered in his ear: "Sometimes things just happen, Brother."

"Cillian!!" I felt Audrey tug on my shoulder, trying to pull me off. But I shrugged her off. Somehow, after the wallop I had just dealt him, Christopher wasn't bleeding. I must have missed the mark of what I was aiming for— knocking the son-of-a-bitch's lights out.

That needed to be fixed. ASAP.

Like a stallion going in for the kill on a foal, I jumped on top of Christopher, pinning him down as I clocked him three times across the face. Then, I grabbed him by the throat, flinging him around like a ragdoll as I squeezed harder and harder.

And that's when Christopher started laughing. Despite the blood streaming down his face, he was just smiling and howling like a hyena hopped up on meth.

His own brother is about to kill him, and he's laughing?

"What the fuck is so funny?!" I shouted at him.

That only made him laugh even harder.

"WHAT THE FUCK IS SO FUNNY, CHRIS?!?!"

He flashed me that campaign-ready smile of his—except now his blood was staining his photo-op-ready porcelain whites. "I'm in love with her. And I'm pretty sure she feels the same. It's been wearing me out, having to hide it for your benefit. And now I don't have to." He motioned towards Audrey's stomach. "And now there's permanent, ever-lasting proof that she chose *me* instead of *you*."

I hesitated for a beat as I absorbed that, and Christopher seized the opportunity, flipping me over, so now I was trapped under his muscular body. It was his turn to whale on my face. His weightlifting-sculpted, toned body was better suited for this type of hand-to-hand fraternal warfare. I immediately felt a tooth knock loose as his knuckles met my jaw on the first go.

"Have you ever thought, Cillian, that it was *you* that drove her to seek comfort in my embrace? That it wasn't some evil misdeed on her part—but just a woman running away from a partner that didn't see her value?" Christopher seethed as he brought his brawny thunder crashing down onto my face. "From a man who had *ruined* her life?"

"Christopher!" Audrey tried the same tactic she had tried with me.

No dice.

Christopher let me have it.

Again.

And again.

"IF YOU TWO DON'T STOP RIGHT NOW, I'M GONNA WALK OUT THAT DOOR, AND NEITHER OF YOU WILL EVER SEE ME AGAIN!" Audrey bellowed.

That worked.

The two of us, each so bloodied that it was near impossible to tell who was who, rolled off each other, panting for breath. I futilely tried to pop my ringing ears.

"Audrey, I—"

"Both of you aren't going to speak again until I've said what I have to say," Audrey stopped me short.

Christopher motioned his hands in the universal "I surrender" position, and I nodded in accord. Both of us side-eyed the other like warring pit bulls vying to be let off their chains.

The silence sat there all quiet-like for a beat before Audrey finally broke the spell.

"I didn't plan for any of this to happen. I didn't *want* any of this to happen. But I'm keeping this baby. That's the one thing I am sure about."

As I saw Christopher's eyes widen, I silently snickered to myself. No way in hell would an old-fashioned place like Middleburg elect a man who impregnated his brother's partner. This isn't Appalachia. And there wasn't any chance that he would give up his political aspirations to be with her.

Audrey knew it, too. We wouldn't have to deal with him. Ever again.

"Christopher, I won't tell a soul. The press won't know anything. It won't affect your campaign at all. It'll be buried forever," Audrey said. "And Cillian—I understand if you hate me. I'd hate me, too. You can be as involved as you want to be—"

"Now, hold on just a minute," Christopher interrupted. "Who said I wanted to bury this?"

Fuck.

"Christopher, this wouldn't be good for your—"

"Fuck my mayoral run. You're more important than that." Christopher pointed his finger at me. "I'll be damned if I let him raise my flesh and blood."

"If you point that finger at me again, I'll make sure you can never lift your arm again."

Christopher simply ignored me as he slowly stood up, approaching Audrey like a coyote circling its prey.

"Think about everything you told me about him that night, Audrey. Do you *really* think he's equipped to be a father? With me, you can have your life back. Everything that you had to give up when you ran off with him? I can give it back to you. I can provide for you. I make more in a month than Cillian has ever seen in his entire life."

I was starting to see spots.

"Audrey, don't listen to him. I *am* ready. I am yours—"

Christopher got closer to my beloved. "You can't tell me with a straight face that night didn't matter to you. That it was just a meaningless night of passion. I know you better than that. *You* know you better than that."

I saw a shift in Audrey's eyes—like she was actively considering what Christopher and the crock of shit his silver tongue was peddling.

"We would be a power couple," Christopher said. "You would have *status*. You would have *influence*. And you could ride as many champion horses as you could stand. There would be nothing that wouldn't be within our means. I want that for you. Don't you want that, too?"

A wave of desperation crashed over me. "Audrey, darlin', look at my eyes," I pleaded with her. "Nothing this motherfucker has told you is the truth. Nothing he's manipulated you to say or think or seduced you to do can't be undone." I had to fix this. Before she put me out to pasture for good.

"Audrey. I've never once lied to you. About anything. Ever." I couldn't see Christopher's face, but it sounded like he was giving an Oscar-worthy performance. Or something a devil would conjure up. Take your pick. "You can read people better than anyone I've ever met. I want you and this baby more than the campaign. Can you honestly tell me that I'm not telling the truth?"

Audrey's eyes started to well up, and I felt myself being sucked into the vortex of nothingness.

Do something, you idiot! Do it now!

And that's when my eyes cycled to the frying pan.

114

There's no way the fucker would survive two direct blows to the head with that thing. It's time to act. Right now. I was going to channel Austin in Sam Shepard's *True West.*

Except I would finish the job.

I grabbed the pan, gripped it with two hands like I was stepping up to home plate, and swung with all of my might.

Somehow, Christopher managed to grab the butcher block cutting board from the nearby countertop and did the same thing as me.

Except we didn't get to each other. Christopher and I were so consumed with rage and hatred and jealousy we had failed to see that—maybe two milliseconds beforehand—my beloved had thrown herself between us to try and break up the melee.

We both hit Audrey with every ounce of ferocity that we had saved up for each other.

And that's when she dropped to the ground like a fawn full of buckshot, her head smacking on the floor with a sickening crack.

It was how I expected the end of the world to sound.

Christopher and I froze.

This couldn't be really happening. There's no fucking chance we just did what we did. No. No. No. No.

Finally, Christopher spoke, his voice cracking as horror rippled across his face. "Oh my God. Is she—?"

I dropped the pan and flung myself down to Audrey's side.

No. No. No. No.

I put my finger to her pulse.

Nothing.

NO NO NO NO NO NO—

"Audrey, darlin'—wake up! Wake up!" In despair, I gave her CPR, pumped on her chest, and breathed into her mouth.

That beautiful mouth. The mouth that breathed life into my soul. The one that made you realize why God gave humans the ability to speak. The one that was the most breathtaking wake-up call a man could ever receive. The one that had made me believe that true love was real and not something made up by Hallmark cards.

"C'mon now, Audrey! C'MON NOW! WAKE UP! WAKE UP!" I checked her vitals again.

Nothing.

I pumped faster and faster and gave her near every ounce of oxygen in my lungs.

NO NO NO NO NO NO—

I desperately checked her pulse one last time.

She was gone.

A guttural, monosyllabic bellow erupted from my chest as I cradled my beloved's body in my arms. Tears seared my face and bathed hers.

Oh my God, Oh my God, Oh my God, Oh My God—

I vaguely heard the distorted voice of Christopher from behind me, trying to get my attention.

Oh my God, Oh my God, Oh my God, Oh My God—

Christopher's voice became slightly clearer.

Oh my God, Oh my God, Oh my God, Oh My God—

"CILLIAN!" Christopher's voice came into focus as he yanked me off her and gripped me by the shoulders.

Through the blindness of my tears, I tried to break from his grasp and grab him by the throat, but he held me firm. Somehow, someway, he seemed totally calm and in control—the ice to my fire.

"Cillian, listen to me!" I thrashed once more, and he slapped me across the face. "LISTEN TO ME!"

And that was when he said the words that ruined both of our lives.

"I can fix this."

"WHAT THE FUCK ARE YOU TALKING ABOUT?" I roared at him.

"Cillian, calm down for a goddamn minute and use your brain," Christopher snapped back at me. "There's no way we can prove this was an accident. We are *both* at fault. We'll both rot in prison—"

"I'm absolutely fucking fine with that!" I shot back.

"You just killed my child, you fucking bastard. You owe me!"

"I DON'T GIVE A RAT'S ASS ABOUT YOU, YOU MOTHERFUCKER!" I started to go for him again, but I couldn't escape from the vice grip he had me locked in.

I saw the shift in his serpent-like eyes. His brain was trying to figure out a tactic that would make me do his bidding.

Fat chance.

"Do you really think Audrey would want you to kill me, Cillian?"

Fuck.

Christopher released me and mockingly invited me to have at him. "If you can look at me with a straight face and honestly tell me that Audrey would want you to murder your own brother, then go ahead."

Fuck.

Sensing my hesitation, Christopher pressed on. "She always talked about how good of a man you were. How pure your heart was. That you would never purposely do anything to hurt her. Do you want to prove her right? Or was she wrong about you, Cillian?

FUCK.

Christopher was inches away from me now. "This is your last chance to show her that you're the man she fell in love with all those years ago. Are you up for it? Or do you want to call the police and ruin both of our lives?"

My entire body went numb. Christopher had broken me—drained me of every single ounce of backbone or resistance. I was a hollow husk.

My Audrey was gone. And it was because of me.

Finally, I managed to croak out, "I'm the man she thought I was."

Christopher's eyes flashed with relief. He put his hands on my shoulders. Like he had done with Audrey minutes before. But I was too far gone to shake him off.

He pointed to the Red Maple tree outside. "We can make this look like a suicide. That she hung herself. I will make this all go away. I will get us out of this. Because that's what Audrey would have wanted. But you have to do *exactly* as I say. Do you understand me?"

I should have killed my brother right then and there.

III

PART THREE: THE RECKONING

"It's picked. I picked it all in the rain. Once it's picked you can't put it back."
—Sam Shepard, Buried Child

Chapter Eleven

Cillian

The worst sound in the world is the cry a horse makes when he knows he's about to die.

I wouldn't wish that sound on my worst enemy. That sharp whinnying of rage from such a majestic, head-held-high creature that comes when he knows his days of rejoicing in this earthly life have expired? That agonized, soul-splitting moan is something that you can't truly understand the devastation of unless you've heard it firsthand. And right now, that grieving was so loud it practically vibrated the ground in front of me.

Cahir. An Irish sport horse seventeen hands tall at least. His name translates to "warrior." It suited him. He was strong and sinewy—the kind of animal that, in his prime, was the embodiment of courage, power, and finesse. The type of creature that would clear five-foot-tall stone fences like they were mud puddles.

But he wasn't in his prime anymore.

A few years back, he had torn his suspensory in a dumb moment of blustery yee-hawing out in the paddock with another horse. It wasn't serious enough to put him down, but serious enough that he couldn't compete anymore. And to Cahir? That was as good as killing him. He was a cranky son-of-a-bitch, too proud to socialize with other lesser horses. He was a warrior, damn it. And now he was a cripple. His spirit had been crushed—he knew he was never ever going to be what he once was. Because of one split moment—a single bad decision, he was now the kind of animal that didn't want to be helped. But he sure as shit needed it now.

And I knew a thing or two about that.

Cahir's leg was bent in ways that no limb should ever be able to go. People can recover from broken legs with surgery. But with horses? It's the kiss of death. The way a horse's leg bones are constructed—willowy thin—they shatter, making the chances of repair slim to none. Lord knows what had happened to him out in the field. We just heard the scream.

"God damn. That's just 'bout the worst break I've ever seen," Rip said just before spitting out a thin, phlegm-like stream of dip.

Rip was my old horse trainer, the man who had gifted me Apollo and made me into the champion that I used to be. A couple years back, he'd finally retired at the tender age of seventy-nine and bought a tiny tract of farm about an hour outside Lynchburg. It's not as pretty as back home—but it sure as hell had been a safe haven for me this past year, a sanctuary from the shitstorm that was my life—and I'd be lying if I said that the James River knifing through the rolling green hills of Rip's property wasn't a sight to behold. And Ol' Blue—the unspeakably gorgeous landscape forever acting as the North Star to my soul—was still within striking distance, just to the west.

When I called Rip on a burner prepaid phone after Christopher's murder, told him everything that happened, and asked to stay with him a while, all he said was 'sounds good, see you soon,' and hung up. He didn't even ask me if I had done it. Rip was that degree of kind—a man who always would take you in, no matter your current state, out of respect for what you once had been.

"You sure you don't want to call the vet?" I asked him.

"Nah. It would take the sum'bitch two hours just to get out here. And there ain't nothing he can do anyway. This ol' boy don't got a prayer at reconstruction." Rip was born and raised in West Texas, so even though he'd been living in Virginia since he was eighteen, that raspy, unmistakable Lone Star drawl never quit. "He's stuck in the mud, and he ain't never coming out. Time to let him lay, sorry to say."

I nodded in resigned agreement at Rip's country philosopher statement of cold, hard truth. Delaying the inevitable with a helpless animal is just about the cruelest thing a human can do. I tugged my trucker hat down low over my eyes—as if doing that would remove the existence of poor old Cahir thrashing around in torment on the grass.

After a solemn moment, Rip handed me the twelve-gauge he'd been shouldering this entire time. "I'm gon' need you to do the honors, Cill'. I've been through too much with this one. Dunno if I could bring myself to do what needs to be done."

Even though he was "retired," Rip still tended six horses on the property. Which is a hell of an accomplishment when you consider how many riding injuries the man had been through. He was like an ancient action figure that had been superglued back together several times over. "Shit, Cill', what the hell else am I gon' do?" was his answer when I asked why he was still doing the grunt work that left him nursing his aching back. And that was the end of that conversation.

The horses weren't anything special—discarded rejects from his old life whose owners didn't want them anymore. Just like Rip himself. So, he had retreated completely off the beaten path—the only piece of "modern technology" he had was an old landline phone that worked maybe half the time. He didn't believe in banks, government, or anything other than you and me and our bootstraps. The only reason I even had his number was he'd sent me a postcard when he moved here telling me how to get a hold of him if I ever needed him. And the nearest sign of any living soul was about twenty minutes off. So, it was the perfect hideout—his libertarian bullshit finally came in handy. He didn't pay me or anything, but he fed me, let me sleep in the barn, and didn't tell a soul. I hadn't left the property once since arriving in the middle of the night, scared out of my goddamn mind. It was raining, and I was soaked to the bone. Rip, without saying a word, plunked me down on his couch and brought me a blanket, change of clothes, and a hot cup of coffee. No questions asked. He didn't need to know anything other than that I needed a caretaker. I was like one of the horses he had taken in. And in exchange, I looked after them.

Which led to me being the one who had to put down poor old Cahir.

I gingerly fingered Rip's rusty, dust-encrusted twelve gauge. "Does this thing even work anymore?" I asked him.

"It'll get the job done." Rip put his worn, callused hand on my shoulder. "I'll come check on you in a lil' while." He patted me roughly before limping off.

I took a deep breath and forced myself to look back down at Cahir. There are plenty of days when I wish someone would do to me what I was about to do to this suffering gladiator.

What if I did it, right here and right now? Put Cahir out of my misery, then turn the gun on myself?

At this point? It was a struggle and a half to think of a reason I shouldn't. Anybody who'd miss me was long dead themselves. And it would save the police the trouble of trying to track me down. Hell, in a sense, it would be a public service. The only person left that gave a shit about me now was Rip. And the way that he drank and chewed dip? It was a goddamn miracle he was still standing—he sure as hell didn't have long left. I wondered if I had the constitution for suicide. Did I inherit that from Mama? Was today the moment I finally packed it in and called it a day for good?

Jesus, Cillian. Quit your goddamn bellyaching and put this poor animal out of his misery. You selfish piece of shit.

I cocked the twelve gauge. Cahir was fiercely pawing the grass, as if he could pull himself up and outrun the agony. His wails of pain were getting louder and louder by the second. This had to happen, and it had to happen now. I had to soothe him somehow, though. Get him to trust me. Give him some sort of peace before I took it away.

I crouched back down so I was eye-level with his muzzle. I took a deep breath and blew some warm air into his nostrils from the deepest crevice of my lungs—a trick Rip had taught me when I was first starting out as an easy way to get a horse to relax.

"Hey there, fella," I whispered. "I'm so sorry. It's almost over. It's gonna be okay, I promise."

I repeated this mantra while gently stroking his mane. I could feel Cahir ease down, which is all I wanted for him. To make him feel that, for one fleeting moment, he wasn't alone.

I stood up. Pointed the barrel to his head. Pulled the trigger.

His fleeting moment—with me, with life—was over.

Now, it was just me who was alone.

Who was gonna put me out of my misery?

I looked at the heap of horse brains sprayed out on the ground. There was a time when this would have made me want to puke. Today, after the year I've had? I'm numb to pretty much everything. And Cahir's unceremonious, tragic end was no different.

What actual purpose did I serve anymore? To anyone?

I gazed down at Rip's shotgun, the cold steel glinting in the afternoon sun.

If I did this thing, right here and right now, I'd be free. No more looking over my shoulder. No more living in fear that the cops, or the people who murdered my brother, would come kicking down the door. No more waking up in cold sweats. And maybe, just maybe, I'd be able to see my beloved again.

I don't know if there's an afterlife. I don't know what to believe anymore. But that chance, that possibility? Of seeing Audrey? I'll be damned if it wasn't one I was going to take.

I cocked the shotgun.

Should I close my eyes? Do people do that when they're about to take their own life?

No. I was going to look straight up at the blue sky—the glorious, cloudless horizon of possible heavens up above. I turned west, so I was facing the Blue Ridge. If Audrey was going to be anywhere, it was going to be there.

I pressed the barrel under my chin.

Right at that moment, a red-tailed hawk vaulted up from out of nowhere about ten feet over my head. I caught my breath. Audrey and I always said that whenever one of us saw a red tail, it meant that the other was sending us a message. A 'love flare' is what Audrey called them.

She was telling me that it was time to come home.

I wrapped my fingers around the trigger.

I'm coming, Audrey. I'm coming to you. I'm coming right now—

Click.

Instead of darkness, all I saw was the same old sky.

Instead of floating towards her, I was grounded in the present.

Instead of just her face, all I saw was everything else.

I looked down at the shotgun. I was out of shells.

After that sunk in for a tick, I burst out in a self-loathing, near-maniacal fit of laughter.

Goddamn, Cillian. You couldn't even do this *right.*

"Cill', what in the fuck are you doing?!" Rip's voice boomed out behind me.

I had totally forgotten he was coming back.

I had been about to blow my brains out without even as much as a goodbye or a thank you. To the man who had trained me for greatness and then given me shelter without so much as one question or ounce of push back when I'd arrived on his doorstep as his one-time Olympic hopeful turned fugitive. No alibi. No money. No hope. No nothing.

And I hadn't even thought to leave a note about Shep.

I tried to think of something to say. But the overwhelming shame prevented anything from escaping my lips. Instead, I just silently handed Rip the shotgun and walked towards the barn.

The other horses needed tending to.

Chapter Twelve

Cillian

That night I hid. Usually at this time, I would have dinner with Rip in his house. But I couldn't face him. Not after what I had almost done. So, my dinner was some stale saltines and a flat, half-drunk bottle of Pepsi. The meal of champions. I had tried to turn in early, but my brain wasn't cooperating.

Up in the rafters of Rip's barn, directly above my cot, there was an owl's nest. The damn thing was as big as a La-Z-Boy. The first couple of nights, the owl's constant *hoo-hoo-hoo* drove me and Shep damn near crazy, but after a while, we had gotten used to it. Shep had started snoring more loudly than usual so he could drown out the sound—and I had become impervious to his perpetually congested snoozing long ago. Neither of us had gotten used to the Owl's face, though—its unnerving, ghostly expression as its unblinking amber eyes fixed on us throughout the night. It was like something out of a horror movie. Shep tried barking at it, but even that didn't deter the damn thing.

So, Shep had taken to lying on his bed upside down so he wouldn't have to look at it. I did the same—even my old goat of a dog had a good idea in him every now and again. My cot was too small for the both of us to sleep in together, which had made Shep real pissed—so I built him a bed out of hay and straw. The damn thing was probably more comfortable than my cot, to be honest with you. He spent near the whole day on that thing nowadays—only leaving to shit and eat. If you include the horses that were underneath me? I had a real farm boy Noah's Ark situation going on.

What a terrific life you've carved out for yourself, Cillian.

Calling Rip's place a "barn" was, well…generous, to say the least. It served its purpose, though, and it was built to last—a testament to good old-fashioned cedar woodworking. Amazingly, it didn't get too cold in the winter—I just layered up with a few extra blankets, and I was okay. But it was about a quarter the size of all the barns I'd ever been in. Most of the square footage was dedicated to the six horses' stalls, all of which were directly below me. So, I got *every* type of smell imaginable wafting straight up to my loft. My area was only accessible by a ladder, so whenever Shep had to do his business, I had to carry him down like a goddamn poohbah. It got to the point where he didn't even have to nudge or bark. He'd just shoot me that tyrannical look, and I knew it was time. My own bathroom was a shoebox—you had to go through the coat-closet-sized tack room to get to it, and it was just a sink, a toilet, and a shower that looked like it hadn't been used in a century. The tack room, which was directly to the right of my ladder, was so small that Rip and I couldn't be in there at the same time. But it got the job done.

Probably my favorite part of the place was the mural on the wall of the hay loft. Rip, believe it or not, was actually a pretty good artist. Just goes to show—never judge a book by its cover. He said it was something he picked up from his mama—she was apparently pretty well known in Texas for her watercolors of prairies. He had gone in for human still lifes, himself. Said that doing them relaxed him. He had painted a 1950s-style pinup model. Her eyes were trained below, and she was flashing a big ol' seductive grin while she winked and did the "OK" sign with her right hand. Imagining old Rip getting on a ladder with his acrylics and creating that in his spare time always gave me a good chuckle.

I let out a loud, aggravated sigh. My insomnia was going full tilt. The owl didn't like that—he trained his fierce yellow eyes right on me. I flipped over to my side to avoid his sniper-like gaze. I had enough happening in my head—I didn't also need the anxiety of whether tonight was when he'd finally swoop down and peck out my eyes the moment I drifted off.

It was moments like this when I got stuck in a tar pit of questions, thinking about what I was running from. And there was no escaping the thoughts.

Mainly, who in the _fuck_ had killed my brother?

Initially, Christopher's murder had stirred up a media firestorm—you would have thought his last name was Kennedy by how much attention it had gotten. And given the frame-up job that had been done on me? I was suspect number one. My personal life was ripped open for all to see—wounds and all. Some of it was true; others were sensationalized bullshit. No, Fox News, I hadn't killed my brother because of gambling debts, and no, CNN, I wasn't a jockey. Goes to show how little the general public actually knows about riding—*he competed with horses, right? That must mean he was Kentucky Derby-bound! Because why do sixty seconds of research when you can just make something up?*

Surprisingly, the one thing that didn't get dragged out under the microscope was Audrey. The only mention of her was that she had tragically taken her own life. No other details than that. I wasn't sure whether to be relieved or horrified about that. Seemingly, no one was entertaining the idea that I *wasn't* the culprit. But, given the "evidence?" Even I could see their point. One day, somehow, I would clear my name and prove everyone wrong. But for now? All I knew to do was stay hidden.

I had been lucky to get away before shit hit the fan—I had a twelve-hour head start on the coverage. I shaved my head, let my beard grow out, paid for things in cash, and had a hat and sunglasses practically fused onto me. I decided to ditch my pickup, and I managed to bribe a semi-truck driver—a good ol' boy if there ever was one—to carry me on his run to Lynchburg, and then I hitched from there to Rip's. If I hadn't acted faster than a knife fight in a phone booth, I'd be rotting in a cell, probably. The first couple of days while I was at Rip's, I kept up with the coverage, out of paranoia, through an old transistor radio I found buried deep in a shed—of course, Rip didn't have a TV or a computer. When Rip found it, he obliterated it with a shovel. He had said that radio frequencies could be traced. I wasn't sure if that was the case, but it was probably for the best anyhow—I was getting obsessed with following the news. So, I have no idea how long it took before people lost interest and turned to the next "hot" story.

The law, though? That was a different matter entirely.

About a week or so after I arrived at his place, the state police detectives came by to question Rip. It made sense—he was basically the only person still alive who'd been important to me. The only other person would be Summer, and that doesn't count for anything. Not like we had a particularly meaningful relationship. Other than our sexual exploits, she wouldn't have much to offer them that they didn't already know. I was somewhat impressed the detectives had managed to track Rip down so quickly. But even he still had to file tax returns—despite his claiming that they were illegal—so I guess it wasn't too hard.

"Looks like the filth is here," Rip had said when he saw the sleek, unmarked police car coming up the hill. "And by the looks of it, it's the fancy type of filth."

My heart started doing a square dance in my chest. "What do we do?"

"Ah hell, don't worry 'bout it. I've been expecting them since you called. Go hide, and I'll get rid of 'em. They don't got shit," Rip asserted confidently. He pointed to the one-way mirror hanging behind the kitchen table that was directly opposite the front door. "Why doncha' take a front-row seat to the action?"

If I wasn't about to combust with anxiety, I would have grinned at Rip's cocksure confidence. The man was a dying breed—an old-school cowboy, if there ever was one. I opened the coat closet, shut it firmly behind me, then wiggled through the hidden door in its wall. Rip's house had been a hideout for moonshiners during Prohibition, so it was still tricked out with a bunch of hidden passageways and dummy doors like that. So, I was now a secret fly on the wall for what was about to transpire.

Please, Rip. Keep me safe, you crotchety old bastard.

There was a knock at the door.

Rip popped in a wad of dip and shot me a *watch-this* wink through the mirror before turning heel to open the door. Two plainclothes state police detectives looked back at Rip. The first one was forgettable. Middle-aged, male, a Budweiser belly, and a high and tight that looked like it had been cut by a kindergartner. His footsteps were louder than most people's voices. The other detective was a younger Black woman who looked to be somewhere around my age—maybe a few years older. In quite literally every way possible, she was the opposite of her counterpart—trim, low-maintenance haircut, and clothes geared for performance as opposed to showy intimidation. She radiated the kind of quiet, steely resolve undoubtedly fostered by years of being a minority in a predominantly White, patriarchal profession. Despite my predicament, she immediately commanded my respect and admiration.

"Mr. Turner? My name is Detective Thornwood," the pudge-ball boomed out. "This is my partner, Detective Rogers." He hooked his thumb behind him. "We'd like to come in and ask you a few questions." Judging by his voice alone, Detective Thornwood clearly wasn't from Virginia. Likely a transplant from up north. Rip hated people who were from up past the Mason-Dixon line. Always referred to them as 'damn Yankees' that wouldn't know good manners if they 'bit them square on the behind.' This Thornwood fellow wouldn't dissuade Rip's theory.

"Are you asking me or telling me?" Rip shot back.

God damn it, Rip. Please don't blow it.

"I think what Detective Thornwood meant to say is that your home is wonderfully...personal, and may we please come in?" Detective Rogers asked as she stepped in, flashing Rip a polite smile.

Now there was a voice that was Virginia born and bred. Melodious, warm, and buttery—just the way the Lord intended humanity to speak.

"Of course, ma'am. Come on in. Make yourself at home." Rip was like me. He had a soft spot for Southern ladies.

I was just hoping to God that wouldn't be my undoing.

The three of them made their way to the kitchen. Thornwood plopped his extra cushion-for-the-pushin' ass right down like he owned the place while Rogers stayed on her feet, eyes scanning over every square inch of her surroundings.

Shit. She looked like the type that wasn't going to miss anything. I was fucked.

"Would y'all like some coffee?" Rip asked.

"No. Let's—"

Rogers gently but firmly put her hand up to interrupt Thornwood. "We'd love some. Thank you, Mr. Turner."

"Rip, please. Cream and sugar?"

"Just black. Thank you, Rip."

"Good, cuz I don't got any cream or sugar."

Rogers chuckled at Rip. Thornwood looked like he was about to pass a kidney stone. The dynamic was becoming more and more clear—Thornwood was Rogers' subordinate, and he seemed to like that about as much as Rip liked frozen yogurt or light beer.

Rip handed Rogers her coffee before sitting down opposite Thornwood.

"Do you know why we're here, Rip?" Rogers queried as she sipped her coffee.

Rip spit out into the homemade spittoon he always kept on the table. "Sure. You're here about Cillian."

What the fuck are you doing, Rip? Are you about to give me away?

"And how exactly did you know that?" Thornwood thundered.

Rip flashed him a bless-your-heart smile. "It's been all over the news. And given that I coached him for near a decade, it only seemed right that eventually you'd come 'round knocking down my door."

Rogers motioned around her. "It's curious, though. You don't have an internet or cable bill in your name. I haven't seen any radios. So, how did you hear about what happened?"

"As much as I hate it, I do have to go into town from time to time. Groceries and the like. Hard to escape anything when you're in civilization. Much as I wish that you could."

Rogers daintily sipped her coffee, belying her razor-sharp stare that was cutting open Rip like a frog in high school biology class, looking for any sign of deception. "You live here by yourself, huh?"

"Last time I checked."

Rogers shot him a half-amused smile. "When's the last time you checked?"

A bolt of sorrow flashed through Rip's leathery face. "Every goddamn morning when I open my eyes."

Despite the tense circumstances, my heart went out to Rip for a moment. When his wife Maggie died a while back, I think a part of him passed on too. He'd never shown real interest in another woman—save for casual, small-talk flirtation—ever since.

My eyes were glued to Detective Rogers. I couldn't get a handle on what she was thinking. There was an indecipherable ambiguity in her eyes. And that scared the bejesus out of me.

"You got a call from a prepaid phone number the day after the murder," Rogers leaned in as she asked. "You want to tell us what that was about?"

My brow was glistening with sweat, and I had to squeeze my hand repeatedly to prevent it from shaking.

C'mon, Rip, hold it together now.

"I think it was some telemarketer trying to sell me God knows what. I don't rightly remember. Call couldn't have lasted more than thirty seconds."

"And what were they trying to sell you?" There was Thornwood, the blowhard, again.

"Hmm, let me see." Rip squinted his eyes, pretending like he was searching for an errant file in the cabinets of his brain. "Insurance for my truck, if memory serves." Damn, Rip was good—if I didn't know he was lying, no way I would have guessed it.

Thornwood gazed at Rip for a half-tick before nodding. "I get those calls all the time, too. For my motorcycle. Even when you take your number off every list known to man, they still find a way to get to you."

Rip arched his eyebrow. I'd seen that look a thousand times before when he was sizing up a horse owner trying to sell. "My uncle was a biker, too. Ran a repair shop in Odessa. Taught me to ride when I was just lil' tyke."

Thornwood's eyes lit up—it was odd to see such a childlike expression on such a fat fucker. "No kidding. What'd he ride?"

I silently breathed out a sigh of relief. One cop was in the bag, at least.

"He had a 1968 Triumph Bonneville."

Thornwood let out a low whistle. "That's a beaut.' Did you ever—"

"Excuse me, Detective," Rogers cut off Thornwood at the knees, resuming her interrogation. "What was the name of the insurance company, Rip?"

"Honestly, ma'am, I'm amazed I remember as much as I just told you. You know how it is. I get so many of those calls, I turn my ears off two seconds in."

That's good, Rip. They wouldn't have the transcript of the call—just the location and the time log. So, on its face, that story was plausible.

"Mind if we take a look around?"

Shit. The question that meant I was dead in the water.

"'Course you can," Rip replied. "Soon as you come back with a warrant."

Rogers clucked her tongue, half teasing, half serious. "And we were getting along so famously," she said. "People who insist on seeing a warrant usually have something to hide. You sure you don't want to show us that's not the case?"

"I understand, ma'am. It's just that my wife was a county courthouse clerk, so I know that you need a warrant to search private property. To get that, you need probable cause. And right now? Well, you don't have anything resembling that. Come back with one of them things, though, and I'll be happy to give you the full VIP tour." Rip winked at Rogers.

Despite my heartbeat knocking so loudly in my ears that I could barely hear, I smiled. Even when Rip was basically telling someone to fuck off, he did it with such charisma.

Rogers laughed. "Fair enough, Rip."

And with that, she got up, motioning for Thornwood to do the same. As she started to walk out, her gaze briefly flickered over to the mirror. She turned back and headed over to it, like a heat-seeking missile.

And they pierced through the glass, looking right into my soul.

My heart stopped. Fight or flight instincts reared up in me.

Stop it. Calm down. Just because she was looking at the mirror doesn't mean she's looking at you. Deep breath.

"What a gorgeous piece, Rip," Rogers said. "I'm a bit of an antique hound in my spare time. What era is this from?"

Rip chuckled. "I have no earthly idea. Came with the house." He gestured to himself. "This may surprise you a lil' bit, but I'm not the man you want to talk to 'bout antiques."

Rogers lingered her stare for a bit, before shifting her eyes back to Rip and smiling. "Of course. I'll be seeing you soon. Thank you for the coffee. Tasted like my granddaddy's—thick as molasses and strong enough to slap you in the face."

Gotta love native Virginians. Even during an interrogation, they'll go the extra mile to compliment their host.

"My pleasure, ma'am," Rip replied, tipping his Stetson to her.

And with that, they left, got in their unmarked, and pulled away.

As the tension started to slowly seep out of my body, Rip turned around to face the mirror.

"See? Easy peasy lemon squeezy," he said with a smile and a wink.

Hoo-hoo. Hoo-hoo. Hoo-hoo.

The barn owl's call slowly brought me out of my memory. Rogers and Thornwood did come back one more time—about two days later, search warrant in hand. But we were ready. We had wiped every instance of my existence clean away, and Shep and I hid out deep in the woods. So, they came up empty-handed. After that, with no official probable cause, they didn't bother Rip anymore.

Still, I didn't think I was out of dodge by any stretch of the imagination. Rogers didn't seem like the type to give something up easily as that. She was probably lying in wait—just holding off until I made one mistake or surfaced in one of the nearby towns. So, that's why it felt like slithering eels had permanently lodged themselves in my stomach. I'll tell you one thing—it's exhausting waking up every morning fearing just getting out of bed. And I was *weary*.

Hoo-hoo. Hoo-hoo. Hoo-hoo.

I sat up. The owl was getting more insistent. There was pretty much zero chance of me falling asleep now. I glanced over at Shep. He was out cold. And judging by the twitching of his legs, he was locked and loaded into whatever dream he was having. No company there.

It was time for one of my walks in the night.

* * *

There was a full moon out. Orion, Taurus, and Aries were glowing above my head in the sky. It reminded me of one of Audrey's favorite Longfellow quotes: "Silently, one by one, in the infinite meadows of heaven, blossomed the lovely stars, the forget-me-nots of angels." The only sound accompanying my wandering was the *crunch-crunch-crunch* of the fallen autumn leaves under my boots. It was absolute perfection, one of those nights that made you believe, even if just for a spell, in Mother Nature's majestic healing power.

Hell, it was the only thing I did believe in anymore.

My breath plumed out in front of me like I was smoking one of Rip's cigars. I hated those things. They ruined the good name of the sweet smell of naturally cut tobacco. I missed cigarettes, but Rip didn't have any around, and I wasn't about to ask him to go get me some. So, I had quit cold turkey. Same thing with my supply of Oxycontin. Piece of advice—never do that. It's about six different kinds of awful.

I exhaled deep, imaging that the fog of my breath was me blowing out the sweet smell of a freshly lit American Spirit. I had forgotten a jacket, and I was feeling it. But I didn't care—these walks were about the only chance for me to free range in the surrounding woods anymore. I couldn't do this during the day. Someone might see me. Rip's property didn't have any neighbors nearby, sure—but there was a park a few miles over, and every now and again, I'd hear the faint sounds of hunters or campers in the distance. So, I had to stick to the barn and the paddocks, frustrated and claustrophobic like a captured mustang out west suddenly caged in a corral.

How long was I going to keep this up? Or was this going to be the rest of my life? A person can't hide forever. And poor Rip—how much longer was I going to put him through this? He was risking jail time for me. If he was caught? He'd live his last remaining years in prison. Sooner or later, I was going to have to figure something else out.

I raked through the state of my finances in my head. It didn't take very long. I only had the cash that was in my wallet when I went over to my brother's cabin—I had stopped by an ATM after I had forked over everything I had to that waitress at the diner—so maybe $100? And it's not like I could use my debit card to make a withdrawal. Maybe I could scrounge up a bus ticket to Mexico somehow? But I would need a new ID. And I had...absolutely no idea how to go about that. I wasn't a criminal—despite what the world may think. Maybe I could go out to California. I had never seen the Pacific Ocean. I could pull a Manifest Destiny and start again. Reinvent myself from scratch. After all, that was the American way, right?

Stop it. You're an idiot. You would last about two minutes in California. And without a new identity or money, nothing's possible anyway. And even if you somehow could wrangle a ticket, what was Shepard supposed to do on a cross-country bus ride? You need to—

I looked up to see I was face to face with a giant fucking Black Bear.

And, from the looks of the cub behind her, it was a mama who'd do *anything* to protect her own. I had interrupted their foraging for a midnight snack. There was maybe twenty feet between us.

Holy shit. This is how I was gonna die. Eaten by a goddamn bear.

What the hell was I supposed to do in this situation? Should I treat her like a riled-up mare? Should I slowly approach her and—

The bear erupted in an earth-shaking roar, as if she read my mind and told me to fuck off.

Okay. We're not doing that.

Pushing my fear down best as I could, I diverted my eyes and started slowly inching backwards. Clearly, I needed to let her know that she was the alpha.

"I mean no harm, ma'am," I said, my voice shaking. "I'm just gonna head on back to where I came. Nice and easy. Nice and easy."

As I started backward, the mama bear padded forward, ever so slightly, but still puffed up full of defensive menace.

"Easy, Mama," I cooed as calmly as I could muster. "I mean no harm. I swear."

Every fiber in my being told me to run. I could feel the mama's gaze boring a hole into my skull. She was ready to rock. This wasn't a battle I was going to win.

"Go on back to your child," I pleaded. "You don't wanna do this in front of him."

Keeping my eyes down in submission, I raised my hands in the surrender position as I continued backwards. In my peripheral, I could see her stop and cock her head at me. Like she just now realized that I was a totally inferior species.

"There you go. See? I don't mean anything. Let's both go our separate ways, now."

I snuck a peek at her. She was sizing me up, evaluating whether I was worth the trouble.

I promise you—I'm not worth the dirt beneath your paw.

A higher-pitched rumble interrupted the standoff. It was her cub, signaling that he was hungry. Finally, the mama turned her back on me and lumbered off with her son in tow.

I slowly lowered my hands and breathed out a long sigh of relief. The adrenaline oozed out of me. I was on the edge of wanting to die, sure—but that wasn't the way I wanted to go.

Would have been a hell of a story to tell Audrey, though.

Audrey.

I did my best to suppress animal-like sobs building in my chest. I was suddenly so bowled over by fatigue I brought new meaning to the phrase 'running on empty.' I needed my bed. And I needed it fast. As I started to turn heel, that's when my knee buckled out from under me.

Of course. This is when my injury would rear its ugly head. Of all times.

I groaned as I managed to pull myself up slowly, gritting my teeth to get through the blinding pain in my knee. I limped forward. My usually twenty-minute walk turned into a forty-five-minute death crawl.

Finally, I got to the barn door, body quaking. I collapsed on the gravel right in front, balling myself up tight as I forced myself to breathe and deal with the lethal cocktail of pain and panic that was convulsing me.

You're alive. You're safe. You're okay. Deep breath. You. Are. Okay.

Just as I finally started to make some headway on putting myself back together, I slowly pulled my head up.

What the fuck?

There was an envelope placed just so on the door's bottom lip, my name in large block letters across the front. My hands trembled as I reached up for it.

Inside was a burner cell phone with a handwritten note: *I know you're here. Press speed dial 1. If you don't, the police will be here to wake you up in the morning.*

I stared at the phone in my left hand.

I should have taken the mama bear up on her offer.

Chapter Thirteen

Cillian

A small part of me was relieved. And strangely calm.

Any equestrian worth their salt knows the feeling. When you're on the back of a runaway horse who's bolted suddenly and is galloping at the speed of the devil's heartbeat? You know there's nothing to do but to ride it out.

But then reality kicked in. And I realized the horse I was on wasn't going to slow down.

Because this wasn't the police.

Detective Rogers or Detective Thornwood would have kicked the doors down and led Rip and me away in handcuffs. Whoever this was? They lived in the shadows—anonymous, like me. Hiding. Which was about ten times more terrifying.

But I couldn't run. Where else would I go? And besides, I couldn't do that to Rip. I had to square my shoulders and take my licks, no matter what kind of hell was waiting for me at the other end of that call.

I flicked open the burner phone and held down the one key until it autodialed. Held the receiver up to my ear. Swallowed down the lump of terror knotting my throat. Listened to the ominous ringing, until—

"How was your waww-uuhk?" The voice on the other end was a sharp, brusque female voice. She sounded like she was from somewhere in New York, judging from the accent.

My walk? Who the fuck was this? Have they been watching me this entire time? God damn it. My safe haven wasn't safe anymore. Fuck. Fuck. Fu—

I gathered myself. I had to act tough, in control.

"Who the fuck is this?"

"Yeeeeesh. Usually, I'm the rude one. But that was pretty rude, Cillian. Where are those goddamn Southern manners that I keep hearing so much about?"

"You didn't answer my question."

"I was a friend of your brother's."

"The same friend that killed him and framed me for it?"

The voice let out a laugh. If a single, emphatically mocking 'HA' counted as a laugh. "If I killed him and framed you, do you think I'd be stupid enough to reveal myself to you?"

Hmm. Fair point.

"Well, you're not a friend of mine."

"No?"

"A friend wouldn't threaten to send me to prison for a crime they knew I didn't commit."

"I had to get your attention."

"Well, you've got it," I snapped. "What do you want?"

There was a long silence. I had a feeling that this woman was trying to stop herself from shouting at me. Finally, she broke the lull. "I want to clear your name. I want to put the actual people responsible for killing Christopher behind bars. And to do that, I need your help."

I thought about this for a tick. It seemed way too good to be true. Like a line from a bad action movie.

"How did you know I was going on a walk?"

"I've been watching you for a few days now from the woods. You walk a lot at night. It's kind of weird if you ask me, but helpful."

Jesus.

"Are you a cop?"

"No, I'm worse. I'm a journalist."

On a different day, I would have laughed at that comment. Today wasn't the day.

"What's your name?"

"There's a Waffle House off Route 221," she replied, not answering my question. "Meet me there in a half-hour. Take precautions that you aren't followed."

And with that, the line went dead.

I snapped the phone shut, my mind racing in about six thousand different directions. I had no way of knowing if this was a trap. The more suspicious side of my brain was screaming—*don't do this, you idiot! Don't piss on my leg and tell me it's raining.* The chances were better than decent that the second I got to this Waffle House, the boys in blue would swarm me and haul me away.

I was about to throw the phone on the ground and stomp it into oblivion when something stopped me. The more hopeful side of me was shouting at me to give it a chance. *What if she IS telling the truth, Cillian? You're really gonna throw that chance away? Have some courage. For once in your life.*

I ruefully laughed at myself. Courage. When's the last time I had shown any remnant of that? Ultimately, though, both sides of my brain could agree on one thing—that I didn't really have much of a choice. My current lifestyle was unsustainable. If this woman even remotely had a chance of helping me—figuring out who killed my brother in the process of clearing my name, I had to know. I had to walk into the fire and risk not coming out the other side. I took a deep breath, mind made up.

Courage, damn it. Courage.

My gaze found Rip's truck. I knew where he hid his spare key.

And despite it all? I could always go for some pancakes.

* * *

Waffle House has never been a restaurant of choice for me. I've always believed places that are open 24 hours a day are usually lacking in the quality department. And this place didn't do anything to dissuade that notion. That yellow neon sign that Waffle House is so famous for wasn't even yellow anymore—it was a faded mustard, like a stain on your t-shirt that had been neglected for too long to be able to fix. Still, though, I saw why my mystery caller had picked this place. Saying it was secluded was an understatement. As I pulled Rip's truck into the visitor parking lot, there wasn't a single other car there. I checked the dash—I was a couple of minutes early, despite me taking a bass-ackwards route to derail any people potentially tailing me.

I took a deep breath, warily exited the truck, and strode through the Waffle House's entrance. The door had one of those stupid little bells that jingled every time it moved a quarter of an inch. To my relief, the restaurant was a ghost town. A ghost town that smelled like cheap, lemon-scented disinfectant and burnt eggs. There was just one salty-looking waitress standing behind the counter, absentmindedly scrolling on her phone.

"Hi there, ma'am," I said, trying to get her attention.

Her eyes flicked up from her screen, piercing me with their disdain.

"We don't allow vagrants in here," she said bluntly.

After getting over the sting of that, I remembered what I looked like. Unkempt beard, a hoodie thrown over top of my trucker cap. If I didn't know better, I'd think I was homeless, too.

You catch more flies with honey than vinegar, Cillian. Audrey's melodious voice burbled in my ears.

"I understand, ma'am. I'm meeting someone here. Just a couple minutes early."

She eyed me for a beat, before finally relenting as she sighed and slapped her phone face down on the counter. "You want some coffee?"

"Some water and a menu would be lovely, thank you very much."

She nodded and disappeared to the back as I set myself down at a table right by the window. I sat looking towards the front door and the start of the parking lot. I immediately glanced over all the exits besides the front in case I had to make a break for it—there was a back door directly behind me and what looked like a side door adjacent to the kitchen. But even if I wanted to run, I wouldn't have been able to with my useless knee. So, I was stuck. Ripe for the picking. My good leg started to bob anxiously. I pressed my palm hard down onto my thigh.

143

Calm yourself, Cillian. Nice and easy does it. Remember your training—if you show a horse you're terrified, it will be scared shitless too. Same principle translates here.

The waitress returned with the water and two menus.

"Know whatcha' want?"

"Yes, can I please—"

Headlights from a cheap-looking rental car flooded the dark parking lot as it pulled up front. A woman stepped out. She was wearing an all-black tracksuit that perfectly matched her midnight-colored, shoulder-length hair. Strode in with the kind of confidence that speaks for itself. She briefly scanned the restaurant before locking eyes with me. I took a calming, deep breath and squeezed the life out of my bouncing thigh.

Here we go.

As the stranger approached, I could see that, even though she was projecting a confident, commanding persona, she was exhausted. Probably running on about two hours of sleep, judging from the bags under her eyes— and that was likely being generous.

"Hello?" the waitress barked at me.

"Pancakes, please. And a cup of coffee for the lady."

The waitress rolled her eyes and set off just as my mystery guest sat down opposite me. We just stared at each other for a long while, as intense as any stereotypical gunslinger from the Old West—the first one to blink dies. Her eyes were different colors—one brown, one blue. I'd only ever seen something like that once in my life before. When I first started working with Rip way back when, he had an old pony named Chocolate who had one blue eye. Rip called it a "moon eye," and said that, in old-timey folklore, it meant Chocolate was marked by Mother Nature as being a wise, mystical creature—one who had a deeper connection with the earth than normal folk like us. Unfortunately, Chocolate died not long after that conversation. I wondered if Rip's theory would apply to humans.

I guess I was about to find out.

"You look different than I thought you would," she said, finally cutting through the silence.

Here we go.

"How did you think I would look?"

"More like Christopher's identical twin."

"Right now, my life depends on looking like anything but."

She slowly put her palms down on the table. I quickly noticed that her left hand was quivering ever so slightly—although she was going to great lengths to cover up the fact.

Thank the Lord. Despite the way she had tried to present herself, she was as nervous as I was—her bluster on the phone must have been an act. Just like mine was.

"How did you find me?" I asked.

"It took a while," she admitted, smirking. "But I did my reporting."

"I don't know what that means."

"It means you'd be amazed what you're able to figure out when you're not tied to procedure and bureaucracy like the police are. I don't need a judge to give me permission to do surveillance."

I shifted nervously in my chair. I didn't like the sounds of that.

"I still don't quite know what that means."

"It means that it's just a matter of time before you get found out by the cops." A wave of sympathetic sincerity flashed across her face. "And that you need to hurry up and take my offer. Before it's too late."

"Forgive me if what you say sounds a little too good to be true."

She studied me for a tick before—

"How badly do you want to prove who really killed your brother?"

"What do you mean?"

"What would you be willing to do to help me if I told you I knew who it was?"

Before I could answer, the waitress came back with my mile-high stack of pancakes and Miss Moon Eye's coffee. She glugged it down in about two seconds flat.

"You want another?"

She pushed away the mug in disgust. "Absolutely not. That was out of necessity, not desire. You didn't answer my question."

I stared into my mountain of flapjacks, avoiding Miss Moon Eye's penetrating look with all my might.

"What if I said I wasn't interested?" I said softly.

Moon Eye shifted in her seat, leaning all her momentum forward. "Then I would say that you're a coward and you're wasting my time. And that Audrey would be disappointed in you."

I snapped my gaze up to Moon Eye, blood pumping hot.

"Don't talk about things you don't know anything about."

"Then you should help me know about it. Listen to what I have to say."

"I don't even know your goddamn name."

Moon Eye took a deep breath and leaned back in her chair. "The people that killed your brother are the most insidious white nationalist group I've ever seen. Before Christopher was murdered, he and I were about to partner on an investigation into them. And I've been trying my damnedest to finish what we've started. But I need help."

I practically felt the heat of her voice—her passion—fly out and slap me across the face. A lump of regret gathered in my throat. My brother had shown some integrity for once in his life. He had been about to embark on something for the greater good—that would have potentially helped eradicate a group of Neo-Nazis—the ultimate scourge of humanity. And I had been planning on cutting him down like it was nothing.

No wonder Audrey had wanted to be with him. He'd shown more backbone in the days before his death than I'd shown...well, shit—ever. Audrey loved conviction. Adored courage.

"And I'm supposed to be that help?"

She shrugged. "If you can name a person who would be more motivated, I'll pack up and leave right now."

"You're awful trusting real fast. How do you know I didn't kill Christopher?"

She arched her eyebrow at me. "Did you?"

"No."

She nodded. "No shit."

"You're about the only one on the face of this earth who thinks that."

"The first thing you learn in journalism school—never believe the narrative being spun without checking the thread to see if it's frayed."

"You don't know me, ma'am."

"Christopher told me that if anything happened to him, I should come find you. That you're the only one I should trust with this. That you would help me. So, was he wrong?"

He said that she should come find me.

I was stunned. Christopher hated me with a capital H. And I hated him right back even more. Hell, I was planning to wipe him clean off the face of the earth with my own two hands. And yet? He told a stranger to find me if things went to shit. That I was the *only* one that she should trust. If that didn't speak to the perverse, unshakable nature of a brotherly bond? I don't know what will.

Fucking 'ey. I was in my own version of a Shepard play.

She leaned forward again, sensing that my resistance was softening. "I promise you if you hear just a tenth of what I have to say? You'll be just as committed to this as I am. And my name is Daniela Langer."

I recognized the name. Daniela had written an expose article about the Klan a few years back that had gotten a lot of attention in my former neck of the woods. Unfortunately, not all the attention was the good kind, as you can imagine. Daniela had to be a tough cookie—I can't even imagine the amount of heat she would have had to withstand to publish an article like that. And given her ethnicity? I can't imagine finding inside sources from the Klan to inform for her could have been a song. So, if someone like *that* says they have something? It's gotta be something worth hearing.

And that's when I heard my beloved's voice in my ears once more:

Inaction is the greatest sin, Cillian. You're better than that.

I twirled the fork in my fingers, watching the faded steel gleam in the slightly buzzing fluorescent lighting above. By this point, I had completely lost my appetite.

What would Audrey do in this situation?

The answer immediately came to me, clear as those angelic morning bells from Trinity United Methodist Church back home. I would do this for her.

Audrey. My beloved—the one who I had failed time and time again. And damn it, for my deceased brother too. The man that I still hated more than anything had sacrificed everything for this. Literally. And despite it all—he had entrusted me to carry on the torch. To finish what he had started. And family business in the Clarke family never goes unfinished. Not for anything.

"I'll hear you out," I said to Daniela.

I was going to do the right thing. For once in my goddamn life.

Chapter Fourteen

Cillian

Her motel room was spotless. I was expecting what I'd seen in the movies when a character was trying to "break a case"—shit pinned all up over the walls, documents and file folders sprawled on the floor, and half-empty boxes of takeout collecting mold on the table. What I saw was the exact opposite—someone who had taken great care to meticulously clean up. To cover up every single shred of her work—and her existence.

This was the room of a person who feared she was being watched.

"Have a seat," Daniela said as she motioned to the dinky table set pushed in front of the curtain-drawn window. "Want anything? I'd offer you a beer, but I think we both know that's a bad idea."

Jesus. What didn't this lady know about me?

"Some water would be great, thank you."

She nodded and headed off to the kitchen—although calling it a kitchen was generous. More like a partitioned section of the room with a hot plate, mini fridge, and a microwave that looked like it had been on its last legs a decade back. The rest of the room wasn't much better—the shag carpets seemed like they were in desperate need of cleaning, the bed's mattress clearly dipped in the middle, and the TV had a spider-web-like crack in the middle. And there was a splotch of God-knows-what on the wall behind me.

This is a place where dreams came to die.

Daniela returned with a room-temperature bottle of water for me and an ice-cold bottle of PBR for herself.

PBR. What Christopher and I were drinking that awful night. When my beloved died by my own hand. The night that ripped out what was left of my soul.

She twisted off the cap and took a long swig, eyes trained on me like a falcon. "It's not a problem if I drink in front of you, is it?"

The way she said it, though, I knew it wasn't a real question. She was testing me. Seeing how fragile I was.

"Of course not." I took a sip of my water, trying not to salivate at the way the bottle was sweating in her hand. The same way it beaded up in Christopher's hand before he ruined my life. Before I ruined it.

Don't fuck this up, you idiot. For once in your life, don't give in to your lesser angels.

Daniela gazed at me, seemingly deciding whether she felt safe to continue. I decided to break the ice first.

"I was expecting something different, to be honest with you," I said, gesturing around.

She arched her eyebrow. "Expecting the den of a lunatic conspiracy theorist, right? Maybe some photos, documents, and maps taped all over the walls? Half-eaten Chinese food on the table? Then I give you some half-crazed monologue about how it 'goes all the way to the top'?"

Get out of my brain, lady.

"Well, I—"

She laughed that short, emphatic *HA* of hers. She got up and reached under the bed. She pulled out a portable reinforced safe and dragged it back to where we were sitting.

"I used to do the kind of thing you were imagining. During my story on the Klan a few years back, I was living out of this fleabag motel in Tuscaloosa—it was even worse than this, if you can imagine—and I had all my research and interviews splayed out everywhere. Someone broke into the room while I went out to pick up a pizza. Set fire to the place. Everything was burnt to a crisp. Had to start totally from scratch. Since then, anything remotely important on paper goes in here, and I also back everything up digitally," she said as she pressed her thumb on the safe's fingerprint scanner.

I nodded. "Smart woman—I don't even know how to set up an iCloud account." I tried on a half-smile to break the tension.

She gave me a half-smile back. "You should take one of those classes they teach at the Apple Store for senior citizens."

"Nah. They'll never get me."

She smiled a full one at me—a real, genuine grin punctuated by that dreamy, almost otherworldly twinkle of her moon eye, and I felt my heart flutter for the first time since Audrey.

Startled by the re-emergence of that feeling, I cleared my throat and distanced myself. "I'm surprised that almost dying didn't scare you off from the newspaper business altogether."

Her smile vanished, and her eyes flared, full of fury, flint, and steel. "Are you asking me that because I'm a woman?"

Nice going, jackass.

"No, no, not at all. Sorry. I'm asking because it would have terrified the shit out of me."

She sized me up, the rage slowly draining out from her gaze as she seemed to recognize that I was telling her the God's honest truth. Finally, she just shrugged. "Nah. It just made me want to get them even more." And with that, she pulled open the safe and removed a laptop and a stack of manila folders. Also inside the safe was a small pistol—the kind you could easily fit in a handbag and still have room left over. Don't be fooled, though. Those damn things can still pack a punch. After all, it's not about size—it's about what you do with it.

Thwap.

Daniela slammed her stack of folders and laptop on the table. The damn flimsy thing nearly toppled over from the weight. Both the folders and the laptop looked like they'd been through a war—the folders were coffee ring stained, the ink smudged to gunshot blood red, and the laptop had enough dings in it to make Steve Jobs cry from beyond. She opened the first folder and slid it over to me.

Once again, not what I expected. The only thing inside was a single photo—

of an older woman talking on a cell phone while she walked down the street smoking a cigarette out of a white holder thing that I thought went out of style in the twenties. This lady was one of those women where it was near impossible to honestly gauge her age. But judging from her perfectly coordinated, designer-chic polished outfit? She had lots of cash to burn. The picture was clearly shot from far off, but with a lens that yielded a good look at her face. Her eyes were a sleek, cold silver—the kind that could stare a shark dead in the face and make it swim away in fear. And yet? There wasn't any discernible trace of life behind them. It was...spooky. The rest of her was a sculptor's wet dream—perfectly angular bone structure, with no wrinkles anywhere in sight. Her hair was severe, dyed a black that 99% of humanity couldn't pull off. But on her, somehow, it looked completely natural.

"Do you know who this is?" Daniela asked me.

I shook my head. "Should I?"

"Her name is Anika Fisker. She's a hotshot political consultant. Gotten all kinds of people across the country elected to office, but she's done the most amount of work right here in Virginia. People in the know call her the Godmother."

I couldn't help but snort. "Do people in the know realize that nickname is real hokey?"

Daniela didn't laugh. "She was running Christopher's campaign for Governor before he was murdered."

My blood ran cold. "This is the woman who killed my brother?"

"She didn't kill him herself. But I know she's the one who's responsible for it."

"And you know this for sure?"

Her face creased with disappointment. "I know it. But I don't *know* it, know it."

"I'm not following."

She took back the photo and put it off to the side as she took out another folder from the pile. Inside this one was a stack of papers about an organization called Fisker Political Consulting.

Gotta love the narcissism of someone who names a company after themselves.

"Looking at those documents, what do you see?" Daniela asked me.

"I was under the impression that you were going to tell me what I needed to know—not the other way around."

"Just do it," she snapped back.

I took a deep breath and thumbed through the pages, trying my best not to let my anxiety get the best of me. Daniela had collated the entire work history of Fisker Political since its inception into studiously crafted spreadsheets and top sheets. From the looks of things, Fisker Political was a firm that was *extremely* selective about the campaigns it worked on, only taking on about one a year. Which didn't seem *that* strange to me. I knew squat about politics—but it would seem that a veteran of that particular circus wouldn't want to do a bunch of races a year, right? From both a financial and a mental health standpoint. At the end of the day, it would always come down to the quality of the candidate.

"I gotta be honest—I don't really know what I'm looking at here, Daniela."

"Keep going."

I pushed ahead to the bottom of the stack. What I found there finally started to sound off some alarm bells. Daniela had bank statements for the company going back as far as ten years. Everything was there, and I mean *everything*—credit card charges, weekly and monthly deposits, and wire transfers. Like with politics, I didn't know a whole lot about the financial world. But I had enough common sense to realize that Daniela having all of this for a privately owned company was about six different kinds of illegal and wouldn't be admissible in court.

Which made me wonder how the hell she got her hands on all of this. Sure as shit would have taken more than a song.

The thing that really caught my eye, though? On every monthly balance sheet, highlighted in bright yellow, was a recurring lump sum cash deposit of $25,000. Like clockwork, it came in on the 15th of every month through various ATMs across the state. There wasn't a single month over the course of ten years where it wasn't deposited exactly on schedule, right to the day— sometimes even to the hour.

"How did you get all of this?"

She reached into the safe and held up a tiny USB thumb drive. "Your brother," she said.

"And how the hell did *he* get this?"

She shrugged, exasperated. "That's the phantom I've been chasing for the past year. I have no goddamn idea. He was murdered before he told me."

I pointed at one of the highlighted cash deposit transactions. "Where is Fisker getting all of this money from?"

Daniela's face clouded. That's when she pulled out the folder that sent a chill down through my toes—one that was labeled "Fourteen Words."

Fourteen Words. The alt-right, Neo-Nazi rallying cry. Until I was a sophomore in high school, I had no idea what it meant. That changed when a couple of yahoos beat the living snot out of the star point guard of our basketball team—Jerome Watkins. Jerome was grabbing a bite one night after a playoff game when two rednecks took him out in the back alley and whupped him unconscious. They wrote it above his head in white chalk: *We must secure the existence of our people and a future for white children.* A lot of people said that Jerome had a shot at going pro one day—but after that, he couldn't walk again.

Jesus. Fucking. Christ.

I took the folder from Daniela. From the looks of her painstakingly compiled research, Fourteen Words was the overarching code name of a Neo-Nazi organization, the "FW Organization," that had its tentacles all over the entire state. The Organization operated in the shadows through legitimate businesses that hid their true purpose—bankrolling the campaigns of politicians who would subtly push their white supremacist agenda. Their ownership was conducted through various shell companies and offshore bank accounts, but the dots were there if you had someone like Daniela to connect them for you. This wasn't a bunch of skinheads with swastikas tattooed on their freshly shaved scalps marching openly on the streets. This was subtle. Exacting. Precise. Which made it even more disturbing.

Reading between the lines of Daniela's research, the Organization was using the "clean" profits from their dry cleaners, convenience stores, and bars to finance the spread of their racism through online campaigns, in-person rallies, and social media. It was the definition of hiding in plain sight. And, surprise, surprise, all the politicians—who conveniently had campaign events in areas where the Organization had some kind of business—were ones that had been elected with the help of one Ms. Anika Fisker.

But I could instantly see Daniela's problem. As horrifying as these allegations were, that's all they were—suggestions lacking in the undeniable evidence department. Far as I could see, there was no concrete, black-and-white connection that proved beyond a reasonable doubt that the Organization was paying Fisker's twenty-five thousand dollar retainer fee, which meant there was no way to prove a link between the Organization and these candidates. Which basically meant that Daniela was sitting on a nuclear missile that she didn't have the launch codes to.

"So, unless you're an idiot, I think you can see my problem here," Daniela said. "Politicians are required to publicly disclose the origins of their funding. Private citizens like Anika Fisker are under no such obligation. And, besides the initial bank statements your brother gave me, all the other research you just read was gathered through...less than legal ways. I have a couple of friends who the NSA wouldn't be happy about me knowing, to put it lightly. And my paper needs something on the right side of legal before they even consider publishing." She took a long swig of her beer, draining its contents. "So...was I wrong in assuming that you aren't an idiot?"

Good Lord, this woman had an uncanny ability to both compliment and insult in one go.

"I'm not an idiot," I replied. "But I still don't see how I'm gonna be able to help you."

She glanced at me coyly. "Fisker has a new show-pony."

This caught my attention. "Another candidate for Governor?"

Daniela shook her head. "Once the business with Christopher was finished, she turned her attention to a congressional race right here in this godforsaken place." She reached for a copy of a local Lynchburg newspaper and pointed to a photo on the bottom fold.

And that's when I finally realized why Daniela needed me. Fisker's new

Congressional candidate was Ada Morgan—Christopher's longtime chief-of-staff and the woman who had helped my brother and me scrub Audrey's real cause of death off the face of the earth all those years ago. The woman who told me to trust her—to treat her like family.

I don't think she really knew what that meant.

Chapter Fifteen

Cillian

Nothing breaks up the monotony of the mid-day lull more than shoveling a steaming pile of horse shit.

I t was one of those brisk autumn afternoons, the kind where the wind whips the falling leaves in a cyclone around you as you walk—where you could see your breath but didn't need more than a jean jacket. The kind of day when Audrey and I would go on long trail rides along the Blue Ridge. Ride until our legs ached, then pick a spot to camp for the night, somewhere that Dolly and Apollo liked, an area where they'd nicker at each other while rolling on their backs—the tell-tale sign of a satisfied horse. Lying on a blanket, Audrey and I would look at the stars, talking for hours before we turned in for the night, squashed together in our one-person sleeping bag. During our happy days, at least.

And now? I was doing my best to avoid the waft of manure of broken-down horses that weren't even mine.

A contented sigh broke me from my memories. Shep had decided to come down from his hayloft throne and accompany me for the day. I guess in his grand prince mind, lolling around watching me do manual labor was accompanying me. Now he was lying one way, his head turned at a right angle. I was always amazed how Shep could contort that way and not be in constant need of a chiropractor. Those big brown eyes of his stared me down as I mucked the stalls and the horses gallivanted in the pasture.

"Don't work too hard, boy," I said. "You don't wanna pull a muscle."

He licked his chops, as if trying to decide whether it was worth expending the energy to respond. Finally, he just snorted and settled back into his sunbeam. I couldn't help but laugh at the look on his face—simultaneous bliss at his surroundings and aggravation at being disturbed.

Good ol' Shep. Always good for a chuckle, even when he was being a dickhead.

Shep was only a momentary distraction for me, though. During my clandestine meeting with Daniela, she had told me the ultimate end game— I was to get close to the Godmother through Ada. Charm her to trust me, to take me into her inner circle—and then feed Daniela every tidbit of information I could possibly dig up. I was going to be Daniela's hoof pick—scraping out every ounce of dirt on the Organization possible. Ada was holding a campaign rally tonight at Riverside Park—and that was where I was supposed to confront her.

"You're going to have to put on a performance—make a real show of it," Daniela had said to me.

"How do you mean?"

"The only way she's going to introduce you to the Godmother is if you kiss the ring."

"Am I supposed to make her an offer she can't refuse?" I nervously cracked.

Sensing my unease, her moon eye twinkled at me. "Something like that. You're gonna have to pretend their killing Christopher was the best thing that ever happened to you."

"What about the whole business of them, you know, framing me for it?"

"You're gonna have to act like they did you a service. Be unflinchingly grateful. Fawning, cloying even. People like this? Show them blind adoration, and they'll give you the keys to the kingdom. These fucking monsters think that they're some sort of lion—alpha hunters leading the charge on their perverse cause of purity. But, deep down, they're more like sheep—they move in packs, desperate for validation from each other. So, get down and be in the herd with them—do and say anything that's in line with their beliefs. And once you're in lockstep with them? We can gut and shear them for everything that they're worth."

Fucking Christ—you weren't the one putting yourself at risk of being trampled, lady.

"I'm not going to lie to you, Cillian—there's a decent chance this ends with you getting arrested or killed and thrown in a ditch somewhere," Daniela said as if she could read my mind. "But ingratiating yourself with them is the only way any of this stands a chance of working. And, unfortunately, this isn't something I'm able to do myself. For obvious reasons," she said, motioning to her face. "So, you're going to have to be the one to play the game."

My blood ran cold at the thought of this being some sort of demented game—a chess match of do-or-die proportions. But I knew Daniela was right. To people like Fisker? We were just pawns—weaklings she needed to vanquish on her way to total domination.

But even pawns can take the queen off the board.

"Cill'!" Rip's voice boomed from the porch where he was perpetually planted nowadays, interrupting my thoughts. "You eaten anything yet?"

That was the other thing—Daniela made me swear to heaven that I wouldn't tell Rip anything. I agreed. I couldn't in good conscience put Rip, the only father figure worth a damn I'd ever had in my life, in more danger than he was already in. And besides, I had to do *something* before the cops caught on. Eventually, everything would come crashing down—it was only a matter of time—and I *needed* to make sure that the damn world didn't fall on poor Rip's head.

Fuck.

I need to get him out of trouble.

I need to get him out of trouble.

I need to—

Breathe, damn it.

It was going to be a trick lying to Rip—even if that was the greater good thing to do. It always ground my gears when people dismissed men like Rip as simple-minded rednecks. Something those asshole, holier-than-thou people didn't understand was that someone could be educated to all hell, but only have one oar in the water. Rip didn't even graduate high school, but his people sense was better than most PhDs.

Moving back to the barn door, I replied, "Nah, not yet."

He waved me over like I was a child. "Well, c'mon then. I got roast beef. The caca'll keep until after lunch."

I smiled, carefully placing the pitchfork against the barn wall. At the mention of roast beef, Shep suddenly came back to life, trotting alongside me as I walked towards the house, his tongue hanging out sideways. Suddenly he had the energy of a puppy.

"Fixin's are out on the kitchen counter," Rip said as he jerked his thumb behind him. "Bring me one, too, while you're at it."

"Sir, yes sir," I mock saluted him.

Rip pulled a big ol' bone out of his jacket pocket—the kind that you see in the pet shops but never actually buy because they seem more suited for dinosaurs than dogs. "Shep, you wanna keep me company for a spell?"

The words were barely out of his mouth before Shep jumped up, snatched the damn thing out of Rip's bony hand, and pinned it to the ground—mauling it like it had called his mother a pig. I sadly smiled as I watched him—this cranky old pit bull was literally the only thing I had left to my name in the whole wide world.

He was the only thing I had left of her.

"Drink?" I asked Rip, determined to not let my demons wrestle me to the ground.

"Coffee black."

Giving him a thumbs-up, I strode through the front door. Sure enough, there on the counter was a three-pound bag of fresh, deli counter-sliced roast beef. I knew what a treat this was. Rip would have had to drive at least 45 minutes to get this—to the one grocery store that actually had a deli counter in it. But he'd never be caught dead eating anything that came from the dairy aisle of the supermarket. I remember once Rip sent me on a grocery run when I was a teenager, and I brought back some pre-packaged honey ham and cheddar cheese, and he looked at me like I had three heads.

As I got to work making the sandwiches and brewing the coffee, my gaze hit the one-way mirror hanging above the kitchen table directly to my right. Where I had seen Rip successfully fend off Detective Rogers' intense interrogation. Despite all the time that had passed since she had been here, I could never shake the suspicion she was lying-in wait at the end of Rip's lane—just biding her time until the moment I screwed up and revealed myself. Which could be tonight.

After all, if Daniela had found me so easily, who's to say that Rogers couldn't?
Fuck.
What if she caught me before I even got to the rally?
Fuck fuck.
What if everything Daniela and I had planned was for nothing?
Fuck fuck fuck.
What if I didn't get the chance to—
Blood spurts all over the counter stopped my anxiety spiral dead in its tracks. Cutting the sandwiches in half, I sliced open the top of my thumb—that's how deep into my stupid "what if" vortex I had gotten.
Calm the fuck down, you idiot.
Miraculously, the blood hadn't soaked the sandwiches. So, I wrapped my thumb in a paper towel and took the lunches to the porch, being careful not to spill the coffee mugs balanced on the plates. Shep, being the goddamn eating machine that he is, was already near halfway done with his bone.

"What the hell did you do to yourself?" Rip gestured at the crimson-soaked paper towel wrapped around my thumb.

"Knife got away from me." I thought it better to leave out the details of my mini panic attack.

"Didn't realize sandwich-making was a contact sport," he guffawed as he gratefully accepted the plate and coffee. "Thanks much."

Chewing silently, all three of us contemplated the sun-dappled afternoon sky—the blue punctured by the vibrant orange maples and the searing, deep red dogwoods. It was Mother Nature's last hurrah—she was strutting her stuff for us one last time before she rode off into the bleak night of winter. For a moment, I forgot my worries and just marveled at her. Lord knows Virginia was a complicated gal full of all sorts of contradictions—but no one could put on a show like her when she was in the mood.

"So. Where'd you get off to last night in my truck?" Rip's voice interrupted my musings.

But the sun had to set on all lovely moments at some point.

"What do you mean?"

Rip looked at me, a mixture of annoyance and amusement forming in his eyes. "What do you mean, what do I mean? The windows were cracked open more than I usually leave 'em. And besides, there was a fresh ol' Cill' sized depression in the seat cushion."

See what I mean? Doesn't miss a God. Damn. Thing.

My mind cycled through the possible yarns I could spin him. But I decided to stick with a half-truth.

"Couldn't sleep, so I went out for a walk. When that didn't do the trick, I decided to go for a drive."

Rip shoved the last of his roast beef in his mouth and chased it down with coffee. "Kinda reckless, doncha' think? That ain't like you."

Ouch. Rip saying that was the equivalent of Mama saying 'I'm not angry, I'm just disappointed.'

"It was the middle of the night. I thought the risk would be low. But you're right, I'm sorry. It won't happen again."

Rip took a long look, silently eyeing me. The only sound was the chainsaw-like, percussive crunch of Shep demolishing his bone.

"That's the size of it?" he asked me.

"Yeah."

Rip contemplated me for an even longer while. Finally, he nodded. "Okay, Cill'. Whatever you say." But he didn't look me in the eyes when he said it—he knew I wasn't telling the full truth and was upset by me playing him for a fool. Hurting Rip made me ashamed. But I was doing it for his own good. All I hoped was that he would understand that one day.

"It's about time for my afternoon snooze, I think," Rip quietly muttered as he rose from his beloved rocking chair, taking both our dirty dishes in the process. "See you at supper." And with that, he lumbered into the house.

I had promised myself I would never lie to Rip, ever. And I had just broken that vow. I'd done a lot of terrible things in my life, but that one is up there with the worst of them.

Time to go shovel some more shit.

Chapter Sixteen

Cillian

I thought I had seen everything—and then Daniela gave me a car key.

I should clarify—a voice-activated digital recorder that looked exactly like a car key. Put the thing in your pocket, and it'll record up to sixteen hours of content. When she handed it to me and told me to use it when I was with Ada, I joked I wasn't James Bond. She didn't laugh.

Up in my hayloft, I looked at myself in the dusty mirror I had rigged up. It was the first time in a good long while I had put any effort into how I looked. It was all hand-me-downs from Rip—the flannel, the jeans, and the Lone Star Beer trucker cap—but they fit me like a glove. That's gotta be a symbol or metaphor for something—but I didn't have the time to figure that out. Wearing Rip's clothes gave me a bit of comfort—it felt like Rip was a wizened, broken-down old knight handing down his sword and shield to me. He would be with me no matter what befell me tonight.

I tucked the fake car key into the front pocket of the flannel. The gadget was clever. If I got frisked, since I just looked like a good ol' boy trucker, the key would seem like it belonged to my rig and nothing else.

You can do this, Cillian. You have to do it. Not just for Audrey. Not just for Christopher. But for humanity, damn it. And if Christopher could do this, I sure as shit could.

An electronic pinging sound from the burner phone Daniela had given me interrupted my self-pep talk. A text from her read: *be there in twenty.* I had told her about my earlier conversation with Rip—that he was suspicious and that using his truck to get around wasn't going to be an option anymore. Begrudgingly, she had agreed to drive me. We would meet in the woods behind Rip's property and take one of the hiking trails to her car. I texted back to confirm. Almost immediately, I got a follow-up: *and be on time. I'm not an Uber driver.*

Despite everything, I couldn't help but chuckle. Daniela was unlike anybody I'd ever met. I'm sure some people found her brusque ways rude or demeaning, but I didn't. Not at all. I found it amusing, but also incredibly commendable—she said exactly what she meant. In my limited time of knowing Daniela, she had told me nothing but the truth, ever. No matter how blunt or scary it might be. I respected and admired that. Audrey had so often hidden what she was truly feeling by saying something that really meant something else entirely, and I'd have to decode what the hell she was actually trying to tell me. It became a frustrating puzzle—one that I was never able to truly solve. That's not to blame her or anything. It was my job to figure it out, right? Maybe some shrink would disagree and say that it wasn't "fair fighting" for her to expect me to do that. I don't know. But I thought that I had failed. So, I completely understood why Christopher valued Daniela as much as he clearly had. In fact, his friendship with her even sparked a little bit of respect for him in me.

Not a whole lot, though—let's not get crazy or anything.

I checked the time—I needed to get going. It wasn't a short walk to where I was meeting Daniela. Luckily, Ada's event was at night—I don't know how I would have explained my absence to Rip if it was light. At this hour, Rip was tucked in and snoring. I looked over at the snoozing Shep—his legs were twitching in his sleep, like he was running. Whatever he was chasing in his dream had no chance. Suddenly, it hit me.

This could be the last time I saw Shep.

That thought sliced open my gut.

And unlike with Rip, I could actually somewhat acknowledge it. Better make it count.

I slowly crouched down so I was at his eye level, being careful not to wake him up. I gently stroked the top of his head. The fur around his eyes had gotten real grey recently. It wasn't just old age running its course—the turbulence of this past year, of my actions, had clearly taken its toll on the old boy. I still remember the way he fit snugly as a bug curled up next to Audrey when he was younger. The way she sang a lullaby she'd made up to him in the car ride back home from the pound.

God, what I would give to hear that song escape from those lips again.

"I love you so much, Shep," I whispered to him, the salty tang of tears stinging my eyes. "I'd be lost without you. Thank you for everything. If you don't see me again…take care of Rip for me, okay? You're my warrior."

Off my last word, his legs stopped twitching, and his eyes opened just a smidge. But instead of shooting me his usual cranky look, his tail started thumping, and he gave me a giant lick on the right cheek before rolling over.

Sleep tight, my Prince.

With that, I wiped the tears from my eyes. It was time now. I shoved the burner phone in my back pocket, climbed down the ladder, and grabbed my coat, closing the barn door as softly as possible behind me.

As I walked, for the first time in longer than I'd like to admit, I thought about Christopher. He'd told Daniela that he trusted me. While I knew Daniela had no reason to lie, I still had trouble wrapping my brain around that notion. For all intents and purposes, squaring off against the Godmother had been the most important thing Christopher had ever done in his life. And he had entrusted *me* to finish the job for him if he faltered.

And I had no idea if I had the stones to do it.

I quickened my pace, futilely trying to outpace my misgivings.

What the fuck was I trying to do here? I'm no hero. I barely even had the courage to meet Daniela in the first place. I'm a coward. I'm a fraud. I'm nothing compared to—

That's when the fox darted across the trail not more than two feet in front of me.

Spooked, I halted, nearly losing my balance.

Foxes never came that close. Ever. Not unless they were rabid.

But this one didn't have that mangy, deranged look. No, this was something else. Mama always used to say that the mysticism of the world was personified to us through animals—that a four-legged creature was the spirits' preferred vessel of communication.

That's when it hit me.

Christopher.

Christopher loved foxes. To the point that he defied dear old Dad over one. Not that I saw it firsthand. But one weekend, he'd been out hunting with Dad, and he came back with a vicious shiner. I asked him what happened, and he told me that he had seen Dad about to shoot a fox for no good reason. Purely out of spite and because he could. So, Christopher pushed the gun away as he fired, so he totally missed the fox. Dad walloped him something fierce. "Some things are just too gorgeous to ever consider killing, you know? And…it would have upset Mom," was what Christopher had said. This was back when we still had normal conversations and confided in one another.

I looked up to see the fox trotting away. But just before it disappeared into the mist, it turned back to look at me. Its yellow eyes nearly blinded me as it illuminated parts of my soul that I had buried long ago. Then, it vanished.

I almost laughed. I couldn't believe I was thinking this. But all the same, I knew it was true, the same way I knew Audrey was my beloved the first time I laid eyes on her.

This was Christopher nudging me forward.

Foxes are deceptive creatures. There's an old country adage that when someone was "dumb like a fox," he or she was beguilingly cunning—much cleverer than what they looked to be on the surface. Christopher was like that. Maybe that's why he liked them so much. Christopher was telling me that I needed to be more like him. That I could act like him—even if just temporarily.

That he believed in me.

I squared my jaw and strode forward. The familiar rush of athlete's adrenaline ran through me—the calm yet laser-focused intensity I would feel entering the start box with Apollo at a cross-country event. I was rearing to go now.

Thanks, Brother.

Before too long, I was at Daniela's meeting spot. A secluded spot at the intersection—if you could call that—of three hiking paths and a creek jutting off the James River. I'd been up here several times before in the middle of the night and had never seen a soul. So, for our purposes? It was perfect.

I checked the time on my burner phone. I was a couple of minutes early still. Just as I started to type out a message to Daniela—

"Keep your shirt on. I'm here," Daniela said as she crunched through the fallen leaves over to me.

"You're early." I slid the phone back into my pocket.

"New Yorkers aren't late to anything. We lose the right to call ourselves that if we are."

I tried to politely smile. Even though I was still riding the high of my fox-induced athlete's adrenaline, that didn't mean that I wasn't still feeling antsy. Daniela must have been able to sense this because she softly put her hand on my shoulder.

"You ready?"

I squelched the instinctual feeling in my gut to run away. "Ready."

And with that, we set off into the night.

* * *

It was a *long* drive to get to our destination—-about an hour or so from Rip's remote farm. So, we had some time to kill. Daniela had turned on the radio in her rental car to a local station—offering the usual Top 40 garbage. I tried my best to tune out the noise by staring out the window at the passing scenery. But in the pitch black, all I could see was the silhouette of the Blue Ridge drenched in moonlight. It was haunting, next-level spooky. People always drone on and on about the eerie bayou swamplands of Louisiana, but in my opinion? Nothing is more unsettling than Ol' Blue looking over your shoulder—lurking in the shadows like a silent stalker ready to strike. Mama used to say on nights like these that you could feel the death lying heavy in the mist.

But I wasn't going to let it suffocate me. Not tonight.

"You know what helps me when I'm feeling nervous?" Daniela asked me without moving her eyes from the road.

"Who said I was nervous?"

She side-eyed me as she flicked her gaze down to my left hand. The damn thing had a death grip on my pant leg, like it was trying to suffocate the denim right out of my blue jeans. "Put your left hand on your stomach and your right hand on your heart."

"I've done breathing exercises before. They don't help," I shot back.

"You haven't been doing them correctly, then."

Daniela must have seen my hesitation because she rolled her eyes. "Fine. Don't. Stay feeling shitty then."

I reluctantly did as she instructed. "Now what?"

"When you take a breath in, imagine that you're inhaling your favorite smell. Then, when you exhale, imagine that you're blowing out a bunch of candles on a birthday cake. Do it three times."

"There's no way that—"

"Just shut up and try it."

I closed my eyes and started the process that I was sure wouldn't do a good goddamn thing. But what the hell?

My favorite smell was easy to conjure up—Mama used to plant lavender in our garden out back when I was a little guy. Even though it was so long ago, that smell has never left my memory. Store-bought lavender scent just doesn't capture the essence of the soothing yet wild sweetness that the actual flowers have. Then, for the cake bit, I pictured a big ol' cheesecake (the best kind of cake in the world, if you ask me) littered with blue candles.

In.

Out.

In.

Out.

In.

Out.

169

When I opened my eyes back up—most every single knotted sinew in my body had undone itself.

Imagining a smell and a cake had actually worked. Fuck me.

Dumbfounded, I turned to Daniela. Before I could even say anything, she cut me off with a satisfied grin. "See? Told you."

"Where did you learn how to do that?" I asked her.

"I used to get awful panic attacks when I was younger."

I nodded, grateful and impressed that she would share that intimate of a detail of her life. Especially someone who clearly put a lot of stock in appearing like a badass at all times. I hadn't even ever admitted my vulnerability to panic attacks to Audrey. "Sorry to hear that."

"Trust me, before I tried it, I was the same as you. Thought it was a buncha' bull. But I'm a full convert now—works every single time."

A comforting lull of silence sat there for a minute as I snuck a glance at Daniela. Last time we'd talked, I was so preoccupied with the circumstances I hadn't really had the chance to look at her—I mean *really* look at her. Her moon eye wasn't the only beautiful thing about her. She had naturally wavy black hair that looked effortless—the kind of gentle curls that I knew rich women spent a lot of money trying to replicate at the salon. Full, magenta lips. And freckles across her cheekbones that looked like they had been gently painted on by a watercolor artist. She was undeniably show-stopping gorgeous—and all without a lick of make-up anywhere.

"Jesus. Cillian, you looking for something or what?"

I immediately ripped my gaze away from her. "Sorry. I…sorry."

Another tick of silence filled the car before Daniela started laughing.

"What's so funny?"

"I just realized that I know basically everything about you, and yet you don't know anything about me. I'm a stranger who's been spying on you. I'm driving you to a potential suicide mission, and yet you've completely respected my privacy and not asked me anything about myself. It's just amusing, is all."

"I didn't want to pry. Your business is your business."

That made her laugh even harder. "Goddamn Southerners. You'll be polite even when someone is pointing a gun at you."

That made me smile. "Yes, ma'am."

"Tell you what—I'll give you three freebies. Ask me three questions. Anything you want, and I'll answer. No holds barred."

"Really?"

"You're gonna have to accept at some point that if I'm saying it, I mean it." *Fair enough.*

"Did you think my brother was as much of a shit-heel as I did?"

There was that distinctively declarative, single-syllable *HA* again. "I don't think there's a soul on this goddamn earth who thought that as much as you, Cillian."

I ruefully smirked. "True. But that doesn't answer my question."

Daniela paused for a moment, pursing her lips as she chewed on that. "He was my friend. I saw him for exactly what he could be—a complete and utter narcissist who loved being the center of attention in every single place he stepped foot in. But I also saw him for what he was deep down—a man who defended what and who he believed in to the hilt. He was also the only goddamn man on the entire campus of the University of Virginia that didn't try to get into my pants or call me some sort of racist slur. He valued my brain—and just wanted to be my friend. Nothing more, nothing less. And I'll always be loyal to him for that."

I had to restrain myself from letting out a scoff of surprise. I honestly couldn't believe that Christopher had never tried to seduce Daniela. But, granted…I was a little biased in my thinking when it came to his self-control (or lack thereof) in that department. "Why are you doing this? Why not leave it be after Christopher died?"

Her answer was quick and reflexive. "Because it's the right thing to do."

Soon as the words came out of her mouth, I knew that was about as true as a horse going oink. "C'mon," I said softly. "The real reason."

She grew quiet for a moment. Finally, she spoke. "My Papi owned a bodega on East 162nd street in the Bronx. It's a nice area now because of the new Yankee stadium, but it wasn't back then. After school, I would ride over on my bike and help him run the store. I'd get there at 3 PM, on the dot, and

Manny, who ran the deli in the back of the store, would have a fresh Cubano made and waiting for me. His family was off the boat from Havana, so he knew how to make it right. Papi would take a fifteen-minute break and have a cortadito while I ate. Manny was his childhood best friend, so they loved each other like brothers. Those fifteen minutes were the best part of my day. Listening to them shoot the shit with one another made me realize that family isn't always connected by blood, you know? One day, my bike chain got tangled up, and it made me a few minutes late. When I got there, the first thing I saw were their bodies. Manny and my Papi had been shot, execution style. Laid out on the sidewalk like garbage bags on collection day. The entire store was trashed. Swastikas and racial slurs graffitied all over. The only thing that wasn't decimated was my daily Cubano. It was sitting right there on the counter, still warm."

Daniela's voice trailed off as she blinked back tears. "If I had gotten there at my usual time, I could have stopped it. I could have saved them."

"You'd probably be dead too, you know," I quietly replied.

Daniela shrugged. "Maybe. But at least I'd have gone down fighting. I promised myself right then and there that I'd never stand on the sidelines ever again. I'll die before I let people like that win."

I let the silence sit there for a moment while I tried to think of the right thing to say. What possible condolence is there for something so disgusting, so horrific? An act so vicious that it defies every single basic law of human decency?

"I'm so sorry you had to go through that, Daniela." Unsure of myself, I started to lightly touch her arm consolingly, but abruptly pulled myself back.

There's nothing you can do or say to make it okay, Cillian. Shut the fuck up.

Daniela took a deep breath, squeezing her eyes dry of any remaining remnants of tears. "And number three?"

I turned to her, surprised. "What?"

"What's your third question?"

"Oh, we don't have to—"

"Please. I need you to ask me."

The way she said it, I could tell she was desperate to change the subject.

But the question I had left wasn't a gentle one.

"Do you think we're going to survive all of this?"

Daniela turned into the parking lot of Riverside Park. It was packed with cars—the venue resembled more an outdoor country concert than a campaign event. Daniela yanked her gear shift into park. In front of each parking spot was an all-white placard. The dark red, all-caps lettering read: VOTE MORGAN FOR A BRIGHTER FUTURE.

She turned to face me. "I guess we're gonna find out."

Chapter Seventeen

Cillian

I had forgotten how much I hate large crowds.

T here were probably about fifty or so people gathered at the park in front of a gazebo, which was outfitted with a podium and PA system. On the lawn in front were a couple of food trucks and a stand offering hot apple cider in souvenir "Vote Ada" mugs. Twinkly lights were strung up all over the lawn, and standing pub tables were strategically placed near restaurant-style space-heaters. Perfectly staged like the "after" shots of one of those home makeover shows that Audrey loved—where the host of the show had spent way too much money transforming some schlub's backyard into space for entertaining he would never actually use.

Remember Christopher's fox. Courage.

I made myself wade through the onslaught of people to get to an unoccupied corner table off to the side of it all—far enough away to avoid Ada's direct eye line while she was speaking, but close enough that I could get a good look at her while she spoke. I finally got through the gauntlet of preppy, Brooks Brothers-clad men mixed in with the rougher, shit-kicker alphas. I spread out my arms and elbows on my table, silently telling anyone who looked at me that I wasn't interested in company. I checked my watch—I still had about five minutes or so until Ada was due to go on.

Ada. I hadn't seen her since that night. When she told Christopher and me that she knew how to handle everything. As she calmly stood over my beloved's body. The color hadn't even left Audrey's cheeks before Ada started treating her like a disposable object—a problem she had to wipe clean from the face of the earth.

"Well, hey there, friend!"

I looked up with a start to see the source of the way-too-perky voice—a bubbly college-aged blonde. She had on one of those campaign pins that was about three sizes too big and was carrying a stack of glossy campaign pamphlets that looked like they just had come out the printer five minutes ago. She probably was a student at Lynchburg College—doing all of this for a course credit and a blurb on the resume. The five-gallon smile she had glued on her face just creeped me out.

Jesus Christ, what if she recognized me?

"Hello," I replied warily, realizing that I had to say something, otherwise, she'd just continue staring at me.

"My name's Annabelle. Is this your first time at one of our rallies?"

Thank God. She has no idea who I am. My dirty unkemptness, bushy beard, and Rip's clothing were serving their purpose. My resemblance to my murdered identical twin was completely concealed.

"It is."

"Well, on behalf of all of us with the Morgan campaign, thank you for coming! We welcome anybody who wants to join our movement to reclaim Virginia's former glory."

Virginia's former glory. That sent a shiver down my spine. Knowing what Daniela had shown me about who was pulling the strings here? It was impossible to not understand what she really meant by that phrase.

"Would you like a pamphlet?" Annabelle shoved it into my hands, not really asking. I forced a nod and smiled.

"Enjoy." And with that, Annabelle moved on to her next target.

I looked down at the thing she had forced on me. On the cover of the campaign booklet was that same chilling, bloodshot red lettering and logo that was on the parking placard. The inside was what I assumed to be "normal" for this type of leaflet—a bunch of gobble-de-gook summaries

175

of the various positions of Ada's Republican platform. My eyes promptly glazed over—they tend to do that with roundabout bullshit where nobody is actually saying anything.

How the hell did Ada devolve into this?

Say what you want about my brother—and Lord knows, I always did—but he never would have gone for all this nonsense. He was a Democrat through and through. A moderate one, sure. But a Democrat, nonetheless. Did Ada believe any of this racist, hate-fueled, doomsday thinking? Had the Devil fully sunk his claws into her? Sure, I didn't really know her. But I knew what Chris had told me—that she was a liberal go-getter. And she was a lesbian, for Christ's sake—something that I knew wasn't exactly on the conservatives' list of preferences.

What the hell did they do to her?

Looking around at my fellow attendees, it was clear who Ada's target demographic was, and it rhymed with "bright hen"—testosterone-drunk, middle-aged white men who felt hot and bothered by the advancement of others and were pissed to no end about it. And, lest I forget—Virginia is an open-carry state. A bunch of them had pistols hanging off their hips. I had to be mindful. Judging by the looks of them, these were the types of animals who probably owned paraphernalia adorned with the Valknut and Deus Vult crosses, were opposed to the removal of Confederate statues, and thought that James Alex Fields Jr. was one of the "very fine people" that Trump referred to that sickening day in 2017. So, I needed to keep a low profile.

But what if one of these yahoos recognized me? Decided to partake in some vigilante justice and take matters into their own hands?

Ear-piercing microphone feedback from the stage split my thoughts. The show was about to begin. A man who was about three sizes too rotund for his suit and bow tie strode up to the mic. He was also sporting the most ridiculous mustache I'd ever seen. I'd always wondered what the Kentucky Fried Chicken man would look like in real life. I guess now I had my answer.

"Thank y'all for coming," he said. "I think everyone here tonight can agree on one thing—this state is in real danger. Danger of falling behind in every single conceivable aspect."

A murmur of agreement rippled through the crowd around me as Mr. Chicken Bucket continued. "The person that's about to step on this stage knows that—she feels your pain. She wants to help bring the Commonwealth back to its former glory. Back to when we were the envy of not just the mid-Atlantic, but the entire country. We must make it a breeding ground for American success—and American success only. For prosperity, for individual freedoms once more. Those know-nothing, latte-sipping, Beltway liberals that have taken control of the state don't know anything about the kind of trouble *you've* been through. They don't know anything about what *you* want and what *you* need. It's time to take our state back! We CANNOT be replaced by the socialist, politically correct, cancel culture agenda!"

The murmur of agreement turned into impassioned hooting and hollering. "Without further ado, it gives me great pleasure to introduce the Republican nominee for the 5th Congressional District of Virginia, Ada Morgan!" Drumstick bellowed as he thundered his meaty hands together.

And that's when I saw Ada.

But the woman I was looking at had left the Ada I once knew in the dust long ago.

The first thing that was different was her hair. For as long as I had known her (and Christopher had known her, for that matter), she had her hair done in a short, efficient, bob. Now? She had her hair long and wavy, almost past her shoulder. Dyed Barbie blonde. They were hair extensions—well-done ones, mind you, but still.

Ada's clothes were different, too—Christopher always joked how he'd never seen her in anything but the most pristine-looking designer clothing. Now? She was clearly going for the folksy, woman-of-the-people look—a plaid flannel tucked into crisp (but not too crisp) denim jeans with a pair of boots that clearly had been carefully scuffed by the manufacturer for just the right amount of rugged. It was like they had put the appearances of Tomi Lahren, Kayleigh McEnany, and Katherine Timpf into an algorithm to create Ada's new look. It was so full-on pandering I wondered how anybody in their right mind couldn't see it.

But looking around? Everyone seemed to be eating her up with a spoon.

The one thing that hadn't changed, though? Those bright blue eyes—the ones that looked like they could power a five-bedroom house all by themselves. The kind of eyes that made your stomach turn inside out before you even knew why.

"Thank you, Mr. Devereaux," she cooed as she took the podium. She put her hands on the dais for a spell, before dramatically shaking her head, taking the microphone out of its stand, and stepping out from the podium.

"I'd rather just talk to y'all directly, if you don't mind?" She motioned to the discarded podium. "That thing's way too formal for my style."

A resounding cheer from the crowd confirmed what she already knew.

Jesus Christ, she was good. The Ada Chris had told me about was formal with a capital "F." This had to be scripted to the last syllable—but she was doing such a great job delivering it, no one else would know.

She smiled as she waited for the cheering crowd to settle down. "By now, I think y'all know my backstory, right?" Affirmations of agreement rippled through the crowd. "For years, I swore to myself that I would never be the one that would be up on this stage. I wanted to be the woman behind the curtain, never the one with the microphone in her hand. After all, it's better to be the one that manufactures the gun than the person who pulls the trigger, right?"

Her joke solicited a big collective laugh from those around me while I tried to figure out what the hell was even remotely funny about that—especially given all the mass shooting tragedies of the past few years. But I suppose this wasn't the audience for that sort of regret.

"That all changed when I got the call about Congressman Clarke. His senseless murder at the hands of his deranged brother. No matter what side of the aisle you're on, I think we can all agree that it was a tragedy. We disagreed on…plenty. But he was my mentor. And a dear friend. And no one deserves to be gunned down in the sanctuary of their own home. Especially by *family*, Lord above."

How the fuck could she say all that with a straight face?

I did the breathing exercise Daniela had shown me in the car to regain my focus.

Ada continued, pacing the makeshift stage like she'd been doing it for decades. "Anyhow, his death made me take stock of what I'd been doing with my life. I had invested years into facilitating Congressman Clarke's rise. And then it was all taken away, just like that," she snapped her fingers crisply. "All of my hopes and dreams zipped up in Christopher's body bag alongside him."

Body bag.

I thought back to the moment I discovered Christopher's corpse. His bits of brain smeared all over the porch. The blood that looked like it had been shot out of a fire hydrant cannon. I had to swallow back the urge to vomit right there on the table.

I'm going to get the people responsible. I swear. Even if it kills me.

Ada paused for dramatic effect before dropping the bomb on the place. "And that's when I realized I had to change my game plan and put my money on a new show pony—yours truly."

A thunderous round of applause surrounded me as I tried in earnest to conceal my absolute disgust.

She was using my brother's tragedy to jump start her political career.

Ada was up there pretending that she was better than us—somehow above the atrocity we three had committed.

After she commanded us to put on gloves so we wouldn't leave our fingerprints on Audrey's body.

After Ada had told us what specific knots we needed to use to make it look like Audrey had done the deed herself.

After Ada told us she would make sure that there would be no autopsy—and that Audrey's family wouldn't request one.

Just get through this. You can do that. God damn it, you <u>have</u> to do this. There's too much at risk if you fail.

I gritted my teeth so I didn't shout out a string of expletives at the deranged hypocrisy of it all.

And that's when she turned her face in my direction.

Even though I knew that she couldn't recognize me from that far off, what she said still sent a lightning bolt down my core.

"And let me tell you something, folks. I know, deep down in my heart, that Christopher would have wanted this for me despite our ideological differences. So, I'm gonna do him proud. And we're going to take this state back and Make America Great Again once more!"

* * *

She absolutely brought the house down with the rest of her speech—by all the carrying on from the crowd, I'm sure people walking past the park thought it was a Bon Jovi concert or something. When she finished, there was a three-minute standing ovation for her. The manipulative power that she so effortlessly wielded over everyone watching her was…something else entirely. She was magnetic. No one could take their eyes off her. Me included. Even despite all the horrifying, disturbing implications her election would bring to Congress.

Now for the meet and greet—anyone who wanted to shake her hand or take a selfie had free rein. Ada was pulling out all the stops to prove her "salt of the earth" mettle. And near everybody in attendance lined up to take part.

I stuck myself at the very end of the line.

My escalating heartbeat rang in my ears, perfectly in sync with the advancement of those ahead of me in line.

Thump-thump.

Thump-thump.

Thump-thump.

Remember everything that Daniela showed you. Ada is not your friend. If she's truly a part of all this, she deserves to be taken down just as much as the rest of them.

Thump-thump.

Thump-thump.

Thump-thump.

Remember your brother and why he was killed.

Thump-thump.

Thump-thump.

Thump-thump.

Remember your beloved and what she would have wanted you to do.

I was nearly at the front of the line now. I was only going to have a few seconds with her. I needed to make them count. Say something that made sure she knew who I was and what I wanted right out of the gate.

What on earth could that be?

Without thinking, I touched the front pocket where the digital voice-recording car key was before chastising myself.

You fucking idiot—you're like one of those morons in a spy movie that touches their earwig repeatedly. You might as well plaster a LOOK AT ME sign on your forehead.

There was just one person in front of me now.

What the fuck could I say to her that would—

My racing heartbeat hit the brakes full stop, and I almost smiled.

Because I had it.

The person in front of me peeled off to the right. It was just me and her now. I kept my head tilted down so she couldn't make me out before I wanted her to.

"Hi there," Ada said, extending her hand for a shake. "Thanks for coming out. Don't be shy."

Taking her hand, pumping it slowly, I raised my face, carefully saying each word like I was shooting poison darts.

"Now, you desperately need me. Now, you can't live without me."

And that's when the color drained from her face as she looked past my makeshift disguise and recognized me and that famous line from *Fool for Love* by Sam Shepard—Audrey's favorite play.

Because that's what Ada said to Christopher and me right before we all dragged away my beloved's body to that Red Maple tree.

Chapter Eighteen

Cillian

"You shouldn't be here," were the first things out of Ada's mouth as she continued to shake my hand. She kept that phony politician smile glued on her face, but the hurricane brewing behind her eyes was telling another story.

There was no way in hell I was going to budge before she did.

"You don't want my support?"

"*You* want to support *us*?"

"Us?" I pretended to play dumb. I knew she would see right through it—which was the point. "Is your campaign not just you?"

Ada looked over my shoulder. Because I had waited until the very last moment, there wasn't really anybody left in the venue—save for a few event people cleaning up and a couple of security guards in the back who looked like they had seen their best days twenty years (and pounds) ago. Ada had made a big show at the start of the meet and greet of instructing the guards to give her space so she could "really converse with her constituents." I wonder if she was regretting that now.

Ada wiped the smile off her face and quickly yanked her hand out of my grasp and squirted some sanitizer onto her palms.

"What is it exactly that you want? You here to do to me what you did to your brother?"

Right down to brass tacks.

"I think you and I both know that's not how things went down." Despite my best efforts, I had trouble keeping a snarl out of my voice.

"Why would I know that?" she said as she folded her arms and stared me down with those blue thunderbolts. "You're a criminal. Why should I—or anyone for that matter—believe anything you have to say?"

"Because I'm telling the truth!"

"Truth. That's rich coming from you—of all people."

Damn it, Cillian. This wasn't the game plan, and you know it.

I took a deep breath and changed tactics.

Switch gears. Put her on the back foot.

"You're all alone right now? Shouldn't there be some version of who you were for Chris running around busily like a chicken with their head cut off?"

"You have thirty seconds to tell me what you want before I start screaming and shouting for someone to call the police," she said, not taking the bait.

I was never any good at lighthearted small talk.

"I came here to thank you and the people that you're working for."

"For what?"

"For having the stones to do the thing that I was never able to."

She arched her eyebrow at me as she looked at her watch. "I don't know what you're referring to. Twenty seconds."

Fuck.

"I'd like to meet the Godmother." I blurted out.

"I don't know who that is. Ten seconds."

This one is for all the marbles.

"If you don't, I'll tell everyone about what I did to Audrey. What *you* helped me do to Audrey."

"I have no idea what you're talking about. But even if I did, it would be my word against yours. A well-respected political insider versus a fugitive wanted for murder. Five seconds."

"I have proof. I have a recording of us three talking about how to get rid of her body."

Her eyes snapped up from the face of her watch questioningly. "No, you don't."

I shrugged, trying to put on my best poker face as I bluffed to kingdom come. "Want to roll the dice and find out? I'll go down, sure. But I'll take you with me. I swear to God."

She studied me for a long tick. "There's no recording." But I could see the uncertainty trickling through her steely façade.

"Okay, Ada. There's no recording."

"Let me see it."

"You really think I'd keep it on me? Geez, Ada—I woulda thought that you were smarter than that."

I could practically feel the heat rising within her as she gauged whether to risk throwing me to the dogs.

Remember what Daniela told you. Lay it on thick. Blind adoration.

"Look, I promise you, Ada. I'm not your enemy. Or the Organization. All I want to do is help. Christopher's death and hiding out this past year have made me realize who the real enemy is in this country. Think about it—why else would I risk exposing myself like this? It'd be suicide unless I meant it. All I'm asking is for you and the Godmother to hear me out. To let me prove myself to you. That's it."

Ada slowly cracked her knuckles one by one. Her eyes never left mine. Not once.

Finally, her body language completely changed. Like she was shedding a skin that no longer suited her. A whisper of regret flickered through her face as she pulled me in close to her.

"They'll kill you, Cillian. Sink their claws into you like they've done with me," she said, barely above a whisper.

Shit. Did I completely play this wrong? Is she just like me—a pawn in all of this?

"What are you talking about?"

She shook her head solemnly. "Right now, no one knows you're you save for me. Turn around and walk away, and that's all it'll ever be."

"The people you work for framed me for Christopher's—"

"You think I don't know that? Lord knows, I know you two had your differences, but I never believed for a minute that you'd actually kill Christopher."

"You seemed to think differently up there on that stage just now."

She motioned behind her. "I never wanted *any* of this—you know that. I *have* to do what they tell me. Say the vile garbage that they tell me to say. I've had to completely sacrifice everything I stand for and who I am. I'm in too deep now. I can't go back. But you can. You can still get out of this in one piece."

Fuck. Was this all one giant mistake? Was Ada telling me the truth? Should I listen to her? Cut and run while the getting is good? Maybe Daniela was misinformed—

"Cillian—I have no reason to lie to you right now. I'm risking my skin by even telling you all of this. I won't be able to protect you if you stay on the path you're heading down. Heed my advice. Get gone while the getting is good."

Inaction is the greatest sin, Cillian. You're better than that.

I caught my breath.

No. I have to finish what I started.

No turning back now.

"Take me to see the Godmother."

Ada gazed at me, a sad recognition of my resolve flooding through her eyes. She nodded and took my arm, pulling me around behind the awning that housed the podium stage. There was a blacked-out Town Car waiting on the dirt road, engine rumbling.

I opened the door and climbed in. If it wasn't a brand spanking new Lincoln that had just been driven off the lot a few hours prior, then whoever had cleaned it did a remarkable job. You could probably lick the black suede leather, and it'd be cleaner than one of the fancy restaurants that Christopher used to love rambling on about. It was even outfitted with a fully stocked bar cart—an art deco piece, from the looks of it, that was bolted to the floor and was adorned with Waterford crystal glasses. Every single type of liquor bottle you could possibly think of was there, too.

Off the sight of the forbidden fruit, my lips started to salivate.

Shit. I needed that temptation right now like I needed a swift kick in the head from Apollo.

Ada slid in next to me, closing the door behind her. The back cabin we were sitting in was soundproofed, a tinted partition window separating us from the faceless driver. She immediately reached for one of the Waterfords. She put it into my hands and then reached into a side pocket of the car and removed an unmarked tube filled with a greenish-yellow colored God knows what. She uncorked it and poured it into my tumbler.

"Drink that."

It wasn't booze—if it was, I had never seen anything remotely that color before.

"The price of admission," Ada said as she sensed my reluctance.

Fuck it.

I swallowed the damn stuff. It tasted like a mixture of seltzer water and cleaning spray.

I started to sweat, and my hands began to quiver.

And then everything went black.

* * *

My field of vision is hazy, save for the pyromaniac colors of that Red Maple tree.

Christopher whispers in my ear frenetically. But I can't make out what he's saying.

Audrey's intoxicating, perfumed scent of honeydew and lavender fills my nostrils.

And then I'm floating, falling into a seemingly limitless abyss—a plunging elevator shaft with no end in sight. Except the walls are painted with Rip's hay loft mural. I fall into a cast-iron tub filled to the brim with Christopher's blood. I try and get up, but I'm weighed down by an immovable, unseen force.

And the pained, agonized yelping of Shep punctures my eardrums.

Is this what Hell is?

I woke up with a start and promptly vomited what felt like my entire soul out onto a snow-white floor in front of me.

186

I'm alive.

The first thing I notice is that I can't wipe my mouth afterwards. My legs and arms are duct-taped to a chair that's bolted to the floor of a white concrete-washed shed that's about as big as a shoebox. No windows.

The kicker, though? I'm in clothes that aren't my own—I've been changed into an all-white sweatsuit.

Which means that my key is gone.

Which means that they might know my real intentions.

Fuck.

The only entrance in or out of the place is through a steel-reinforced metal door. The only light source is one of those cheap work lamps that you buy at Home Depot and immediately regret doing so when it craps out after only twenty minutes.

This is where I'm going to die.

I hear footsteps from outside. The door swings open. In walks the Kentucky Fried Chicken lookalike from Ada's rally. In one hand, he carries a folding chair, and in the other, he pushes a gleaming gold drink trolley. The thing probably costs more than most mortgages around here. On it was a shaker filled with ice, a cocktail glass, and what looked like super precise measurements of gin, triple sec, lemon juice, and egg white. KFC placed the trolley right next to the folding chair, which was positioned about two feet in front of me. He left and closed the door without a word or glance in my direction.

What the fuck was happening?

I heard the clacking of her heels first.

The door swung open to a woman dressed in a platinum pantsuit that perfectly matched her titanium-colored eyes. The only pop of non-chromatic color anywhere to be found was her crisp, cream-colored button-up and bone-white painted nails. She acknowledged my existence with a prim tightening of her lips—one that couldn't quite be called a smile, but it wasn't a grimace either—before she settled down into the folding chair opposite me.

"Hello, Cillian," she said. "I was told that you wished to speak to me?"

This is the Godmother.

The way she spoke was unlike anything I'd ever heard before. It was barely above a whisper and yet had unmatched power. If it hadn't been for the restraints, I would have automatically leaned forward in my chair the second she opened her mouth.

I motioned to our surroundings and my chair-bound predicament. "Is this how you normally treat your guests?" I tried my best to say it in a light-hearted, confident way.

She released a laugh that didn't do that word justice. "Well, as I'm sure you could imagine, certain precautions had to be taken. And besides—I haven't decided yet if you're a guest or something else."

Was she toying with me? Did she already full well know my intentions and was just letting me dangle? Or was she actually feeling me out?

"I promise you that I'm not an adversary."

"Just because you're not an adversary doesn't mean that you're my brother-in-arms, either."

She reached over to the bar cart next to her and, with the dexterity of a seasoned barkeep, mixed, shook, and strained out her cocktail and took a precise sip. I had to make a conscious effort to swallow back the drool-like saliva that was pooling in my mouth.

"What is it that you think I do, Cillian?"

"Make the world a better place," I quickly said, remembering Daniela's instructions to butter her up at every opportunity, even despite the disgust and fear knocking around my brain.

"And how do you believe that I do that?"

Fuck. I hadn't thought this far ahead.

To ingratiate myself with her, I was going to have to spew out the filth that they believed in like it was my own set of ideals. But even despite my mission, I was only going to say those putrid words as an absolute last resort.

"Finding and backing candidates like Christopher and Ada as vessels for the true cause," I said, thinking on my feet. "It's brilliant, really."

She arched her eyebrow at me. "I would have thought that you would have been upset with us."

"For framing me, you mean? I was, initially, sure. But I realize now that it was all for the cause. You needed a fall guy. I was the easy choice. I understand that."

The Godmother took another exacting sip of her cocktail. "I had high hopes for Christopher. It was a shame, really."

"What was a shame? Having to kill him?"

A flash of impatience flared through the Godmother's eyes before they were quickly replaced by that icy calm once more.

Careful, Cillian. Don't spook her off, you idiot.

"It seems like there's something you'd like to accuse me of, Cillian. Why is that?"

"Nothing like that," I replied, backpedaling furiously. "I'm just making conversation. And to be honest with you? Y'all beat me to it—if you hadn't gotten there first that night, he would have died by my own hand."

She coolly nodded. "I'm aware."

"Then you're also probably aware of—

"How the two of you murdered Audrey together? Yes. Cillian, you'll soon learn that there is *nothing* that I do not know."

My face flushed. "It wasn't murder. It was an accident."

"Sure. I would imagine that's why Ada had to go to such great lengths to cover it up."

"You weren't there," I said as my voice quaked. "You don't know what happened."

"I know enough."

And that's when she reached into her pocket and removed my car key recording device.

God fucking damn it.

"I know enough to know that a horse-riding bumpkin like you has no business carrying around something like this unless you had a hidden, ulterior motive."

Did she know about Daniela? Did she know about Ada trying to warn me off?

"I don't know what you mean. That's how I start my truck."

She shook her head and clicked her tongue. "You're such a bad liar. It's adorable."

"I swear. I'm not lying."

The Godmother took a third sip of her cocktail before she dramatically dropped the key into her half-finished drink. She stared at me, her eyes practically glowing as she watched me process the weight of this. Even though I'm not a tech expert, I knew that was probably enough to fry the thing.

"How about you extend me the courtesy of not treating me like an imbecile? You're not interested in my work. You're probably naïve enough to think that it's repulsive or some other nonsense buzzword that the left or CNN likes to brand it. I know that. You know that. Let's clean our hands of that. I'll give you one last chance to level with me. Tell me why you're here and who put you up to this."

She could be bluffing—don't give in, Cillian. Not yet. It's time to bring out the big guns. The indescribably vile phrase that would make her think I was a real believer.

"We must secure the existence of our people and a future for white children."

She eyed me for a beat before squeezing my shoulder and giving me a wicked smile. "I admire your persistence to the charade. Christopher was the same way, you know. Once he stuck his mind on something, there was no putting him off it. I loved that about him. But unfortunately, it was also his undoing."

The Godmother swiftly turned around to face the metal door. "Bring her in!" she yelled, as if she was trying to rouse someone that was living in between the walls. Compared to the quiet, controlled way she had been speaking previously, it was a concussive grenade.

Then I heard the clopping of steel-toed boots.

Then, the ominous *woosh* of the metal door being forcefully swung open.

Then, the sound of dripping blood splattering the pristine floor.

And that's when I saw him—the Budweiser-bellied male detective that came to Rip's house that day, Thornwood—enter through the door.

And he was dragging an unconscious, bound, and gagged Daniela beside him by the nape of her neck.

And the blood on the floor was hers.

Chapter Nineteen

Cillian

Thornwood roughly dumped poor Daniela next to me. The piece of shit didn't even have the decency to give her a chair.

Jesus Christ. How many cops did the Godmother have under her thumb?

"Wake her up," the Godmother said to him.

Without thinking twice, Thornwood reached into his pocket for some smelling salts and shoved them in front of Daniela's nose. With a sputtering, blood, and snot-filled cough, Daniela came to, staining her white jumpsuit identical to mine.

"Miss Langer—what a pleasure to make your acquaintance," the Godmother said.

Daniela shouted something in response—but her gag reduced it to just a collection of muzzled, incomprehensible syllables.

"Shut the fuck up!" Thornwood bellowed as he viciously backhanded Daniela.

"That's quite enough, Detective Thornwood," the Godmother commanded.

Thornwood straightened his shoulders and spat dejectedly on the ground but did as he was told. Daniela, struggling through her pain, defiantly brought herself to a cross-legged sitting position.

God damn it, Cillian. The jig is up. Another poor soul is going to meet their maker because of you. Do something.

"Leave Daniela out of it," I yelled. "She has nothing to do with this."

"You and I both know that's not true. And besides, I don't think you're in much of a position to bargain," the Godmother retorted.

"It's me you want," I replied, trying another tactic. "She didn't do anything."

"Yeah, she didn't do anything except act like a little cunt when I tried to be reasonable with her," Thornwood cuttingly remarked.

I turned to face Mr. Beer Belly, no-holds-barred rage flying through me. "Hey fat fuck—Daniela has more courage and integrity in her pinkie finger than you've got in your entire goddamn body. So, close your fucking mouth before I do it for you."

"Oh yeah, big man? And how exactly do you intend on doing that, you fucking moron?" he said, motioning at my restraints. "You're as goddamn stupid as your brother."

"At least he wasn't a half-brained lackey who took orders from deranged white supremacists—"

The Godmother loudly banged her fist on the drink cart beside her. "ENOUGH!"

The skinny legs on the cart rocked violently with the force of her fury. Finally, she cut through the silence, snapping her fingers to the standing-at-attention Thornwood. "Arthur, provide me with your service weapon."

Thornwood quickly and obediently complied. The Godmother locked her sniper rifle sight directly on me. "I am not deranged."

Then, without an ounce of hesitation, the Godmother pulled back the hammer on Thornwood's gun and—

BAM!

The bullet careened out of the gun and mushroomed in Thornwood's temple, drenching us in his blood like Daniela and I were on a water ride at Six Flags.

The Godmother's heels click-clacked as she stepped over to Daniela and undid her mouth gag. "I told the Detective not to hurt you any more than necessary. It irritates me when people don't listen to me."

And with that, she sat down back in her chair, crossed one leg over the other, and laid the gun in her lap as she reached into her pocket and squirted some Purell onto her palms.

"Now, Cillian. You were saying?"

Fuck this.

I tried to Hulk-burst out of my restraints—but I didn't get very far.

"That's not going to work, I'm afraid," she said to me.

"If you're going to kill us—stop pleasuring yourself and get it over with already," Daniela snapped at the Godmother. "Neither of us has anything to say to you."

I nodded in agreement as I tried not to retch at the sight of the blown-to-bits Thornwood lying a few feet from us, his detective's badge shimmering in the dim lighting. I could tell Daniela was feeling the same—but, admittedly, she was better than I was at acting tough.

Seemingly sensing this in both of us, the Godmother motioned over to Thornwood. "Yes. I know. Horrible, right? The stench is only going to get worse, too. Luckily, I lost my sense of smell years ago. I regret not being able to smell the full bouquet of a glass of wine, for instance. But in times like this? It has its advantages. And yes—to answer the question both of you are thinking. He is not the only policeman I have on the payroll. The reach my people and I have would...astound you."

That dripping-in-ill-will smile spread across the Godmother's lips as her gaze cycled over to Daniela. "I've read your work, you know. You should be proud of yourself. You've accomplished so much—against what all rules of natural order intended for you."

Daniela's eye twitched with fury. "Am I supposed to thank you for that?"

Bemused, the Godmother smiled. "No, I wouldn't expect you to. Just an observation."

"What's the point of all of this?" I spit out. "Why are you doing this to us?"

"That's a fair question, Cillian," the Godmother responded as she pushed aside her chair and paced in front of us like a feral jungle cat. "The thing is, we thought we nipped this whole problem in the bud when we eliminated Christopher." She raised the gun at Daniela as a way of pointing to her. "Then your friend over here had to keep digging into me and my organization. Frankly, given the meager breadcrumbs Christopher had given her, which I still have no idea how he managed to procure, the fact she was able to put together what she did was impressive. But she couldn't leave well enough alone. Everyone that worked for me said I should just kill her and be done with it. But my grandfather was a journalist—and no matter how tainted her bloodline, I didn't want to murder a good reporter without reason— especially one as high-profile as she. But when she managed to resurrect you, Cillian? That I couldn't ignore."

A chill ran down my spine. "How did you know where I was?"

The Godmother laughed sympathetically, like a grown-up explaining taxes to their child. "Oh, my dear, every single step you've taken since your brother's unfortunate downfall we've monitored. We know how Rip takes his coffee. How lazy Shepard has become in his older age. The color of the paint the old man used when painting his barn. The deli counter he went to when he bought that roast beef. Hell—even Thornwood knew you were there. Why do you think we sent him to question Rip? If it wasn't for his partner, we would have solved everything right then and there."

God fucking damn it. No-no-no-no-no—

As if reading my mind, the Godmother raised her hand to stop my train of thought. "Don't worry. I don't intend to lay a finger on your precious Shepard and Mr. Rip. Assuming you two cooperate with me, of course. I need to know everything that you two know. Tell me that, and I'll make sure your deaths are quick and painless."

"Fuck you!" Daniela shouted out as she tried to break out of her bondage, to no avail.

"I don't think that's any way to treat someone who avenged your cruel treatment and ungagged you, is it?" The Godmother replied coolly. "Showing some manners would be appreciated, Daniela."

"I'm not going to show you jack shit, you racist monster—"

BAM!

One of the Godmother's bullets whizzed by my head, missing my cheek- bone by maybe about two millimeters—the heat of the bullet singing off a couple of sideburn hairs.

That rocked both Daniela and me into stone-cold silence.

"Let's get one thing straight, please. I am not deranged. I am not a monster. I am not a crocked old white man with delusions of grandeur while he tries to squeeze his fat behind into the folds of a white hooded robe. I am not a redneck farmer that wears a Confederate flag on his ill-fitting motorcycle vest while chanting and hollering in the streets. I am not a computer geek hiding behind a web forum while typing with Cheeto-encrusted fingers. I am not anti-Black, Hispanic, Asian, or anything else. I am pro-White. That's all. I am everything that my ideological predecessors failed to be. I've been doing what I've been doing for the past twenty years without anyone batting an eye. I am sought after. I am corporate. I am well-spoken. I am well-groomed. I am powerful without being ostentatious. But most importantly? I am *invisible.* Members of both political parties seek my support and are terrified of me in equal measures."

The Godmother, eyes ablaze once again, crouched down so she was on eye level with Daniela. "All that is to say—I think I've proven now that I don't respond well to disrespect. You should keep that in mind. When I come back, I expect you two to be more forthcoming with what you know about my business. Or I'll make your deaths excruciatingly slow…and unimaginably painful."

And with that, the Godmother strode out, slamming the door behind her with a clang.

I met eyes with Daniela—both of us silently apologizing to each other for our predicament. Neither of us had to say anything to know what the other was thinking.

The silence in the air hung thick like Rip's cigar smoke before—

"I'm not telling her or anyone else she brings in here shit—even if they torture us for days," Daniela proclaimed to me. "You know that, right?"

My beloved's voice crackled through my brain like a radio broadcast.

Inaction is the greatest sin, Cillian. You're better than that.

"Neither am I. No chance in hell."

"Good."

Another moment of silence. Finally—

"An ex once told me that my workaholic nature was going to kill me one day," Daniela cracked. "I guess I proved him wrong, huh?"

We both burst out laughing. I marveled at her wisecracking courage. Daniela's nerves of steel were nothing short of miraculous. Audrey would have admired the hell out of her. Lord knows I did.

I haven't been able to prevent the deaths of practically everyone in my life. My mother, my beloved, my brother—all of them slipped through my fingers. I was not going to let the same fate befall Daniela. No matter what I needed to do. No matter what it meant for me.

Determination flushed red through my face. "You're not dying here, Daniela. I promise."

"I didn't realize you were secretly Harry Houdini, Cillian. That's really something."

My eyes darted around the room, looking for something, anything, that could be of any help to us.

Fucking Christ, this place was as threadbare as a buzzard-devoured carcass.

As my gaze went back to Daniela, Thornwood's corpse with his stupid badge gleaming as bright as ever, and back to Daniela again, that's when it hit me. The obvious fact that had been sitting in front of me this entire time.

Literally.

"Wait a second. Daniela—they didn't strap you into a chair like they did with me."

Daniela arched an eyebrow at me. "So?"

"So…that means you can move, right?"

A slow smile spread across Daniela as she started to catch my drift.

I quickly did a once-over of the entire room. "I don't see any cameras in here, do you?"

She shook her head. "No."

And with that, my eyes went back to Thornwood's detective badge.

"I think I have an idea."

* * *

Clearly, the Godmother leaving us alone to stew was a tactic to try to get us to turn against one another. Little did she know that was the exact opposite thing she should have been doing—it gave us more than enough time to put our plan into action. After probably a hundred dozen awkward kicks, Daniela was able to dislodge Thornwood's badge from his belt. My guess was correct: there was a sharp, metallic pin-clip holding it in place. Daniela managed to roll herself over to the badge, pry it open with her fingers, and then use the pin clip to cut herself free from her duct tape restraints. Then, she was able to free me from mine. Now, Daniela and I would wait on either side of the door until the Godmother reentered and then ambush her. It was a crude plan, granted—but it was all we had.

For the initial spell of time, Daniela and I stood at attention like soldiers, adrenaline pumping through us like the diesel I used to put into my truck. Neither of us said a word to one another. Each of us pressed our ears up to the snow leopard white wall probably about six zillion times to see if we could hear anything. No dice. Wherever we were had been soundproofed to the umpteenth degree. When the minutes turned into hours, though— exhaustion started to settle in.

Which is exactly where we were now—about three hours in.

I squeezed my eyes shut and then opened them back up again, willing my body to stay coiled and ready. I looked over at Daniela—she was doing the same thing.

But the cuts and gashes on her face were slowly starting to seep blood down her cheeks.

Without thinking twice, I ripped off a section of my sweatsuit and moved over to dab the blood off Daniela.

She immediately jerked away. "What are you doing?"

"Oh, sorry. I didn't mean anything by it. It's just—your face. It's bleeding again."

She touched it and saw the fresh crimson on her fingers. "Oh. I guess it is."

I motioned to hand her the ripped-off portion of the sweatsuit so she could do it herself, but she waved me off. "No, it's okay. You can do it. I just didn't know what the hell you were up to before."

I stepped back to her and gently dabbed at her wounds. As I tenderly wiped away both the crusted and the fresh blood, I couldn't help but notice, once again, her stark beauty. Even though she was beat to hell, she was still…breathtaking.

I gently chuckled.

"What's so funny?"

"Nothing—I just realized that this is the most intimate thing I've done with a woman since Audrey died."

"Well…you're welcome. I set all this up so we could have this moment. It was an incredibly elaborate scheme."

"A dinner date would have sufficed just fine."

"I'll keep that in mind next time."

We both wryly smiled at one another before I pulled away the sweatsuit rag. "There. Good as new."

"Thank you," she replied.

I silently gazed into her moon eye as she looked right back at me. There was something I hadn't seen from her before—an unguarded, unadulterated vulnerability.

Last time I'd seen a look like that, Audrey told me she was pregnant.

And then she'd died.

"Daniela, I—"

And that's when it happened.

My knee gave out from under me, buckling my lower half with blinding pain as I collapsed to the floor.

God damn it. This can't happen right now.

Fuck.

Fucking.

Fuck.

"Cillian, are you okay?" Daniela asked as she bent down to try and help me up.

"It's an old riding injury. It's…aw, God fucking damn it, it doesn't matter."

I took her outstretched hand and tried to pull myself up—but I only got about a few inches off the ground before I couldn't take the pain anymore.

"What can I do to—"

And that's when we heard footsteps.

But when the door swung open, it was something different than what we were expecting.

The Godmother was standing there, gun raised at us.

But she was also joined by Ada—who was wielding a firearm, too.

"Hello, you two," the Godmother said. "I'd like you to meet my daughter, Ada."

Chapter Twenty

Cillian

Daughter.

"So, you're—"

"Yes, Cillian," Ada said before I could finish my thought. "My birth name is Ada Fisker. But my mother and I thought that it would be better if I went by my middle name, Morgan."

Was she the one that—

"And yes, before you ask—I'm the one that killed Christopher. Usually, we have people who take care of that sort of thing for us, but given the... delicacies of the situation? I needed to handle it personally. And besides—Christopher was never going to suspect me. No matter how paranoid he had become."

"So, everything you said to me after the rally—"

"Yes, Cillian. It was a double bluff. A trap. One which you fell into miraculously easily. Because I am a lion. And you are a lamb."

Ada. The woman who had made me string up my beloved in a tree was the murderer who had killed my kin. And dug my own grave in the process by framing me. God damn it all, how did I not see this coming?

Out of the corner of my eye, I could see Daniela slowly reach towards her pocket, where I knew she had stashed Thornwood's badge. Off this, the Godmother menacingly cocked her gun at Daniela. "Hands where I can see them."

Daniela slowly raised her hands in the surrender position. "Okay. Easy."

Ada pointed her gun at me. "Get up."

"I can't."

She arched her eyebrow at me—just like I'd seen the Godmother do to me. "Your knee acting up?"

I nodded.

"I don't care. Up."

I gritted my teeth through the excruciating pain and slowly brought myself to my feet, raising my hands in the same surrender position as Daniela.

"I guess I shouldn't bother asking you why you did all of this, right?" I asked Ada.

"You're not a stupid person, Cillian," she said. "Don't waste my time with a stupid question."

"Christopher didn't do anything to you. He gave you a job, and—"

Ada laughed. "You think I *needed* that job? I could have gotten any job I wanted in the country. No. My mother anointed your brother for a very specific reason. He was to be the chosen one, and I his guardian angel. But we didn't have anything on him to really set the hook in. Then, things changed. *You* happened. And then Audrey."

The color drained from my face with my beloved's name in this lunatic's mouth. "Don't you dare talk about her, you fucking sociopath."

Ada laughed even harder at that. "You think we didn't know about her and your brother? About the night they had together? Once that glorious morsel of information came to light? We knew it was only a matter of time before we would have what we needed. Especially with your temper, Cillian. You're what we call in our line of work easy money—a ticking time bomb if there ever was one."

"Fuck you!"

"And the moment my daughter stepped in to help clean up your two's... mess...with Audrey?" the Godmother interjected. "We had the leverage we needed. We just sat on it for a while, biding our time until Christopher got to the level of political influence we needed. But then he had to go and grow a conscience with *this one."*

The Godmother sneered at Daniela as she offhandedly motioned towards her.

"And besides, Cillian," Ada chimed in. "No one asked you to leave Rip's farm. You—and you alone—put yourself in this situation. Not us. No one made you listen to…this," she said as she wickedly pointed at Daniela.

"Fuck you, puta," Daniela spat out.

"Charming." Ada turned to face the Godmother. "Mother, shall we dispose ourselves of these two, once and for all?"

"I think that's a grand idea, darling," the Godmother replied.

As they cocked their guns—

"You're not going to want to do that," Daniela quickly countered.

"And why is that?" the Godmother asked.

"Because the FBI will close in on this place faster than you could ever imagine."

That stunned the room into a submissive silence. I did a double take, swiveling my neck to Daniela in disbelief. The Godmother and Ada squinted their eyes at Daniela, sizing her up—weighing whether to believe her.

"The FBI?" the Godmother replied.

"That's right."

"I think you're lying," the Godmother said as she gestured over to me. "And from the looks of Cillian, I'd bet all the money in the world that I'm right in my assumption."

"You think I would have told Cillian anything about this?" Daniela snorted. "Yeah, right. Cillian is about the worst liar I've ever seen in my life. He would have given it away in about twenty seconds."

"Prove it," Ada shot back.

"Every Thursday morning for the past month and a half, I've been meeting with a Special Agent Cooper to tell him about the findings in my investigation. We go for breakfast at six AM. Which, correct me if I'm wrong, is about a half-hour from now?"

Ada checked her watch and held it up to the Godmother. "Shit, she's right."

"You've correctly guessed the time," the Godmother said. "Congratulations.

Still doesn't mean that you're telling the truth."

"Cooper and I have agreed that if I ever miss that meeting and don't tell him why, he should assume the worst and go investigate my last known location." Daniela leaned in conspiratorially. "And this is just a hunch—but I don't think the Feds finding out about this place would be very good for you."

"How would they know your location?"

"I have a GPS tracker embedded in my shoe."

Ada's face went white. And while I could tell the Godmother was skeptical, there was undoubted concern splashed across her usually stoic face.

Jesus—could that actually be true? Was Daniela about to pull a miracle out of thin air?

"I know—it sounds ridiculous. But it's 100% true. You. Are. Fucked."

"Mother, let's kill them and be *done* with this! Let's cut our losses and move on."

"Ada, be quiet. There's no way she's telling the truth. She's bluffing!"

"But if she's not, we've got a very finite amount of time to get out of here—"

"This is your problem, Ada. You don't have the foresight that you need—the calculated sense of risk and aggression that separates the queens from the pawns. You're always on the defensive—"

"I wasn't aware that I had a problem, *Mother*—"

"I've always told you that, *Dear*—"

As the two of them turned to face one another while their squabbling became more and more heated, I finally realized what the whole point of all this was: Daniela reached into her back pocket, grabbed Thornwood's badge, and quickly nodded at me.

And that's when she whipped that badge with all her might at the Godmother's face.

And we bum-rushed them like rabid banshees.

Daniela got to the Godmother just in time, pushing away her weapon as a bullet discharged loudly, skyrocketed up into the ceiling. Adrenaline surging through me, I followed Daniela's lead—I lunged towards Ada, knocked the gun out of her hands, and pinned her to the ground.

"Get off me, you fucking half-breed!" the Godmother shouted as Daniela wrestled the gun out of her grasp.

"Gladly," Daniela responded.

And then she pulled the trigger.

And the Godmother's brains splattered all over those pristine white walls.

"Oh my God!!!!" screamed Ada. "What the fuck are you—"

Daniela turned to face her. "Cillian, get out of the way!"

I threw myself down to the ground.

Daniela pulled the trigger.

And Ada was no more.

Daniela and I stood in stunned silence for a tick before Daniela finally spoke out, stuttering with shock.

"I couldn't not…I just…they—"

I put my hand on her shoulder. "Don't you feel bad. Not for one second."

She nodded in agreement, but I saw the opposite in her sickened expression. The horror of this wasn't something she could unsee or forget. It was a part of her now.

I knew that better than anybody.

"There's no Special Agent Cooper, is there?" I asked her.

A small smile spread across her lips as she breathed again. "You've never seen *Twin Peaks* before, Clarke?"

"I've never gotten around to it."

I gently took the gun from her and tucked it into my waistband. "And I'm assuming you don't actually have a GPS tracker in your shoe?"

Her small smile got wider. "No. But I have something better."

She reached down and peeled open the tongue of her left boot. Inside was a microdot recorder the size of a pea.

"You really think you were the only one with a recorder on you? I've kept this on me every single day—kind of an insurance policy ever since the Klan took their first pop at me that time in Tuscaloosa. And it's never actually been worth a damn…until now."

"So that means—"

She nodded. "We have them, Cillian. We can burn these fuckers to the ground."

Salvation.

"So…does that mean all of our conversations were recorded, too?"

"You bet."

"I'm not sure how I feel about that."

"Do you really think now is the time to talk about that?"

"You're right. We gotta get out of here."

I reached out for the metal door and opened it for her.

We stepped outside into one of the most beautiful sunrises I'd ever seen. The stunning golden pink streaked across the sky looked like a signal from God. I felt hope flood me.

But then reality crushed it.

We were smack dab in the middle of a rural militia survival camp.

Daniela and I ducked behind a line of bushes and took stock of our surroundings.

A ten-foot-tall "Don't Tread on Me" flag flapped between two trees, overlooking a target practice field. Paper dummy outlines of Joe Biden, Hillary Clinton, and Kamala Harris were riddled with bullet holes.

Two lookout towers loomed on either side of the camp.

A row of bunker cabins. Each of the cabins had Blood Drop Crosses painted on the side of them. A hop and skip to the left of the shed we just walked out of were six men sitting around a campfire, dressed in paramilitary fatigues with AR-15s holstered across their backs.

Fucking shit.

Daniela pointed to our right to the surrounding woods. "If we can get there without those fuckers seeing us, we should be okay. It looks like it's about a hundred-yard shot from here."

"Yeah."

She glanced at me and then down at my knee. "Think you can manage it?"

I shrugged. "I'm going to have to, right?"

She nodded. "Follow me. We'll bear crawl through these bushes and then make a break for it."

"Got it."

I got down on my hands and knees and trailed behind Daniela, both of us moving as stealthily as humanly possible through the cold, damp dirt. We got about halfway home before—

BWAH-BWAH-BWAH-BWAH!

A deafening siren blared through the camp.

Daniela and I looked at each other in horror and then down at the ground.

We had set off a pressure-sensitive, hidden trip-wire alarm.

The paramilitary men snapped to, cocking their guns as they barreled directly at us.

And that's when Daniela and I did what I knew best.

We ran, thanks to the adrenaline supercharging my bum knee.

Zing!

A bullet whizzed by my ear.

Crack!

A bullet splintered a branch hanging over Daniela's head.

Thunk!

A bullet careened off a rock next to my foot.

Miraculously, we made it to the tree line in one piece.

But we were now being hunted.

In a terrain that neither of us knew how to find our way out of.

I pushed my legs as fast as they've ever gone to keep with Daniela's frenetic pace. My lungs felt like they were going to pop at any moment.

Inaction is the greatest sin, Cillian. You're better than that.

My beloved's words ringing through my ears, I kept pushing.

Faster.

And faster.

And faster.

Daniela and I went all out until we reached a babbling creek. The animalistic cries of the survivalist militiamen weren't far behind. We had maybe thirty seconds before we were in their sights again.

"What's the plan here, Clarke?" Daniela asked.

The paramilitary assholes were closing in.

These fuckers will know these woods like the back of their hand. It's only a matter of time before we get caught. We're not going to be able to outrun them. Not unless—

And that's when I saw it.

Another fox a few feet away from us.

Christopher.

I locked gazes with the fox—its unblinking yellow eyes piercing me, guiding me resolvedly towards the right thing to do. The only thing to do.

Inaction is the greatest sin, Cillian. You're better than that.

"Cillian—"

Crack!

A gunshot sliced the air, sending the fox running and locking me into my plan.

I turned towards Daniela and pointed to the creek. "Listen to me. Follow this creek. Creeks lead to rivers, which lead to towns."

Daniela's eyes widened as she quickly picked up on my meaning. "No—"

"Stop. We don't have enough time. Creeks lead to rivers, which lead to towns. I'm going to go in the opposite direction and draw them out. You'll have to be quick. I'll only be able to buy you a few extra minutes head start. When you get somewhere safe, call Detective Rogers. She's a Virginia State Police Detective. She was Thornwood's partner and might be the only honest one in the entire department. Show her that recording in your boot. Tell her *everything* you saw and heard tonight. Show her what you showed me back at the motel."

I removed the gun from my waistband and gave it a quick but thorough rubbing on my clothes to remove any signs of Daniela's fingerprints. "And you have to tell her that I'm the one who killed Ada and her mother."

"I can't let you do that—"

"You can. There's no sense you going down for something that needed to happen by every God-given sense of right and wrong. Go write that story. Expose these monsters for what they are. Stop them from doing any more damage."

"Cillian, we still might be able to get away together—"

I shook my head. Put my hand on her shoulder. "Diversion is our only chance. I've long run out on my purpose here on this earth. You haven't. You saved my life. My turn now. Go be the light the world wants you to be. The light the world *needs* you to be."

Her moon eye teared up.

"Do me one favor? Find Rip and Shep when this is all over? Tell them I love them?

Daniela nodded.

"Go on now."

And she took one last look at me before hightailing it.

The yelling got louder.

And louder.

I waited. Waited until they were almost on me.

Louder.

I could see them now. And they could see me.

It was time.

Gripping the gun, I ran in the opposite direction from Daniela, firing into the air. "Come and get me, you fuckers!"

Please, God, let this work. Let them take me. Not her.

I snuck a peek back over my shoulder. All six of them followed me like bloodthirsty hunting dogs, hot on the trail of a wounded animal ripe for the picking. Beyond them was the faint outline of Daniela, escaping to freedom.

Praise be. She was safe.

I pushed onwards.

Pop-pop-pop!

The bullets were a sea of hellfire all around. But I didn't care.

I was happy. Excited for the first time in years.

Because I was going to see my beloved again.

Audrey, I'm going to wrap my arms around you once again. Tell you everything that I should have told you when I was alive. Tell you how you made my life worth living. That you were the only real home I ever had or needed. How sorry I am for every single goddamn thing I did. And hell, maybe I'll even make peace with Christopher, once and for all. I know that would make you happy.

She smiled at me as she sat the trot on Dolly. That glorious, euphoric smile that made me weak in the knees.

I yee-hawed Apollo into a canter, laughing with delight as the sun blasted my face.

Audrey and I were headed right for one another. At long last.

And that's when one of their bullets hit the mark and lodged itself right next to my spine.

I hit the ground face-first.

I felt the blood gushing out of me.

It was only a matter of seconds now.

My vision blurred—the six militiamen's voices garbled. But I saw one thing above me clear as day.

I had been slain directly under a Red Maple Tree.

This is what I deserved.

I felt the footsteps, heavy and labored, approach me from behind.

Heard the reloading of one of their guns. Felt the cold steel of the barrel pressed into the back of my head.

Audrey's voice.

I want you forever, Cillian.

I had finally made things right.

And going to where I belonged.

Audrey and I galloped off, romping through the hills of Heaven. For now and forever.

I was finally free.

Acknowledgements

First and foremost, I'm incredibly grateful to the incomparable team at Level Best Books for publishing this novel. Without y'all, Cillian's story would be languishing untold in a file on my laptop. I am forever in your debt.

I'd also like to thank:

My *New York Times* bestselling mother, L.M. Elliott, for not only the stellar editorial guidance you provided me with while I drafted, but also instilling in me the belief that I could even write a novel to begin with. You are my inspiration in all things, and I love you so much.

Ciara, my brilliant beta reader, for her developmental eye and helping me polish up *Blue Ridge* into what it is today. I value your insights—and friendship—dearly.

Phoebe, for your steadfast support of me throughout this turbulent process—and for helping me believe in love again.

Matt, for being an unwavering mentor and champion of my work—and encouraging me to continually push myself and grow as an artist.

And finally, you—the person who bought and read this book. I hope that you enjoyed the novel and that it resonated with you.

About the Author

Peter Malone Elliott is an author, screenwriter, and developmental editor. Born and raised in Virginia, he now lives in Brooklyn, but still holds the magic of the mountains and Southern living near and dear to his heart. *Blue Ridge* is his debut novel. Other notable writing achievements include a Leo Award nomination for "Best Screenwriting, Motion Picture" and winning the Grand Prize of the Script Pipeline Screenwriting Competition. Peter is also the founder and owner of Fortiter et Recte Literary, where he offers bespoke editorial consulting for manuscripts and screenplays.

SOCIAL MEDIA HANDLES:
  @pmewriter (Instagram)

AUTHOR WEBSITE:
  Author Site: https://www.pmelliott.com/

Developmental Editing/Consulting Site:
  https://www.fortiteretrecteliterary.com/

Printed in the USA
CPSIA information can be obtained
at www.ICGtesting.com
JSHW081111011223
52896JS00001B/2